"First your mouth, Domini," Luke said. He brushed his lips against hers, his eyes narrowing when she turned to follow his lips. He took her lower lip between his teeth and flicked his tongue over her lips. She leaned into him, closer, wanting more.

"You feel it, too, don't you?" he said. "Like a storm that's gathering strength." His thumbs coasted up from the curve of her hips, shaped her waist and then slowed to measure each quickened breath as he raised them to gently press the sides of her breasts.

"Frightened?" he asked.

"Yes," Dominica said. "But not of you. The things you make me feel."

She tilted her head back as he kissed her. Her fingers caught the back of his head, entwining in the still-damp length of his hair. Luke gathered her closer to the heat of his body. He cupped her buttocks, bringing her up against his hard, aching flesh, making sure she was certain of how much he wanted her.

"That's it, Domini," he harshly whispered, "Give yourself to me."

**As a child, Dominica had loved to watch storms breaking in all their fury. But now the storm was within her very core. . . .**

ANNOUNCING THE

# TOPAZ FREQUENT READERS CLUB
## COMMEMORATING TOPAZ'S 1 YEAR ANNIVERSARY!

### THE MORE YOU BUY, THE MORE YOU GET

Redeem coupons found here and in the back of all new Topaz titles for FREE Topaz gifts:

Send in:

- 2 coupons for a free TOPAZ novel (choose from the list below);
  - ☐ THE KISSING BANDIT, Margaret Brownley
  - ☐ BY LOVE UNVEILED, Deborah Martin
  - ☐ TOUCH THE DAWN, Chelley Kitzmiller
  - ☐ WILD EMBRACE, Cassie Edwards
- 4 coupons for an "I Love the Topaz Man" on-board sign
- 6 coupons for a TOPAZ compact mirror
- 8 coupons for a Topaz Man T-shirt

Just fill out this certificate and send with original sales receipts to:

**TOPAZ FREQUENT READERS CLUB-1ST ANNIVERSARY**
Penguin USA • Mass Market Promotion; Dept. H.U.G.
375 Hudson St., NY, NY 10014

Name_____

Address_____

City_____State_____Zip_____

Offer expires 5/31/1995

This certificate must accompany your request. No duplicates accepted. Void where prohibited, taxed or restricted. Allow 4-6 weeks for receipt of merchandise. Offer good only in U.S., its territories, and Canada.

# Whisper My Name

Raine Cantrell

A TOPAZ BOOK

TOPAZ
Published by the Penguin Group
Penguin Books USA Inc., 375 Hudson Street,
New York, New York 10014, U.S.A.
Penguin Books Ltd, 27 Wrights Lane,
London W8 5TZ, England
Penguin Books Australia Ltd, Ringwood,
Victoria, Australia
Penguin Books Canada Ltd, 10 Alcorn Avenue,
Toronto, Ontario, Canada M4V 3B2
Penguin Books (N.Z.) Ltd, 182–190 Wairau Road,
Auckland 10, New Zealand

Penguin Books Ltd, Registered Offices:
Harmondsworth, Middlesex, England

First published by Topaz, an imprint of Dutton Signet,
a division of Penguin Books USA Inc.

First Printing, June, 1995
10  9  8  7  6  5  4  3  2  1

 Topaz is a trademark of Dutton Signet,
a division of Penguin Books USA Inc.

Printed in the United States of America

*For special friends who always believe—*
*Fran, Gayle, Maggie, Rogenna, Suzanne, and Terry*

# *Prologue*

∾

The mountains waited, as did the messenger beyond the small pool of light the single candle shed on the gleaming wood writing desk. Within its light lay a letter, sealed and ready to begin its journey.

The letter was to arrive at the mission off the California coast in weeks; it was the final link that would bring the events of the past together. When the letter's demand was answered—and it had to be answered—there would be no turning back, no stopping what had to be.

Fingering the soft doeskin bag of coins that would make the journey possible, the writer's thoughts drifted back in time.

This was the only way.

*Vengeance is mine, sayeth the Lord.* But the Lord had not brought vengeance. He had rewarded the secrets kept with riches. If the Lord would not move to do what must be done, it belonged to another who had waited and planned. Too many years, hard lessons of patience learned, and willingly paid, to see justice served. Soon . . .

A motion brought the messenger forward to receive both the letter and the coins. When the door closed softly behind the man, the write was once more alone, as it had ever been.

There was only one who could destroy this plan for revenge: the wild card. Never controlled. Always returning. Drawn by the land, and linked, as they were all linked, to the tragic events of the past. But the deed was done. Too late now . . . much too late.

# Chapter One

❧

Dominica Kirkland forced a show of bravery and stepped off the stage in the mining town of Florence. It was night and the drunken male voices raised in song made her anxious. She felt as if her bones had been rattled loose and knit back together with aches and kinks a permanent part of her body.

The letter which had drawn her here, and the money provided for the trip, had been stolen as she purchased her stage ticket. The thief had been quick in the press of bodies, for she hadn't known of her loss until seated on the stage. She had almost turned back to the only home she knew, but the chance of putting to rest the mystery surrounding her father's death tapped a well of determination and she had finished her journey. There was a lesson she had learned at a tender age that stood her in good stead now: if she revealed fear, strangers would prey on her.

Domini trusted her instincts. She saw nothing to fear in the kindly face of the man at the stage depot who opened the door and helped her down. She clung to the thought that he might help her and ignored the stares that sent a shiver walking up her spine.

Saturday night in Florence was no place for a lady. It was no place for Luke either, in his present mood. He took another, longer look at the woman arguing with Chay Booker in front of the stage depot, ever mindful of the wide berth miners and ranch hands gave him. A loner by nature and circumstance, Luke knew it was just as well that no one tried to crowd his space in front of Long Tom's saloon. He was restless, bored, and drunk enough not to walk from whatever came his way.

Swigging a drink from his bottle of whiskey, he targeted a flint-eyed gaze on the woman again. First impressions could save a man's life. Luke had learned early on to size someone up quickly and coldly. And the woman he watched was no lady.

She touched Chay as she walked with the ease of a woman familiar with touching strange men. Most ladies wouldn't put their lily white hands on a man unless they had to. And then only after they had trapped him into marriage. She appeared to ignore the whistles and catcalls that came her way. Ignore them as if she didn't even hear the miners bent on inviting her to celebrate while they stood drinks for their less fortunate brethren, or the cowboys with a week's pay burning holes in their pockets, more than ready to raise hell and break anything else that got in their way.

She didn't even glance up and around to see who was speculating about her riding ability.

A lady would have been hollering for help if someone told her they'd like to ride her hard and put her away wet. That his own thoughts were as crude didn't matter to him. He was watching her reactions. Weighing. Judging.

She'd come off the stage alone, something else that no lady would do unless she didn't have a reputation to protect. Eyeing her willowy build again, Luke found himself adding that there weren't many ladies who turned a man's thoughts to how she would feel accommodating the fit of his body and for how long.

The constant creak of the swinging batwings and the shouts and laughter within the saloon faded from Luke's hearing. Just as the once held thoughts of being a part of it had faded over the years. He stashed his whiskey bottle between his knees and built himself a smoke. As he brought the match tip to light his cigarette, he looked up and found that she was watching him. He didn't even feel the match burning down until the singed leather of his glove warned him. The light and the heat were gone in the same instant, but Luke wouldn't forget.

She was tall for a woman, topping Chay by a

good three inches. She had some to go to come near his own six foot two inch height. But then, he reminded himself, he had never paid attention to a woman's height. His business with them was concluded prone and willing, satisfying a need like eating when hungry and drinking when thirsty.

In the light spilling from the lantern hung near the depot door, he couldn't see much of her face, half hidden by the shawl she had wrapped around her head and shoulders. She certainly wasn't dressed like any lady he'd seen. No bonnet, no fancy hat, no parasol, no high buttoned shoes. The hem of her gown was ankle-length, revealing a pair of moccasins. White women didn't wear them.

Curiosity kicked up his interest another notch. Not many women made the rough and dangerous hundred-twenty-five-mile trip into this part of the Idaho Territory. She wasn't someone's wife sent for after a big strike, or a left-behind sweetheart come to be married. That kind of news spread fast and there hadn't been any. But there was another kind of woman drawn to a place like Florence.

Jimmy Jack, the town's half-breed drunk, wove his way through the milling horses being led down to the livery since the hitching posts were crowded with mounts, heading for Luke. The fact that Luke couldn't keep his eyes off her for more than a few seconds sent a shaft of annoyance through him. No corset cinched her waist or hips. She moved with the supple grace of an Indian

maid, following Chay back and forth as he un-
loaded the boot of the stagecoach.

"Got a drink, Luke?"

He took another drag of his smoke and handed
it to Jimmy Jack. "Want my makings to save one
for later?" A nod sufficed for Luke to hand them
over, but he held onto the bottle. "Aloysius should
be done shoeing my grulla. You go check on it for
me, an' I'll leave you the bottle."

Once more Jimmy Jack nodded. Luke saw half
his tobacco spill from shaking fingers trying to fill
the thin paper. He removed them from the old
man, built a cigarette, and tucked it in his torn
shirt pocket.

"Molly's got food for you. You make sure to
sweep up for her, an' she'll let you sleep in the
kitchen tonight. Go on now, see about my horse."

If his grulla hadn't cast a shoe just outside of
town, Luke wouldn't have bought another bottle
of whiskey. He wasn't about to leave Jimmy Jack
more than a drink or two, so his swigs were hard
and fast until less than a quarter remained in the
bottle. At least the old man wouldn't get his belly
rotted out drinking swill.

The liquor, added to what he had already, set
fire to his blood. It set him to thinking about the
last, quick tumble he'd had with Tassy that afternoon, before the sweat and leavings of other men
couldn't be hidden by the lilac water she favored
as a washup between customers.

This only brought him back to thinking that the

woman across the street was here to make money from hungry men. Since he decided for sure that she was no lady—for he knew firsthand all he had ever wanted to know about ladies—odds were she was a new nickel-a-ride-mattress-back. He'd never had any truck with virgins, the territory didn't have many, and there was something about her that attracted him. Attracted and aroused him enough to think about plunking down a few silver dollars for her time.

Jimmy Jack reappeared at his side. "Mornin', grulla ready." He reached out and touched the rawhide strips that hung from Luke's gun belt. "You keep?"

"Always. I never forgot what you taught me, Jimmy Jack. Go eat at Molly's." He handed over his bottle, wiped his mouth with the back of his hand, and moved.

Luke paid no attention to the men coming and going across the street. Two things made most of them step aside for him: his reputation and his name. He had earned the first, and he hated the second.

He sauntered at an angle to where the woman stood, idly noting that most of the families who came into town to buy their monthly supplies and pick up their mail from the stage were already off the street.

He gave thought to the fact that he might be piling up grief for himself like the thunderheads in the sky above him, building grief for anyone caught in the open when the storm clouds burst. Thought about it and dismissed it. Luke rarely denied himself anything he wanted. He only had to want it badly enough. He'd learned early on that everything and everyone had a price.

And he could buy whatever he desired. All it took was a whisper of his name.

Chay disappeared inside the depot office just as Luke came to a stop behind the woman. Tension rolled off her body and collided with his. No cloying fragrance reached him, just the warm, clean scent of a woman. He was struck by the strange thought that there was a wildness in her, as deep and dark as the currents of the Salmon River. Gut feelings were about the only things Luke trusted, so this one came and settled. Fast and hard. The same way his body was urging him to take her.

He was damned to figure why. He hadn't even seen her face. And when she leaned close to the doorway and spoke again to Chay, Luke found that her voice ran through him the same way: deep, dark, and fast. He felt his nerve ends sizzle as if lightning strikes had hit them.

A loud clap of thunder sounded and he looked up, a frown tightening his brow. Storms were wild in these Idaho mountains. A man had to outwit and outrun their fury. For all the arguing she was doing with Chay, there was no anger in her voice. There was a liquid, throaty quality to her every word that drove itself into his senses like a miner's pick sinking deep into rock. Liquid as hot honey, the slightly accented voice hit him with the same potency as the fancy aged brandy that his brother favored. For the moment, Luke chose to listen.

"There must be someone willing to help me, Mr. Booker. I told you both my money and the letter were stolen in Lewiston once I had my stage ticket. I can't spend the night here. Someone has to—"

"Look. I done tole you once, done tole you too many times, there ain't no one gonna make that trip tonight." Chay came to the doorway. "If I could figure a way to help you, I would. Can't, though. Ain't my job to see to folks once the stage gets 'em here."

"I was assured that the Colfax name meant something—"

"Does. Sure as hell does." Chay stepped out. "Luke? That you standin' there?" Chay ran a hand over his thick red beard, his head jutting forward on his long neck like a turtle coming out of his shell. "By damn! Can't tell where you begin and the dark ends."

Dominica Kirkland whirled around, nostrils flaring like an animal scenting danger. She was unsettled that someone had stood behind her without making a sound. Her first thought was that Chay Booker was right; there was no telling where the man began and the night ended. She was not accustomed to looking up at many men, but he was taller than her by a half foot at least.

With his presence came a deep sense of darkness, not only from his clothing as he stepped forward, but with a darker, powerful force impacting on her as she looked upon his face. Domini wondered if he had been named for Lucifer, the most handsome of the fallen angels. His features were hard-edged, and there was a consuming blaze of unexplained anger in his eyes.

"You can help, Luke. This here gal's lookin' for—"

"I heard her, Chay." Luke motioned to the man, and Chay slipped back inside the depot office, closing the door.

Domini glanced from the closed door back to the man who stood watching her. There was a dangerous stillness to him, bringing a feeling that nothing going on around him escaped his notice. Including her.

The ensuing silence was meant to make her uncomfortable and it did. She bore with his scrutiny for a few moments more, then spoke.

"Since you heard my request, you know I need to reach the Colfax—"

"He send for you?" *It would be just like Matt to order himself up a new woman. Arrogant bastard that he was.*

"Yes, I was sent for. The letter that was stolen—"

"Well, it don't matter none. You're here." Luke tilted back his hat brim with his thumb. He looked her over from bottom to top, then focused on the way the freshening wind pressed the cloth of her gown against her legs and the flare of her hips. The legs were long, the kind men could dream about, and her hips had a womanly invitation to cushion a man's ride with ease.

"You'll do," he announced.

"Do? For what? I'm only interested in a ride—"

"Same here. No sense in wasting time." He reached out with his left hand and caught hold of her chin with his thumb and forefinger, lifting her face up toward the lantern light.

Her brows and lashes were as black as his own, framing green eyes that tugged at his memory. She wasn't pretty. It was too soft a word for her. Her features were strongly molded on smooth golden skin that didn't owe its color to the sun.

He thought her a breed, then dismissed it. There was a delicate refinement to the angles and planes of her face. Striking was the only word that came to his mind, for he had the unshakable feeling that a man would never tire looking at this woman through all the seasons.

The very fact that she stood still, and silent, while he took her measure confirmed his earlier assessment of her. Somehow having his opinion verified didn't dim his interest. If anything, seeing her up close, touching her skin, only brought out tiny claws of need inside him. He brushed his thumb across her bottom lip and released her.

"Let's go."

"Just a moment. Who are you? And why are you willing to give me a ride out there tonight?"

"I'm Luke. An' it's too late to start out there tonight, just like Chay told you. I'll get you a room at the hotel." Luke glanced around and saw the single carpetbag near the door. "That all you got?"

"Yes, that's mine." Domini watched him scoop up her bag. "Mr. Booker said there wasn't a room to be had."

"There's always a room for me." He eyed her ruffled expression. "You coming? There's about three minutes before the storm hits. I've already had my bath an' you'd shiver in the cold slash of this mountain rain."

"Why are you willing to help me when—"

"Sometimes Colfax's interests an' mine ride the same road. That's all you need to know." He caught hold of her arm.

"I'm not sure I want to go—"

"It wasn't ever meant as an invitation. Colfax sent for you. That makes you Colfax property. 'Sides, this town ain't no place for a woman alone tonight."

Domini stared up at him. The warning and the threat were there in his voice and the still blazing anger of his eyes.

"Do you work for him? Mr. Colfax, I mean."

"I've done some troubleshooting for him in my day."

Her gaze lowered to the gun he wore low on his left hip. She hadn't missed the knife sheathed slightly off center to the left of the small of his back. Domini was no stranger to men and their weapons of violence. If Sister Benedict hadn't believed that she could take care of herself, Domini knew she would never have allowed her to make this most important trip on her own.

Even with anger shimmering in his gaze, there was the awareness that she was a woman. She sensed no evil for all that he guarded himself. What frightened her was the desire she had to feel his gentle touch on her face again. Strange how she felt its loss.

"Two minutes and counting until the storm hits."

"I can't pay you."

"Yeah, right. The money got stolen. We'll figure out something."

"All right. I'll come with you."

A loud clap of thunder capped off her agreement. Domini watched him walk away, expecting her to follow. He walked as if he were alone, and she wondered why men simply stepped aside for him. Too exhausted to think about it, she began to follow him toward the far corner, where the wind swung the post sign announcing Tanner's Hotel. Luke took the steps lightly, moving with a grace that drew attention to his lithe, powerful body.

A fat drop of rain hit Domini's cheek and she looked up. She loved the first moments before a storm—when the wind rushed and the clouds piled and billowed before spilling their precious, life-giving rain. Exhilaration filled her as lightning split the sky and lit the undersides of the dark clouds. Here was raw power as only nature could unleash. She was distracted by curses as the door behind Luke was flung open and four men staggered out to the wooden porch.

Since Luke stood dead center, and showed no inclination to move, the men split to go around him. Domini saw that Luke didn't even turn to acknowledge being told that he couldn't get a room here; they were full. He just remained where he was, waiting for her.

Domini could smell the incoming rain now, and with it the stench of unwashed bodies. Two on each side of Luke, the men came down the steps toward her. She caught Luke's gaze on her, but sensed he was very aware of the four men. She glanced at the two nearest her, then back at Luke. He had set her bag down, but it was the only move he had made.

"Bless my bleary eyes! We got ourselves a woman."

Domini stilled, as a fawn hiding in a thicket would still when a hunter approached. Only she had nowhere to hide. To run would have them on her like a pack of wolves. She never once thought to call out to the man who waited for her. She had been on her own for so long that she depended upon no one but herself.

They wouldn't expect her to fight. Violence was against her beliefs, but she had been trapped by men like these before, and the Lord didn't need another lamb. Domini closed out the sound of their voices, blurring in her mind their crude words, just as she had done with the other men when she arrived.

Luke, snared by a fierce hunger that flooded his loins with heat, was caught up in her obvious enjoyment of the coming storm. The four men were circling her now. He waited for her plea. It took a few moments for him to realize that the plea was not coming, and he was filled with an explosive possessiveness.

"Caully."

One man turned at the soft murmur of his name. "That you, Luke? Thought you were gone."

"Well, I'm right here, Caully."

"Didn't mean to cut you out. Plenty to go 'round since we're sharing."

"That's not how I figure it." Luke came down the steps and never once looked at the woman.

But Domini couldn't take her eyes from him. He moved with a mountain cat's grace, supple, primitive, and dangerous. A shiver walked up her spine. She stood forgotten when Luke reached out his right hand and gathered up Caully's shirtfront, and with a twist of the material he lifted the man up on his toes.

"Now, Luke—"

"Now, Caully. Just listen. You don't look. You don't touch. An' you never make the mistake of thinking that I share. Ever."

"Nooo sireee, Luke. Caully ain't gonna make

that mistake again. Just let him go and we'll leave, Luke."

"Always said you were a smarter man than some, Ramsey. Take him an' get the hell out of my sight."

"Com'on, Caully, he's wild tonight," Ramsey muttered as he grabbed hold of his friend's arm and hurried with the other men past Domini.

"Who are you?" Domini rubbed her arms, ignoring the rain and staring up at him.

"About the only man who can get you out of the rain tonight. Coming?"

*Never share.* Domini heaved a weary sigh. So the battles were not done. But one was better odds for her. Still caught in the tension of the past minutes, Domini hesitated. He removed his gloves, tucking them into his gun belt, and held out a hand to her. Rain pelted them both. She knew as she reached out to take his hand and looked into fathomless black eyes that on some deep, instinctive level she trusted this man.

He didn't say a word as he opened the door and ushered her in before him to the hotel desk.

"Sorry, we're full up—"

"Harold, I need a room."

Domini saw the flustered look of the desk clerk when Luke reached over and spun the register around.

"You never stay in town on Saturday night, Luke."

"I'm here tonight."

"If you're just looking for a place for a few hours, I work all—"

"Harold, you ain't writin' no newspaper. An' room six is no longer occupied by Lagen. Don't bother going up. I'll explain to him."

"But he just checked in. . . ." Harold Doverville's voice trailed off. He wasn't about to argue with Luke. He didn't like arguing with anyone. If Luke wanted to dispossess one of the Gold Bar C hands, that was his business.

"Send up some hot water." Luke glanced at her. "Make that later, Harold. Much later."

"You can't do this." Domini would have said more, but the cynical twist of his lips silenced her. She had her first look at him in the light. His hair, the little she could see of it beneath his hat, was as black as her own. There was a scar on his right cheekbone, a jagged mark that hadn't been stitched before healing. His eyes were for a woman to lose herself in, and against the sudden racing of her heart she heard a warning.

Abruptly he headed for the stairs, carrying her bag. Domini took one step, then another. There was no choice. All the doubts she'd had about coming here surfaced, but as she climbed the stairs behind him, the certainty that she could trust him returned.

"Wait here." His order was given in the same soft voice he had used all the while. She glanced down at her bag, which he had set beside her, leaned against the wall of the dimly lit hall, and closed her eyes.

"Lagen. Lagen, open the door. It's Luke." He had to repeat it twice before the sounds of swearing revealed that the man had heard him.

Domini did not open her eyes when she heard Luke's order for him to get his gear and leave. The protest from Lagen that he had a woman with him brought Luke's suggestion that Harold had offered his room for a few hours. She didn't want to see the knowing looks of the man and the woman with him as they left.

She sensed his nearness, although he hadn't made a sound. There were his scents that she had marked without knowing, of damp leather and horse, of whiskey and smoke, of power. All masculine. All intriguing. The rain slashed against the window at the far end of the hall, and she heard its force drumming on the roof. The room would be dry and, once she explained his mistake about her, safe. Domini went inside.

Luke had lit the lamp and stood holding the still smoking match. "I want to see you in the light." He saw the delicate twitch of her nose as she caught the reek of sex and liquor from the tangle of sheets on the bed. Luke walked past her to close the door, securing it with a straight chair wedged beneath the handle.

"Are you giving me a choice?"

"About the light? Sure. It's the only one." He

came to stand behind her. But he didn't touch her. Not yet.

"You're wrong about me."

"You're not a woman? Fooled me but good," he whispered, smelling the rain that mingled with her clean scent. She stepped away and reflex made him grip the end of the shawl, stripping it and whirling her around to face him.

Straight and smooth, her ebony hair was coiled in a thick knot at the base of her neck. "These have to go." He reached out for the combs and pins. Hunger to taste her lips made him catch her head between his hands, dragging her close.

Domini went still as his fingers touched the delicate flesh just behind her ears. She was suddenly afraid to move, afraid she would lose the shimmering anticipation that trembled to life. It was not submission to his greater strength. His eyes bore into hers, drawing her into his need. There was a natural hard edge to his temptingly handsome features that whispered of hunger and darker passions. Hard-edged, yes, and filled with a simmering promise of danger.

"I've wanted to touch you from the moment I saw you," he murmured.

Domini closed her eyes and saw again his face in the match's flare against the night. Something wild inside her cut loose from its mooring. Shocking, dizzying longing to answer the hunger in him intensified with the slow brush of his body against hers. Stormy excitement rose, each sensation sharp and exquisite. His mouth was closing over hers, and she had her first taste of a man's hunger. It would be so easy to stop him. She had to stop him. But her will, that indomitable strength of will that helped her survive, was dissolving with the emotions colliding inside her.

The generous shape of her mouth was soft beneath his. *Soft enough to ease a man's pain.* Luke rejected the thought even as it formed. There was nothing soft in him. Not anymore. There was only a need to know her mouth, to savor its taste and feed the sweet, hot ache that filled him. He'd think later about the strange yearning for her mouth. Luke had never kissed any woman, whore or lady. He had thought it an intimacy that gave away too much of himself. But he wanted her kiss. There was no soft, coaxing touches—he captured her lips with his, and felt her explosive answering need meet his demand.

Domini let his kiss take her on a wild, potent ride for long moments. He was a storm, flooding her with a torrent of emotions that had no names. Their harsh breaths mingled like the rush of the wind in a dizzying force around them. But she could not let this be.

Luke pressed his body to hers, his tongue delving deep in her mouth, passion a hot, driving force that took him right to the edge. His hips ground against her softness and for seconds before she struggled, he was aware of the pliant yield of her body against his. Her hand slid around his waist, the move a warning flare, but she rocked her hips and he thought she was trying to climb into his skin.

It was seconds before he realized that the cold press on the side of his neck was his own knife blade. He eased his mouth from hers but didn't move. "Honey, you just made the biggest mistake of your life."

"No. It's you who made the mistake. And"—she pressed her point home with knife tip and words—"your life that's at risk." She knew how awkward her position was. He could easily twist away and be free. There was no time to think, or be weak. "I'm not what you think. I tried to tell you—"

"Like hell you ain't." He saw within the darkened green of her eyes that she would use his knife on him. Her hand wasn't shaking, only her lower lip gave a betraying quiver. Luke brought his arm down hard, slamming into the crook of her elbow, and twisted free. She didn't release the knife. It ripped down his shirt, blood welling to fill the long cut.

"You bitch!" The words were without heat, but then the heat had disappeared and cold fury had replaced it.

"No! I'm protecting myself. You think I'm a whore for sale. I'm not." She backed away from the murderous look on his face, knowing the knife against his gun offered no protection at all. The brass bedstead brought her up short.

"You're not?" he repeated. "Like hell. You trotted after me willingly enough back on the street. Do I look like some fool samaritan ready to pay for a room and not get something in return?"

Domini remained very still, studying him. "No, you don't look anything like a samaritan. But I believe there is good in everyone and—"

"Never mind! If you're not Matt Colfax's whore, then who the hell are you?"

He made no move to stanch the blood dripping down his arm, or to take the knife from her. Domini couldn't help herself. "You should wrap your arm," she whispered, wary and holding the knife out before her.

"The hell with my arm. Answer me. Who the hell are you?"

"I don't know Matt. Toma Colfax sent for me. I'm Dominica Kirkland."

"The devil you say." Luke shook his head, staring at her with disbelief. "Kirkland? You're Jim Kirkland's wife?"

"No. My mother is dead. I'm his daughter."

He threw back his head, flooding the small room with laughter. There was no joy, no welcome at all when he ceased abruptly and looked at her. "Welcome to hell."

# Chapter Two

❧

It wasn't a welcome at all, and Domini didn't mistake it for one. She wanted to deny the absolute certainty in his voice, but couldn't do that, either. But she could use this as an opening to have some of her questions answered.

"You sound very sure of that. Why? What is it that you know? Who are you really?"

"I do know exactly what I'm talking about. That's all you need to know. You bought yourself a ticket to hell."

His look was forbidding and Domini heeded it. Her questions would have to wait a while longer. But she could not just stand there and let him bleed.

"Hell might be where you'll head if you don't take care of that arm."

Luke glanced at the bleeding wound, then back at her. "I've had worse and survived." He eyed her wary stance, the way she still held the knife. It wouldn't stop him, but she didn't know that. She didn't know him at all. And from the anxious way she questioned him, he was for keeping it that way.

With her shawl gone, the lush curves of her body were revealed despite the high-necked gown. As quickly as the cold fury had come, it left him. The heat was back, and with it the need to take her down beneath him until he had his fill of the wildness he had tasted. Nor did it make sense that he was having this strong a reaction to her.

Drink had only blurred the edges for him; boredom still ranked high. That might explain it. He didn't often give in to curiosity, but it bothered him that she didn't react to what he had said.

"You heard me, didn't you? You've put yourself in hell's own caldron coming here."

"Have I?" Domini refused to let him see how much his words disturbed her. Her gaze skimmed over the jagged scar on his right cheek. *"I've survived worse."* She didn't doubt it.

"I've already explained that I was sent for."

"Yeah, right. Stolen letter. Stolen money."

"You don't believe me." She didn't ask it, so she was not surprised that he ignored her. "Just so you know, I've learned to be a survivor, too."

She saw his dark eyes, as black as the thick, wavy hair that brushed the collar of his coal dark shirt, narrow. A frightening shiver of awareness coursed through her.

Taking his time, he let his gaze drift down from

her green eyes, straight nose, expressive, generously shaped lips to her hair. The plain dark blue gown with its long sleeves was travel-stained and confirmed his earlier thought that she wasn't wearing a corset. His attention lingered on the flare of her hips before he looked back at her face.

"I'll just bet you have."

With a tension burning like fox fire, a charged silence filled the room. Domini knew her strength, and it was ebbing quickly. She was desperate to distract him from another bold pursuit.

"If you won't take care of that arm, let me."

"Feeling guilty? First rule of a survivor, honey. Don't have pity for anyone."

"I couldn't live that way."

"Then you won't survive."

"Your arm?"

"What the hell makes you think I'd trust you? Take a peek in the looking glass, innocent. Your eyes give you away. You'd as soon as cut me again as take another breath."

"No. You're wrong about me. Again." Even as she spoke, Domini shifted her hold on the knife, balancing the blade between her fingertips. She brought her arm back to throw the knife. His look was level and challenging. He didn't move or flinch, didn't take those black, fathomless eyes from hers.

There was little risk to her. He couldn't know that she had a knife of her own. Perhaps the gesture was foolish, certainly dramatic to prove him wrong—although she didn't understand why it mattered to her—but she threw the knife.

The blade whistled close to Luke's head before landing with a solid *thunk* in the door behind him. "Nice throw. But the wrong move. What's to stop me now?"

His overpowering maleness filled the room. Domini had to reach behind her to brace herself by gripping the bedstead. His voice held a low-pitched timbre of sensuality that stroked her. She didn't understand what was happening between them. She listened to an instinct that warned her to be still.

"Forget it. It was a good throw. You plannin' on using a knife on Toma?"

The breath she had been holding escaped her lungs with a swift release of tension. "Why would I want to kill him? I told you he sent for me."

"Funny how I keep forgetting that. Maybe it's because I know him and you don't."

"Then tell me!"

"I only paid for the room for one night. And it wasn't to waste time talking about him."

She bowed her head for a few seconds, allowing this second refusal to talk about Toma to stand.

"There's whiskey left in the bottle on the chest."

Domini looked at him. Anxious to be done with feeling pinned in place, she released her grip on the bed. She wanted to make amends for cutting him. Starting for the chest, she faltered when the knife sailed by to land in the center of the top drawer.

"Just so you know I favor my left hand but there's nothing wrong with my right."

She whirled and faced him. "Don't you trust anyone? I gave up the weapon to defend myself. Didn't that prove anything to you?" *God, forgive the small lie. It is one of my necessary ones.*

"Like I said. Look at yourself, honey. You've got a regular army's arsenal of weapons to use."

"No." She went quickly to the chest, levered the knife out of the wood, and grabbed hold of the bottle. "Sit on the bed and I'll clean that up."

When she turned, he was already sitting near the headboard. She shook her head. She had not heard a sound.

"You told the clerk to bring up hot water. I'll tell him we need—"

"Don't bother. The whiskey is enough."

She came toward him slowly, masking her fear of being too close, of touching him again because of the feelings he stirred to life. Thrusting the bottle at him, Domini looked at his face.

"I'll use the knife to cut away the shirt. If you can't trust me, say so. You can do it yourself."

Before she realized his intent, he had his right hand on her hip, pulling her into the V of his thighs. He lifted the bottle, tore the cork out with his teeth, and spat it aside.

"First one's for me. You can use the rest of it."

Domini set to work quickly. She cut away the

ripped sleeve, feeling the buttery soft linen weave. The hand-stitched seams showed exquisite work, expensive work, and she wondered again who he was. She removed the material as gently as she could, trying not to think about the heat of his body that surrounded her. Her gaze remained on his arm, but she felt him watching her face.

He lifted the bottle for another drink just as she stepped away. His fingers tightened for a moment, then slid down the flare of her hip and over her thigh.

"I'll get something clean from my bag to wash it with."

"Bet it's something soft, virginal, and white."

"How did—" She stopped herself the moment she saw the knowing look in his eyes and the cocky grin on his lips. He had tricked her into the admission, and there was no point in trying to deny it now. Her carpet bag held a choice of two sets of drawers and chemises. Both had been worn during her journey. There was the new nightgown that the nuns at the mission had made as a parting gift for her.

Domini had no choice. Working with Sister Benedict among the poor of the village had shown her how important cleanliness was for proper healing of all wounds.

Luke figured there wasn't much in her bag. There'd been no heavy weight, and the way she opened it and rose moments later with something white in her hand told him he was right. Soft and virginal. He took another sip of the whiskey as she laid the nightgown on the bed beside him.

Without a word Domini opened the seam on one side with the knife, and set about cutting a good portion of the hem off all the way around. Once she had two pieces, she took the bottle and soaked one cloth, standing outside the spread of his legs.

"Don't you trust me?"

"I'm still here. Now, hold still. You know this will sting."

She bit her lower lip, begging for forgiveness from the Lord for having caused the wound she quickly cleaned. She was uneasy with the truth of his observation about her, uneasy with the way he watched her, uneasy with touching the warmth of his flesh. His skin was dusky, nearly as golden as her own.

The cut ran from behind his smooth, muscled shoulder to nearly his elbow. She hadn't realized that she had stroked him with a trembling hand until he spoke.

"Curious, are you?"

Domini snatched her hand away. She cut the remaining piece of cloth into strips, hesitating a few seconds before she made herself start to wrap his arm.

Bending over to catch the cloth end behind his arm, she felt the weight of her hair slip free. She closed her eyes briefly.

"Why?"

"I wanted to see it down." Luke tucked the empty bottle between his legs and gathered up a handful of her hair. It was heavy as satin, black as night, and smooth as silk. "Take down the rest of it."

"No." She whirled away, one hand reaching out to tug her hair free. "I'll finish the bandage, but you must promise not to touch me again."

Both their glances went to the knife lying on the bed.

Luke looked up first. "Or?"

His expression was tense, waiting, and when she didn't immediately answer him, it changed, communicating a desire so intense she caught her breath.

"Would it give you pleasure to take from me?"

"I'm not Toma Colfax. I don't *take* unwilling women. Finish my arm."

She knew the danger had passed. Still, she hesitated.

"I don't bite."

Her gaze went to his mouth, to the white teeth that flashed in a grin.

"All right."

Luke waited until she was beside him. He dug the fingers of his right hand into the mattress's edge. "That is, I don't bite unless you do first."

Her fingers were clumsy tying off the bandage. She repeated his words to herself, then wondered if they were true. Her loose hair fell like a curtain between them as she gathered up her nightgown and fled to replace it in the carpet bag.

When she rose and glanced at him, he had stretched out on the bed. One hand rested beneath his head. "It will be best if I sleep here, on the floor."

"Suit yourself. There's plenty of room here."

Eyeing the space between his body and the wall, Domini shook her head. "There's room, but not safety."

"If safety's what you're after," he noted softly, "you've come to the wrong place for it."

"I'd like my hairpins and comb back."

He ignored her outstretched hand. "Answer me."

Her hand fell to her side and she shook the loose hair back. "Toma Colfax sent for me. He's been kindness—"

"Kindness? Toma? The man wouldn't know kindness if it sat up and bit his ass, honey. You can't be talking about the Toma I know."

"Because you see darkness in everyone, you expect others to do the same?"

"Because I *know* that bastard." He began to realize he'd had it all wrong. It wasn't Matt, but the old man who'd brought her here. Intended to take her onto Gold Bar C land. Into *her* house. His gaze was cutting. Jim Kirkland's daughter? After all this time? It didn't make sense. And Toma always had a purpose for everything he did.

But Luke understood that he had made a mistake with her. She wasn't going to tell him more unless he changed his way of asking.

"If you're gonna insist on sleeping on the floor, take the blanket from the bed. I never use one."

"I've done without before."

"From all you've said, I gather you haven't had an easy time of it."

Domini nodded, then walked to pick up her shawl. She wrapped it around her shoulders and returned to her place near the door. Knowing that he was watching her made her awkward as she sat with her back against the door.

"Will you tell me where you met Toma?"

"I've never met the man. Over the past ten years he's paid for my keep at the mission of San Gabriel."

"Paid for your keep?" He'd have sworn that she was lying, but her gaze met his, as level and direct as any man's. Yet the doubt was hard to bury.

"It was only a few weeks ago that I found out about him. Sister Benedict showed me his letter demanding that I come here before taking the vows of a novice."

He didn't make the mistake of telling her it would be a waste to see her locked in a convent. He remained very still, waiting as she was waiting. He'd made the right choice, for she continued.

"At first I didn't want to come, but Sister reminded me that I owed him so much that to refuse was wrong. And he was my father's friend."

"Toma doesn't have friends. The man counts his enemies and owns everyone else."

"If you bear such dislike for him, why do you work for him?"

"That's likely Harold with the hot water I ordered."

Domini threw him a startled glance. Then she also heard the footsteps coming down the hall. She rose quickly, stepping back and away from the door.

"He'll think—"

"He doesn't get paid to think. Just open the door."

Domini did as he ordered. Harold stood holding a bucket of steaming water in one hand, soap in the other, with washcloths and towels folded over his arm. She set the bucket inside the door, took the other things from him, whispered her thanks, and closed the door.

The cool air from the hall had chilled the room. She once again listened to the sound of the rain. It was softer now, but her gaze locked on the steaming water.

"Go ahead. Use it."

She looked at the washbowl and pitcher on the chest. Tempted, Domini slowly shook her head. "If you'd like to wash, I'll pour the water into the bowl for you."

He lifted his wounded arm. "Ain't much chance I'd manage. Now, if you were to do the honors, I'd consider it."

Bending over, she dipped her fingers into the water. "It's hot."

"So am I."

"Hot enough to scald a man if it were flung at him."

"You or the water, honey?"

"I thought you wouldn't bite unless I bit first?" But the words were no sooner spoken than another, deep shiver of sensual awareness flooded her.

His gaze swept her from toe to head. Her cheeks hinted of color beneath the golden skin. "You don't know, do you?"

"Know what?"

Luke felt gut-punched. She watched him with a combination of innocence and curiosity. She had the kind of willowy, long-legged body that made his blood run hot and thick. Solemn eyes met his returning gaze. And in them he saw confusion. He wanted to unpin the other coil of her hair, then wrap the wealth of black silk over his body.

He remembered watching her enjoy the coming storm and felt the fierce hunger that had swept his body. He ran the tip of his tongue over his lip, tasting the soft, explosive heat of her mouth again. His fingers tightened over the mussed sheets beneath him. He felt himself harden as he had in the seconds she had been pliant against him, rocking her hips against his, the seconds before she pulled his knife on him.

His head burrowed deeper against the pillow. "Christ!" he muttered. "You don't know. But I do."

When she realized he wasn't going to continue, she came nearer the bed. "If you know, then tell me what it is so I won't do—"

"Honey," he stated coldly, harshly, lifting himself up on one elbow and wincing from the pain. "I'm not gonna *tell* you anything. But I'll show you right quick if you don't stay the hell away from me."

She spun around, ready to run, then heard him groan. A glance over her shoulder revealed him lying on the bed, his eyes closed. She felt the tension seep out of her. She had to trust her own instincts to be right. Whatever it was had passed. He would leave her be now.

Only the thought of being in a strange place without any money and a chilling rain falling kept her there.

She watched the rise and fall of his chest, fascinated by the sense of power that came from him even at rest. There was a masculine grace to his big body. She stared at his scuffed boots, the frayed edges of his pants, the muscular legs, narrow waist and shoulders broad enough to carry whatever burdens the Lord sent his way.

Her gaze returned to his narrow hips and the gun belt he still wore. She had a feeling it was never far from his hand. Seeing the stark bandage on his arm brought the appalling realization that she had cut him.

Rubbing her arms, Domini turned away and was again tempted by the curls of steam that rose from the bucket of water.

She sniffed the soap, surprised to find it faintly scented with pine. Turning the bar over in her hands, she knew this wasn't the coarse milled soap that the nuns at the mission favored.

Darting a glance at the bed, and the man in it, she knelt on the floor and opened the top few buttons of her gown. Wetting, then soaping the cloth, she sighed at the first touch of heat to her skin. With one hand she held her loose hair to the side, slipping the wet cloth inside the gown.

It wasn't enough. She could smell her own musky odor. Tomorrow would see her arrival at the end of her journey. It was bad enough that she couldn't clean her clothes before she met her benefactor for the first time. But she didn't need to meet him smelling like a hundred-mile journey either.

Luke hadn't moved. There was only the even sound of his breathing. From the spot where she knelt, she could see the lower portion of his body. She set the washcloth on the rim of the bucket and slid the comb and pins from her hair. Shaking it free down her back, she used its thick, concealing curtain to open her gown to her waist, then slid the long sleeves off.

It wasn't the bath she longed for, but it would have to do. *Listen to yourself, going on about a bath when there were weeks that water didn't touch your skin. When you had no clean clothes to wear. When hunger cramped your belly and you couldn't close your eyes for fear of having the rats bite you. And if the threat of rats wasn't enough, there were worse animals to keep you sleepless.*

A cold trembling overcame her. She knew it was her exhaustion that allowed those fears of long ago to surface.

Hurrying now to finish, she nevertheless took the time to fix her bodice before lifting her skirt. It was awkward at best, trying to wash and remain decently covered at the same time, but Domini managed to her satisfaction.

When she was done, she rose and carried the bucket to the corner close to the chest. She reached up to lower the wick until the light went out.

Settled near the door, wrapped in her shawl and using her carpet bag for a pillow, she closed her eyes.

And from the darkness came Luke's sensual, husky whisper:

"You were right. Hot enough to scald a man."

Domini didn't answer him. But she was shocked by the soft, deep explosion that rocked through her.

"Don't lose any sleep over it, honey. We'll leave at first light. I can't wait to see what other surprises you have in store for me."

It was both a challenge and a threat whispered in a room alive with a dark, dangerous, shimmering excitement.

# Chapter Three

❧

"I can't ride a horse."

"You what!"

Shivering in the pre-dawn chill, Domini repeated it. With sunrise still a good hour away, she couldn't make out Luke's features as they stood in the yard in front of the livery. She glanced at the lantern lit and hanging near the stable doors, but its light didn't reach them.

Her eyes had the gritty feel of having had sand rubbed in them. She hadn't slept well. Luke's last words to her had preyed on her mind. *Well, he shouldn't be complaining then, for here was another of her surprises for him.*

"Well, ya want the mare or not, Luke?"

Luke shot a murderous glare at Aloysius Fraser. The man was obvious in his enjoyment. He stood scratching his belly through the gaping hole of his union suit. Snapping his suspenders, Aloysius began whistling. While it annoyed Luke that he was enjoying this, at least it was a change from the man's grumbling for the past two hours since Luke had woken him.

Restlessness and a throbbing in his arm had sent Luke out of the room so early. He had intended to surprise her with his choice of a young, spirited sorrel with a gentle mouth and the intelligence not to shy from his grulla. Devil stood nearly seventeen hands of raw, muscled power, tame enough when led by a halter, but let anyone but Luke get on his back and the horse was dynamite and fury.

A real surprise package, as more than a few men had found out. But Luke was being given a surprise of his own as Domini sighed and repeated again that she couldn't ride a horse.

His own words came back to haunt him. He couldn't wait to see what other surprises she had in store for him.

"Luke? Couldn't we rent a buckboard? I'm sure that Mr. Colfax would reimburst you."

*"Mr. Colfax? Pay you?"* Aloysius's laughter turned to a fit of coughing, and Luke slapped his back so hard that the man stumbled.

"Luke? Did I say something wrong?"

"No." The word was curt, sharply bitten off. Luke felt that soft voice of hers, husky with sleep, liquid with warmth, sizzle through him like lightning.

"Everything has to be packed in by mules to reach the Gold Bar C. There's no way to use a wagon. You want to get there, you ride. Now, you've got the choice of gettin' on that horse an' coming with me, or stayin'." He slapped the rein ends into her hands.

"We had mules at the mission," she said with an eager note that more than hinted she would prefer one.

"Ain't one to be had. An' that's a fact," Aloysius answered. "Mule's worth his weight in gold. On account of the miner's needing 'em."

"Oh." Domini tried to tell herself that her fear was foolish, but fear, she had learned, could not be easily explained away at times. Unfortunately, this was one of those times.

Luke's growing impatience reached out to her as she struggled to find another solution. Looking from Luke to his horse's powerful built, she voiced her thought.

"Couldn't we ride together on yours?"

If he had suddenly turned to stone, Luke couldn't have been more still. Put her up on Devil? Torture himself? In his mood, he'd likely set her up in that saddle facing him and slide his aching flesh into that sweet body that didn't know when to quit teasing a man. *But she doesn't know what she does to you.*

"Luke?"

"No."

His curt refusal left her no choice. Domini glanced at the leather she held, then at the mare who had craned her head to lip her shawl-clad arm. Stroking the white blaze on the horse's face, she nodded acceptance of his terms, then realized that he wasn't looking at her.

"All right. I'll try. I only ask that you be patient with me."

"Sure."

"And since I can't ride, you'll have to help me, Luke."

*Help her? He was the one who needed help.*

"Luke, you'll need to teach me what to do."

He was still imagining the smooth, gliding ride Devil would give them. He'd like to teach her how to ride. Him, or the damn horse.

"If you were so set on leaving a few minutes ago, why won't you help me up now?"

"I will." But he took his time sliding on his leather gloves before he turned to face her. "Lift your arms and put your hands on my shoulders," he ordered, setting his hands on her waist beneath the shawl. Even through the leather he could feel how little cloth separated him from warm skin.

"Spread your legs." He lifted her, swearing that his words came out a soft, dark, sensual command. She wasn't supposed to react with a trembling awareness that coiled around him. She wasn't supposed to smell faintly of sweet pine, or catch her breath when he repeated his order.

"Spread you legs, Domini, or I'll do it for you." Without a sound he bore the bite of her fingers digging into his shoulders, sending a shooting pain down his arm as he set her on the saddle.

He'd made the stirrups too short. To adjust them he'd have to touch her again. She'd asked him for patience, and Luke didn't think he had any left. He looked up at her and let out a long breath of cynical acceptance.

"Bend your knee." While he worked the strap, lowering the stirrup, he distracted himself by thinking that he had made a good choice of the sorrel. The mare stood quietly, as if she sensed her rider's fear. Reaching for Domini's foot, Luke's hand slid up the supple hide of her moccasin, and he found out that not everything about her was soft. There was strength in her calf, and while he'd never walked when he could ride, he knew that wasn't true about her.

Once he'd adjusted the other stirrup, he took the reins from her hands. He lifted her bare hand to the saddle horn, and before he thought about it, he stripped off his gloves.

"Put these on. Hang onto the horn and leave the rest to me."

The cutting edge in his voice brooked no argument. Domini swallowed. Once, twice, harder each time. She was trying to rid herself of the anger that rose with every bite he took out of her. *No, don't think about that.* It wasn't her fault she'd had no horse to ride. He had no reason to make her feel as if she had committed some unpardonable sin.

He had likely learned to ride before he could walk. Damn him! *No. Lord, forgive me for that.*

The strength of her anger shocked her. She had learned to control her temper. The lesson had been difficult, but with the nun's help, long talks with Sister Benedict, hours of prayer, and enough penitent tasks, she had thought she had accomplished it.

Luke made a mockery of her belief. She wanted to snap back in kind, but she held her tongue.

The supple leather gloves were still warm from touching his skin. Domini put them on, hoping he would move away from her. The gloves were too large, but he didn't seem to care.

She maintained her rigid posture as he secured her carpet bag with the strips of hide hanging from the saddle. The mere brush of his chest against her leg was enough to set off the tiny tremors that she couldn't seem to control around him.

And he knew it. He had to, she decided, feeling the curve of his fingers over her calf, but with his touch she in turn felt the increased anger and tension rolling off him.

Using every bit of her formidable strength of will, Domini refused to look at him, refused to give in to the need to talk to him. But when he moved away to his horse, she couldn't take her gaze from him as he stepped into his saddle with a smooth, fluid grace. Maybe she had been wrong. Luke had not learned to ride before he could walk. The man appeared to have been born in a saddle. She chided herself for the petty thought.

"Ready?" he called back, and without waiting for her answer, he neck-reined the grulla to move out of the livery yard.

Luke barely resisted the urge to set his heels into Devil's sides to ride out the restless wildness he couldn't shake. He wasn't insensitive to the fact that if she hadn't lied to him about not knowing how to ride, she'd be sore as a throbbing toothache after an hour in the saddle.

He had throbbing of his own to contend with, so he kept the grulla to a walk, feeling Aloysius's speculative gaze follow them. Before one Gold Bar C hand headed for home, he'd hear talk about Luke and the woman. He wondered if the old man would have apoplexy knowing that he'd snatched her from under his nose.

Dominica Kirkland was a trusting fool. But that didn't stop him from casting a quick look over his shoulder at her. With regret he'd noticed that she had already coiled and pinned that glorious mane of hair up by the time he'd returned to the room. He could have told her that her rigid seat was going to be hell on her body. He already knew she could move like a blade of grass bending to the wind.

"Sit easy," he yelled at her. "Move with the horse, not against her. You'll be stiff as a corpse by afternoon. And then I'll have to touch you again to take you down." He shot her another look. "We both know you don't want that to happen, do you?"

Domini didn't answer him. She tried to do as he said, but it was a long way to the ground.

As if he knew she hadn't obeyed him, Luke called out again. "You'll learn. A damn painful lesson, too. One I might find pleasin', but you sure as hell won't."

That low-pitched timbre of sensuality underscored his words, and Domini reacted with a curl of warmth stroking through her.

The threat had released some of his tension, although Luke couldn't figure out why. He was ready to make the reluctant admission that he admired the way she controlled her fear. He couldn't say the same for other young women that got hauled by overanxious parents to the ranch.

The Mayfields' daughters, Bonnie Sue and Patty—a bookworm and a giggler, would have been whining by now. Netta and Maude Warren had the mistaken idea that their timidity appealed to a man. And Celia Tanner, with the rigid code her mother imposed on her, would never have found herself riding out alone with any man.

If Luke believed he had a conscience, what he felt would have been a prick to one. He hadn't given her time to eat. He wouldn't have minded a cup of Molly's black brew himself. His saddlebags were already packed with the supplies he had bought yesterday before the grulla had thrown a shoe.

He had told her last night that he didn't think she had had an easy time of it. But he wondered now how many times she had gone hungry. He was no stranger to the hollow, empty feeling. But he'd been too young, too stupid to understand what defiance earned him. He couldn't even explain to himself what kept drawing him back to that mountain ranch time and again, hoping things had changed. They never had.

It was in the past, the far past, and it remained buried like the nightmares that sometimes plagued him because he'd wake shaking with a cold sweat and never remember what they were about.

He took a bracing breath of cool mountain air. He'd taken her out so early simply not to share her with anyone.

And he didn't need another slip like the one Aloysius had made. She had no idea how ironic her remark was that Toma Colfax would reimburse him for expenses. The old man was likely to take another piece of his hide for interfering with his plans.

He wanted to avoid thinking what those plans might be. If Toma had made them, there couldn't be any good to come from them.

Christ! She was an innocent and he, the bastard, more than ready to lead her. Lamb to slaughter. Dominica Kirkland to the Gold Bar C. It was all one and the same. Why had Toma raked up the past by bringing Jim Kirkland's daughter here?

Instinct said she didn't know why Toma had sent for his old partner's sole heir. The greedy bastard couldn't be thinking of giving her a share of the mine claims or the land their gold had bought.

Toma never gave anything away. He sold things. It was a lesson that Luke never forgot. And Toma's prices were steep. He had to own you body and soul.

He recalled her telling him that she had wanted to take vows and become a nun. She'd need her faith and the Lord at her back to survive Toma's brand of deviltry. He knew it wasn't a fanciful term to describe Toma. The man had been born in hell, raised by and forever guided by the devil himself. Him and his wife.

And Matt? Who could figure which way Matt would bend? That he would benefit from whatever choice he made was a foregone conclusion. Matt was for Matt, first, last, and always. Luke had swallowed that bitter knowledge a long time ago, too.

He allowed the horses to pick their own way over the rock-strewn trail. They were heading for high country, a place where he felt at home. The sky was already breaking the night's hold, turning pale in the far distance. He wondered if Domini would find the same peace that filled him in this land.

This time he didn't bother to look back, just settled himself deeper in the saddle. Time would give him all the answers he needed, and maybe a few he didn't want.

Domini shivered as the morning's chill lingered.

She was used to a burning rising sun that brought unbearable heat to sear land and flesh alike.

She was feeling the ache of her spread thighs. Holding onto the high saddle horn with one hand, she used the other to tuck more skirt beneath her legs. Within the soft, supple skin of her moccasins, her toes curled with tension as she pressed down on the stirrups.

"Do we have far to ride?" she called out.

Until that moment Luke hadn't really made up his mind. He urged Devil off the wide trail and into the lodgepole pine forest. "Two or three days if we're lucky. Depends on the weather."

"Two or three days?" she repeated.

Her gaze swept the tall, thin trunks of pine trees and rose straight as ship's masts. Their yellow-green branches curved upward at the tips. Cones were clustered at the ends, surrounded by a tight bundle of reddish knots. The growth was dense, so crowded that the branches were entangled from one tree to another.

The sound of the horses was muted here. She forced herself to look down at the thickly carpeted ground. Brown pine needles soaked up noise, and she felt as if they were alone in the world.

The sudden ripple of bird cries through the pines startled her. She hadn't realized she had made a sound until Luke spoke.

"What you're hearing is the warblers and—"

"That *whee-twee* noise?"

"Yeah. And the jays. Whatever happens, never

cry out like that. You never know what animals might be around. And they don't all have four legs."

"I'll remember." Birds? She'd been frightened of small birds? The repeated *klak-klak* made her seek out the bird that sounded as raucous as the old village women at market. The noise was unpleasant, but Domini smiled when she caught sight of the rich blue plumage and ebony crest of the jay gliding from one tree branch to another above them.

"And the trees, Luke, what are they called?"

He drew rein and the mare stepped up close to the grulla. "These are lodgepole pines, named because the Indians use them as the lodgepole for their tepees."

In a deliberate move, he crowded the mare. "I told you to keep your voice down. You keep your questions till we make camp, and even then you wait for my word. Voices carry. You don't want trouble, you don't invite it. I'd have a time protecting you if we get jumped."

"Jumped? I'm not a mining claim."

"Honey, where we're heading you're worth your weight in gold." His gaze roamed over her, and the ache that had barely subsided rose with double force. He was tempted, so damn tempted, to sweep her off the mare and show her the kind of trouble she courted in a man.

The small hitch in her breathing told her she was very aware of the danger she faced. Luke backed Devil away from her. "Just remember what I said."

"Yes. This time I will." Two or three days alone with him? Alone with a man whose heated touch set off a storm of seething emotions she couldn't name and couldn't control? Domini glanced at the darkly clad body ahead of her. She was riding off alone with a man who wanted her, made no effort to disguise it, and was angry that he did.

The hunger she had been feeling disappeared as fear took hold. Knowledge settled in its place like a cold, hard knot in her belly.

*Had her instincts been wrong? Had she made a terrible mistake in trusting him?*

# Chapter Four

❧

Matthew Colfax listened to the masculine laughter appreciating his father's brag that the only pleasure they could find missing from his office on the Gold Bar C was an accommodating woman.

He smiled with the rest of them as Toma led the way inside and wondered what their reaction would be if he told them what he had learned late this morning. Luke was back. After five months of no word, he'd been seen in Florence last night. Matt wasn't about to share that information with these men, least of all his father, but he knew laughter wouldn't greet the announcement.

Matt had to agree with his father's assessment of the room. But he couldn't watch Toma swig down another glass of the raw whiskey he still insisted was the only drink for a man.

One corner of the room was dominated by a

card table with places for five chairs. Any more, Toma declared, and a poker game lost its edge.

The floor-to-ceiling book-lined walls boasted the fortune he'd spent on books. It was a shame that their leather bindings had never been opened. Red cedar paneling had come from the trees felled on their land, milled by Colfax saws and installed by a small army of carpenters that Toma had personally hired on a trip to Seattle.

Butter-soft leather chairs built to take a man's weight were quickly filled by the same men who gathered for these monthly Sunday suppers with their sons.

The company would be pleasant enough, the aromas rich as cigars and cigarettes were lit to satisfied murmurs, and the thickness of the wood insured that no words spoken here would pass these walls.

Matt poured himself a brandy from Waterford crystal, and slipped his gold pocket watch from his vest pocket. He'd remain an hour and no more. Supper had been the same long, leisurely meal it always was. Lavish praise had been politely whispered to both Josie, their housekeeper, and Ellamay, the cook, as they left the dining room.

From the belches released the moment the doors had been closed behind the men as the women continued down the hall to his mother's gold and white drawing room, Matt didn't doubt that the compliments were sincere. Toma enjoyed playing host. He was generous with his hospitality.

But Matt knew why. It made him feel powerful, and power was the only thing that mattered to his father.

Matt couldn't quite figure out what these monthly suppers meant to his mother. With her sharp tongue that was quick to criticize and slow to praise, he knew she thought herself above the wives and daughters of the men liberally indulging in the liquor that Mr. O'Malley served.

Matt refused to have his glass topped by the bandy-legged Irishman who had come west with a younger son of Irish gentry hoping to make his fortune in the gold fields and ending up dead over a questionable poker hand.

Toma had been present, and promptly hired the man to work for him. Matt wouldn't have been surprised to learn that his father had done the questioning and the shooting that followed. When Toma wanted something, he went after it. Nothing and no one was allowed to stand in his way.

At twenty-eight Matt was the oldest of the sons in the room, Frank and Marty, sons of Martin Mayfield, a man whose wealth in mining and land almost equalled Toma's, were both in their mid-twenties. Vincent, at twenty-five, was the oldest of the Warren sons. Sinclair was younger by a year, and Kenneth had just passed his nineteenth birthday.

Moving to stand near the glass-fronted walnut gun case, a recent addition in a room already over-crowded with testaments to his father's wealth,

Matt did what he did best. He watched and he listened.

The talk was general, of yields and stocks, and his gaze roamed the room. No one would claim that Toma did things by halves. Shelves had been cut from the upper levels of the bookcases to display Toma's hunting trophies. Two massive heads of bighorn rams were mounted on opposite walls, side by side with a dozen antlered racks of moose, elk, and white-tailed deer.

His father stood in front of the native stone fireplace, commanding the attention of everyone in the room, one arm resting on the mantel, standing as straight and tall as a lodgepole pine. The gleaming polished black boots were a perfect match for his eyes. A tailor in Boise City custom-made his clothing from the finest materials available. Toma had come a long way from the saddle tramp who couldn't put together a miner's outfit.

Matt glanced at the grizzly bear's skin beneath his father's boots. It lay over the thick Turkish carpet, and a black bear's fur cushioned the boots of Martin Mayfield and his sons where they sat on the long sofa built to accommodate Toma's six-foot height.

Peter Warren was giving a heated accounting of the latest failed attempts by the army to get the Nez Perce Indians to move to the reservation lands at Lapwai. The whole issue bored Matt. It had been going on for over a year. War, he believed, was the only way Chief Joseph would give up his claim that he'd been promised he could move his people to the Umatilla Reservation.

Ray Tanner jumped into the argument of what was to be done to insure their safety. By virtue of his placer miner yielding nuggets worth between fifty to seventy dollars each, Ray had bought up the hotel, café, and freighting line in Florence. Two months ago he had taken title to land that bordered the Gold Bar C, where he was building himself a house and ranch to rival the Colfaxes's. And he was dangling the prospect of marriage to his lovely daughter, Celia, in front of him.

But Matt had his own agenda. It didn't coincide with his father's, but then, they rarely saw eye to eye.

He smiled at the man he hated, the one whose blood ran inside him, and savored the withholding of his news. He knew what Toma's reaction would be if he found out that Luke had been sighted this close to the ranch. He knew it, and he had insured that Toma wouldn't know about Luke.

Not until Matt was good and ready to tell his father.

And he just might wait until hell froze. His smile deepened with the thought. He tossed back his brandy and decided that he would remain and have another drink.

Domini bit back a groan. She wouldn't waste the energy. This was the second time he had called a halt since breakfast. She knew he expected her to get down, and she mentally went over the moves he had made to dismount earlier.

Clinging to the saddle horn with her left hand, she forced the screaming muscles of her right leg in a wide swing over the mare's rump. She grabbed hold of the raised back edge of the saddle seat and hung suspended, unable to kick her left foot free of the stirrup so she could collapse in a heap on the soft, pine-carpeted ground.

Fear streaked through her as the mare side-stepped. She prayed for the strength to force her body to do her bidding and get her out of this awkward position.

The heat of his body warned her how close Luke was before she heard him.

"Useless as teats on a boar."

"Maybe not. A traveling circus would pay handsomely to display a freak of nature."

"Ridin' hasn't curbed your tongue." He slid one arm around her waist. "Let go. I've got you." He took her full weight against him and used his hand to free her foot from the stirrup.

"Your arm," she murmured in protest.

"Hurts like hell's on fire, but I'd bet you're hurting more." He was thankful that she couldn't see him. Her slender waist felt good beneath his arm. He had all he could handle not to slide his hands to her hips and pull her against his thighs, easing and arousing rigid flesh that pressed the black cloth of his pants.

"You'd win, Luke." The smile on her lips at finally being off the horse died. She unconsciously moved closer to the warmth of his body. He'd told her the sun had risen, but within the dim light filtering down through the thick pine branches, Domini couldn't tell.

This time she didn't hold back the groan as he lowered her to her feet. The chafed skin between her thighs burned. From her toes to the small of her back, bones and muscles refused to cooperate and hold her up. The feel of his breath on her bare neck sent shimmering sensations flooding from her breasts to her knees.

The sudden move he made to snatch her off her feet and swing her up into his arms made her cry out.

*"Quiet!"*

She closed her eyes as the world tilted and swirled. She could remember her father picking her up, swinging her around to shrieks of laughter, but she had been a child, not a woman far too conscious of the man who held her in his arms. She turned her face against Luke's muscular chest, her fear of falling eased. Releasing the breath she held, Domini tried to fight the feeling of helplessness. That, too, was a haunting memory from the past she needed to keep buried.

Luke found a deadfall, the trunks nearly three feet wide, and set her down. He stood there, looking at her, absently rubbing his chest where her breath had slid beneath the cloth and warmed his skin.

Domini sighed deeply and looked up at him. "Thank you. I don't think I could have—"

"Save your thanks. I didn't do it for you. The horses needed the rest." Clipped and sharp, his voice echoed the hard look in his eyes. "Rub your legs, then get up and walk. If you want coffee, there's some in my canteen. But you'll have to get it."

She hadn't realized she had already obeyed him to knead her thigh until she followed the lowered direction of his gaze. Just like that, her body was suddenly alive with a quivering, sensual awareness that she couldn't fight. She looked at his hands and knew the strength in those long fingers would have her tight muscles soft and screaming with pleasure, not pain, in minutes. The mere thought of having him touch her sent warmth curling through her. Her hands stilled as she looked up at him again.

"Wasn't the bacon and beans we ate enough for you?"

"What the hell are you talking about?"

"Your look, your voice, Luke. You're tearing strips out of my hide, and I don't know what I've done wrong."

"Back to that?"

"Answer me. If you explain, I'll stop." She stared into his eyes, seeing for herself the flare of hunger within the black depths.

"You gonna stop breathing?" he whispered, " 'cause that's what'll take."

With his abrupt turn she almost called out to stop him. Almost. She had finely honed instincts to protect herself. Teasing a long wolf was not in her best interest. But as she worked her sore muscles as hard as she could, her gaze strayed time and again to where he was stripping off the saddles and rubbing down the horses.

Domini stood up and made herself walk, knowing that he was right. If she didn't keep moving, she would stiffen up just like a corpse. The area wasn't exactly a clearing, for the sun was shut out by the tangled growth above her. The lowest limbs of the sweeping pines were man-high, measured against Luke's height.

She avoided walking near where he stood leaning against a tree, sipping from the canteen. He had made the coffee this morning, thick and black, but despite its bitterness she had welcomed its heat. She wouldn't have minded a little of that warmth now. She realized they were steadily climbing, and the air was thinner and colder.

But she wouldn't go near him. *"Can you stop breathing? 'Cause that's what'll take."* Even silently repeating his words reinforced her decision. Luke would have to wait until the sun stopped rising. She had to find out why she'd been sent for. Sister Benedict had been vague about the reason. She had accepted the nun's word that Toma Colfax had paid for her keep all these years out of friendship for her father. And perhaps that was part of the reason she had agreed to come and meet him.

This was the land that had captivated her father. The land where he had come hunting gold to give them a better life. Only it hadn't worked out. And . . . With an abrupt turn of thought Domini remembered Luke's reaction when she had told him who she was. *"Jim Kirkland's daughter?"*

With a whirling turn that made her wince, she forgot her decision not to go near him. "Luke?" she called, heading for him. "Did you know my father?"

She stopped short a little behind him. He had stood there listening to every whisper of sound that she made, and now he stalled her by handing back the canteen.

"Have some. It's still warm." When she didn't take it immediately, he added, "Bother you to drink from the same canteen?"

"No. No, it doesn't." But as she closed her hand over it, Domini knew she lied. It did bother her, but not the way he meant. Placing her lips where his had been was sharing an intimacy with a man who didn't want any. *Not true. He's made it clear enough that he'll share a far greater intimacy any time you let him.* But Domini countered her own thought. Luke would share his body, but it would be an empty mating. Even animals came together to create life.

Despite the temptation he offered, she had to keep her vow of chastity or she would make a mockery of what she had learned to believe. A rueful smile curved her lips. If Sister Benedict could meet Luke, she wouldn't have instructed her how easy it was to remain chaste. But the gentle-tempered nun was far away, too far to help Domini now.

"Finished?" he asked, still without turning to look at her.

Domini shook the canteen. "There isn't much left. Not that it matters. I want an answer this time, Luke. Did you know my father?"

"I met him." His voice was guarded. "He was real easygoing, and he laughed a lot."

"That's not the answer I wanted."

"Too bad. It's all you're getting. Time to mount up."

She glanced from him to the saddled horses and back again. His forbidding expression challenged her to push him. Domini had learned that pride was a sin, but she summoned every ounce of pride she possessed to walk away from him. She consoled herself with the thought that if she had waited this long for answers about her father, she could wait to meet Toma Colfax to hear them.

She made two attempts to mount before he came up behind her and lifted her up, setting her on the saddle. She bit her lip to stifle the cry when her inner thigh met the hard leather.

"If I didn't know better, I'd swear you do it on purpose."

"What? What am I doing now? You told me to mount up. I'm up."

He smiled at the flare of temper lighting her green eyes, and inched the brim of his hat back. "Every time I've turned around I've had to put my hands on you. If I was another man, I'd take it as an invitation."

"But you're not another man, are you, Luke? And you do know better."

"That's the hell of it, honey. I do."

Domini closed her eyes. *Two or three days? Dear Lord, help me to survive him that long.* When she opened them, he was taking a thick wool shirt from his saddle bags, walking back to her.

"Lift up."

"What are you doing?"

He slipped the shirt sleeves around her waist, tying them in a bulky knot. He had just slid his hand to her thigh when Domini bolted upright, all her weight resting on the stirrups. To keep her balance she had to grab hold of his shoulder.

"Now sit," he ordered, sliding his arm across her stomach to match action to word.

Domini snatched her hand away and gripped the horn. Her seat was considerably eased.

Luke seemed to think so, too. "That cloth's heavy enough to cushion that sweet, curving bottom or come nightfall you'll have so many blisters I'll be forced to handle you again."

"Your kindness is touching. But animals get handled, not women."

"When you've been handled by a man, honey, try telling me that again."

*Don't answer him! Not one word. Not a sound.*
Domini took her own warning to heart. But the
curl of heated awareness surged deeper. She was
tantalized by the thought of Luke holding her as
he had last night, kissing like a wild storm unleashed, and she the sapling bending to its fury.

Without another word Luke went to where
Devil waited. Using the same fluid grace as he
had this morning, he stepped up into the saddle,
and with a touch of his blunted spurs he set the
big gelding moving.

Domini started to call out and stopped herself.
She eyed the knotted reins draped on either side
of the mare's neck. She had managed to conquer
her fear of being so far off the ground, but wasn't
ready to handle the horse on her own. Luke, already disappearing down a path he alone could
see, wasn't giving her any choice.

"Well, honey," she snapped in imitation of his
sarcastic tone, "let's see if I can handle you."

As she lifted the reins in one hand, she thought
she heard the faint sound of masculine laughter.
The raucous cry of a jay overhead made her dismiss the thought. Luke hadn't given her one genu-
ine smile, so how could she think he'd heard her
and laughed?

Like the burning memory of the kiss they'd
shared, the idea of handling Luke continued to
tantalize her. She found that the mare needed
very little guidance from her, and she quickly
caught up to the black-pointed horse he rode.

Domini grew tired of trying to stare a hole in his back. The added padding of his shirt lessened the pain, and she found herself taking more interest in her surroundings. There were so many questions she wanted to ask him, but kept his order in mind that there would be no talking on the trail.

She caught brief glimpses of a cobalt sky, the color intense, and the line between shadow and sunlight as sharp as the cut of a knife. A low line of clouds smudged the far horizon, and abruptly they were once more riding in the shadows of the giant trees.

There were men on the ship who had called this God's country, and she understood a little better why they had. The land had not known the touch of men. She found no signs to mark the trail he followed, and she looked hard for them.

They were soon climbing again. Domini had found that the horse would pick her own way, and she clung to the saddle horn as the path grew steep. A dulling numbness overcame her, and not even the land drew her attention.

Just hang on, she told herself. He'll have to stop soon. He wouldn't care that she couldn't feel her legs, but he'd stop to rest the horses again. And when he does, I'll show him I'm not as useless.

Clinging to the thought, Domini never saw Luke lift his head and catch the faint curl of smoke rising from a campfire. She wasn't aware that he changed their direction deeper into the forest of pines, or that he looked back and saw not a woman too tired to care where he was heading, but a green-eyed little girl with the same infectious joy that had filled her father's eyes.

Luke knew the debt that he owed Jim Kirkland. He had thought long and hard about it. If it wasn't for Jim, he would have run and kept running, likely riding the outlaw trail and ending up in jail or swinging from the gallows. It had been Jim who gave him the secret hope that someday things would change. Luke often wished he could bury that hope.

As he added another two hours to their riding time, he wondered if it was the debt or his desire for Domini that brought a surge of possessive protectiveness to keep her safe.

*But who's going to protect her from you?*

He'd silently voiced the question. And silence was all that came in answer.

# Chapter Five

~

"Suppertime, honey. Your mare wants to eat even if you don't."

Chilled to the bone, Domini barely lifted her head. There was a faraway sound to Luke's voice, and it took her long moments before she realized they had stopped. She repeated his words, but all she smelled was the ever present scent of pine. It could have been dusk or the middle of the night for all she could tell. Not that it mattered. She couldn't move.

"You've been mumblin' for the last hour that you'll show me you're not useless as teats on a boar."

She was too exhausted to hear the teasing, almost compassionate tone in his voice. "Don't believe me. I lie a lot."

"You do? That's something you'll have to tell me about. Guess you're not gonna show me anything, so let's get you settled."

He had to pry her hand from its grip on the horn, and untangle the reins she had twisted around her fingers.

"Easy, girl. Easy there."

Domini couldn't decide if he was murmuring to her or the mare. She struggled against a leg tingling with a hundred needles pinching it to kick her right foot free of the stirrup when Luke asked. He coaxed her with a gentle voice that soothed, and there wasn't an ounce of pride in her when she felt the caressing glide of his hands closing around her waist to lift her out of the saddle.

Held against him, she snuggled close to his shoulder.

"That bad, huh?"

She managed a murmur, sinking into the heat of his body. His masculine scents were on every breath she drew, horse and leather, and something more that she couldn't name.

But the longer he held her, the more her senses came alive with a curious weak feeling that overtook the pain of blood flowing again to numb, aching body parts.

"Luke?"

Her husky, warm whisper tore through him, and he couldn't fight the swift rise of hunger to hear her call his name after he'd pleasured her and himself and neither one of them could move. His lips hovered above her mouth. It would be so easy to cover her mouth with his and slide his tongue inside for a taste of sass and honey.

She burrowed deeper against him, giving him total trust and sighed a blend of contentment and discomfort.

He knew men who'd call him a curious kind of fool for not carrying her over to the bed he'd made and claiming the wild feminine heat that waited. He clenched his teeth against temptation and carried her to a place beneath the sweeping branches of pine. He'd made a nest, thick and warm, of the dry pine needles covered with his blanket.

Lowering her down, he slipped his arm free, to her sleepy protest. Luke couldn't wrap the blanket around her fast enough or tight enough. But as he walked away, he knew he'd only hidden her from sight for now. Too bad he couldn't hide the scent and feel of her from his mind.

He stripped the gear from the mare, using the tall grasses he'd picked near the hip-wide stream to dry her coat. He grabbed the coffeepot and led her to the rope picket fence he'd made using the saplings on both sides of the stream. Devil lifted a dripping muzzle from the water, a soft nickered greeting welcoming the mare. Luke retied the rope and walked upstream to fill the pot.

Domini woke to the scent of sizzling bacon and the tantalizing smell of coffee. With a barely stifled groan she struggled to sit, rubbing her eyes and sniffing with a smile of appreciation.

"Suppertime," he whispered.

Domini glanced at a fire no bigger than a pitcher's opening. Suspended above it was the coffeepot hanging from a tripod of branches. Luke lifted the crisp bacon from the black frying pan, setting it aside on a slab of rock. While she watched, he mixed flour and water into the drippings and set it back on the fire to bake.

Beyond the small scurrying sounds coming from the forest behind her, Domini listened to the wind high above them. She shivered as she came fully awake. There was no sign of the horses. She saw that Luke had chosen to make their camp beneath two close-growing pines. Someone would have to stumble upon them before they would be seen.

She glanced at him, seeing the play of light and shadow over his hard-cut, handsome features, and remembered vividly the moments when he had held her. Her stomach rumbled with hunger, and he looked up then.

"There's another camp about a mile upwind of us. Keep your voice soft and low, honey. I'm in no mood to fight off three men."

She crawled from the warm nest and instantly wished she had stayed there. The bite of cold mountain air cut through her clothes. Trying to untwist her shawl, Domini found that she still had his thick wool shirt tied around her waist. A quick look showed that Luke had donned a hide vest, as dark and unadorned as everything else he owned. He also appeared as warm as the bed she had just crawled from.

"Would you mind if I wore this?"

He had to look at her again. Some of her hair

had escaped its pins and fell on either side of her face as she struggled with the bulky sleeves. Her fingers were stiff and awkward. *Would he mind? Hell, no. He wasn't about to torture himself by wearing a shirt that had absorbed her heat and scent for hours.*

"Sure, put it on." And he listened to her deep, appreciative sigh as the wool cut the cold, thinking of other hotter, more pleasant ways he could have warmed both of them.

With narrowed eyes Luke watched her roll up the cuffs. He knew the ride would be hard on her, and he wondered who it punished more, her or himself. If he had been alone he would have pushed on until he was certain there wasn't another man within shooting distance, but she had been about to fall out of the saddle.

Despite aching, sore muscles Domini came to sit beside him. She had known he was a big man, and she measured his shirt against her own body, from where the shirttails hung to her knees to the shoulders that slid down to nearly the crook of her elbow. Domini had always felt awkward about her height and size, but wearing his shirt made her feel small.

Her mouth watered for hot coffee, and her stomach rumbled as the dough baked in the bacon drippings. "Luke, why should it matter that other men are camped—"

"I told you. You're worth your weight in gold. Or a bullet for me."

Keeping her voice to the same husky whisper as his, Domini leaned closer to him. "Then why risk a fire to cook if you're worried?"

"I've been wondering that very thing. Fact is, I didn't think you'd make it any farther without rest and hot food."

"Oh." She hadn't really showed him that she was stronger than he thought.

"Soon as we eat we move out."

"Move out? Why can't we stay here? You said—"

"We've been here almost four hours."

"And I slept all the while."

He could almost sense the turn of her thoughts to him calling her useless. "Don't be so hard on yourself. I let you sleep. Otherwise I'd be packing you prone across that saddle." He shifted forward to give the pan a half turn. "Won't be long now. While we wait, why don't you tell me why you lie a lot."

Domini shot him a startled glance. She pushed her hair back from her face, but didn't attempt to repin it.

"I told you that? Yes, I must have. Or how else would you know?"

"I told you, your eyes give you away. I could also say that I can read your thoughts like my own. But then, I might be the one lying." Slick as water sliding over moss strewn rocks, the words and the lie beneath them fell from his lips. Luke looked away from her. He had a feeling that Domini did a little deep looking herself, and he didn't want to know what she saw in him. He'd learned a long time ago to stop looking. Rage wasn't a comforting sight to see.

The pan dough was beginning to brown and he leaned forward to poke one finger in its center.

"Almost done." He paused, then pushed her. "So, you gonna tell me?"

"They're only little lies. I always ask the Lord's forgiveness for them now. But the nuns worked very hard to cure me of the habit."

"Did they?" His voice sharpened against her reminder that she'd intended to make her vows before Toma sent for her. He didn't want to think about her shut away, bound up in a stifling head-to-toe-covering black habit. Not when he couldn't stop thinking about peeling cloth off inch by inch to taste the storm wild skin that trembled at his touch.

"A lie's a lie. The reason doesn't matter. But why did you ever start?"

"Survival."

It was so soft, so unexpectedly a tiny sound that he was compelled to look at her. The stark truth waited like a snare in her green eyes. *Survival.* He knew everything about it. The easy lies told to others, and the worse kind, the lies you told yourself.

"And the knife. Did its skill help you become a survivor, too?"

She closed her eyes against the commanding blackness in his. "Yes." The word hissed out between clenched teeth as she fought the terror he had brought to life.

"Why?" He didn't understand himself badgering her for answers she would rather not tell. He knew he was right. Her body no longer appeared pliant, but ready to spring at any danger that neared. "Tell me."

"It was the only way they learned to leave me alone."

"The nuns?"

"No. They were my refuge."

Like the stark truth in her eyes, the words revealed memories of nightmares. He looked away from her flushed cheeks and pale lips, feeling something close to shame for pushing her. But he *had* to know more.

"Who were they?"

Domini wrapped her arms around her waist. She began to rock back and forth. "It was a long time ago. Leave it be."

"And if I won't?"

She closed her eyes briefly, fighting shivers of terror. "Why should my past matter to you?" She stared at his back. "Don't you have things in your past, Luke, that you won't talk about because remembering hurts as much as what happened?"

"We're not talking about me. We're talking about you. And when I ask you a question, you answer."

"You don't ask. You demand."

"Same thing." He rocked back on his boot heels, pivoting to face her. "Since I'm the one risking his life to take you up to the devil's caldron, you'll make it worth my while. Since the only thing you'll give is talk, talkin's what you'll do."

"Risk your life? What are you saying? I don't want—"

"Ain't your choice now."

"Tell me what you meant."

"Last ruckus I had with Colfax, he said he'd kill me if I set foot on his land again."

"Kill you? Why? Why didn't you tell me? I thought you worked for him."

"I never said that."

Domini paused, thoughtful for a moment. "No," she finally admitted, "you never did."

"It's nothing to get worked into a lather over. The old man's made threats like that at least twenty times that I can recall."

"What kind of a man makes threats about killing people?"

"Colfax. The devil's own. A law unto himself. Like I said, forget it. Let's go back to where you learned to use a knife. Somehow I can't swallow the nuns teaching you how. And I want to know why."

"It's not important."

"I say it is. Tell me."

He was as hard and unyielding as the stone of the mountains surrounding them. Domini saw it in the slant of his jaw, the steely determination in his eyes that raked her from head to toe, and heard it in the relentless intensity of his voice. She stopped rocking to curl her legs tighter to her body.

"I'm waiting to hear. I'm not real high on patience."

"I c-can't." Her hand inched toward the knife hilt hidden in her moccasin. He wasn't going to leave her be. But she had taught others the lesson of leaving her alone.

"You're hiding something. I want to know what it is."

She couldn't hold his gaze. Her eyes darted to the fire, but all she saw was the black pan. It had been very dark, almost as black that night, too. Trying to hold the caged memory in place, Domini shook her head in denial. The pins began slipping from her hair as the shaking grew faster. The straight, heavy weight whipped back and forth over her face as she heard within her mind the whispers.

"No. No," she repeated, refusing to allow him to pry open the lid on the memories she had buried as deeply and as surely as she'd seen her mother in her grave.

Without thinking, Domini withdrew the blade.

Luke eyed seven inches of gleaming steel, and the way her hand wrapped the slender handle, with her thumb extended, pressing on the blade. He couldn't see all of her face through the black curtain of hair, but he had no doubt that she would use the knife on him again.

Her body was tense, coiled to spring at him if he made one move toward her.

*"Don't you have things in your past that you won't talk about because remembering hurts as much as what happened?"* He repeated her words, heard the desperation when she had spoken in his mind again. He wished he could remember. Then the stalking nightmares would have a name, an ending he could put to rest.

"Please, Luke, don't force me to hurt you again."

Her hot-honey, husky voice drove itself into his senses. He looked up. She had pushed her hair back from her face. The plea in her voice was repeated in her eyes. But there was more than a plea within her dark green, narrow gaze. She watched him as a wary mustang would, ever alert to the danger of a man's approach, nostrils flaring in fear of a man's touch, ready to lash out against any loss of freedom that touch would bring.

As he stared at her, a faint smile that had nothing to do with amusement curled his lips. There was a wild, untamed, passionate willingness to fight to protect herself and her secrets from him. He wondered if she would ever bring such passion to a man's bed. The thought of being the man to draw that primitive passion from Domini brought a hot rush of blood that shocked him. The ache that had never subsided made him curse his masculine vulnerability.

"Keep your secrets," he whispered in a voice

gone dry with need. *For now.* He swung back to the fire and removed the pan. As if the past few minutes had never happened, he slid his own knife from its sheath to cut the pan-sized biscuit and began filling its steaming inside with the bacon.

Domini sat frozen in place. She had heard him, even repeated his words to herself, but she couldn't take her eyes from his back, couldn't believe the danger had passed.

Her ragged breathing filled her ears. Her heartbeat refused to slow, for blood still rushed with sizzling tension through her body. He had pushed her, pushed her hard into a corner where she had no choice but to show him what she would do to protect herself.

She didn't understand why. Was he testing her? But what reason could Luke have for doing that? It made no sense.

She had to accept that it was over.

Domini wasn't sure how long she sat there with her fingers still clenched around her knife, watching him.

He finished with the bacon-filled biscuits and set them on the slab of rock. The coffeepot had been emptied into his canteen, and he was already scooping handfuls of dirt on the fire.

She blinked rapidly as the last ember was smothered. The darkness was absolute. She strained to hear him move.

"L-Luke?"

"I'm right here. Filling my belly. Something you'd better do. Soon as I'm satisfied, we're riding out."

She closed her eyes briefly, willing herself to complete calm. With a sure motion she replaced her knife in its sheath and came to her knees.

"I can't see."

"Hold out your hand." He counted the seconds she made him wait. "Can't trust me now?"

"Can I?"

His answer was to wave the tantalizing smell of bacon under her nose. "Take it and eat."

She forced herself to eat. His swift change of mood left her unsettled. His night vision was better than hers, for the moment she licked the last crumb from her fingers, he handed over the canteen of coffee. It was hot, thick, and strong, but she welcomed the liquid heat that curled down to her belly.

Domini drank again, realizing that she could make out his shadow separate from the night that enfolded them. She handed him the canteen.

"Had enough?" he asked before drinking deeply from the warm place her mouth had rested.

"Yes. I promise I'll be better tomorrow. You won't have to make camp and cook." To reinforce her promise, she sat back, stretching out one leg and bending the other so she could knead the sore muscles of calf and thigh.

A scream like a woman in pain filled the night.

Domini felt the hair on her back rise in alarm. "Luke!"

"Cougar's cry. Too faraway to bother us." When it came again, Luke added, "That's a mating call."

"Mating call? Lord spare the poor female. Sounds like she'll be ripped apart." She tried to make sense of her instinctive trust in his word that the continuing cries were those of an animal about to mate and not a woman in agony. She switched legs and resumed her kneading.

"For some animals a violent mating is nature's way of insuring the survival of the strongest."

Domini's hands stilled. She looked up to where he sat. It was only the night, she told herself, that added a soft, heated intimacy to his voice that awakened a new, more dangerous tension inside her. *Please, let it be that.*

"And for some men. Violence is their way of proving how strong they are."

"Not always. A stallion in the wild chooses only the strongest mares to mate with. She'll snort and squeal, kick and bite, forcing the stallion to be just as relentless until she's ready to stand, quivering and willing to take him. But she knows he's conquered her challenge. When he runs from danger she'll follow him because he is the strongest, and survival's bred in every living thing."

She blamed the dark that she couldn't see him and stop the image coming to mind. Only it wasn't the scene he had starkly created. Domini saw

Luke and herself. A mating born of a wild storm's fury, burning down everything in its path.

With the image came a frightening excitement. Need like a hunger too long denied coursed through her. The chill of the night disappeared from the burning inside her body. She didn't know how to control the vivid sensations that he so easily brought to life.

And he hadn't even touched her.

She felt empty, and aching, and wanting all at the same time.

Domini denied it. But she couldn't speak the words. She could almost touch the heavy, aroused waiting tension in him. It sharpened her senses. The sweet smell of the pines grew overpowering, cutting off the air she needed. Every scurrying noise in the forest around them seemed too loud, too close.

She licked her lips, memory quick to supply the heated taste of his hungry mouth closing over hers.

"L-Luke?"

Her husky, trembling whisper of his name slid through him. Hot. Fast. Deep. Just the way he had wanted to take her.

"I'm here. Right here. Say it, Domini. All it takes is one word and the way you whisper my name."

# Chapter Six

～

*All it takes . . . one word . . . just one.* The air thickened with tension until Domini couldn't draw breath.

There was no need to see him. Her mind supplied the image of the hard-edged features that made her think of Lucifer, the most handsome of fallen angels. Black as the night was, Luke was the darker, more powerful force impacting her senses. Everything about him was dark, from the unadorned clothing that bore no flash of silver or brass to his boot-blacked blunted spurs, from his hair as black as her own to the eyes that drew her to discover the dark, seething emotions stirring within them.

The dangerous stillness in him whispered to her of hunger and dark passions. She fought to remember more than the first sharp, exquisite sensations he had awakened with a kiss. She had to force herself to remember how easily her strength of will had dissolved.

He had thought her a fancy woman to be bought by whoever had the price. The mention of her father had stopped him. And that's what she had to remember now, her reason for being here, of her need for answers about the man who had abandoned her and her mother.

*One word. That was all it would take.*

"No."

He had his whisper. Not his name. Not the word he wanted. He came to his feet in a controlled rush.

"Then we ride."

Domini realized the heat and tension were gone as if they had never been. "Luke, wait. I want to tell you, to explain—"

"Honey, there was one thing I wanted to hear. You didn't say it."

She knew he was up and moving by the sound of his voice. She ignored the soreness of her body and rose. Starting toward him, she stopped.

"You don't understand, Luke. I made a promise. One I can't easily break. But more than that, I couldn't give myself to a man who cares nothing about me. And that's all it would be, Luke. An empty satisfying of a need, like eating when hungry or drinking when thirsty. The hunger comes back, so does the thirst. Because they're needs of the body.

"They don't satisfy the needs of the soul, Luke.

They don't make your inner spirit rejoice. That's why I say they're empty. And that's what I'd be if I said yes to you. Just someone you'd use to satisfy a need and leave empty—"

"Empty? Hell, no, honey, you've got that all wrong. If I wasn't a careful man, I'd leave you with a belly full of—"

"And still walk away," she finished softly, sadly, but an accusation firm with the conviction that she was right.

Silence answered her. Moments of silence when she believed that he wouldn't answer her at all. Moments when she prayed he would deny her accusation. Moments more when hope she didn't know that she harbored rose within her that Luke wanted more than a body to slake his lust. With the stretching silence came her answer long before he finally spoke.

"And I'd walk away," he answered at last. "Like I said, we ride out."

A wash of relief that the danger had passed left her shaking. Domini remained where she was, knowing he had moved off to get the horses. She didn't understand why she had wavered, even for a little while. She knew what she wanted. A man like Luke had no place in the life of a woman who would take her vows and live behind the protection of habit and convent walls.

Domini, about to turn to get the blanket, stopped dead. *What was she thinking?* She had never admitted protection as the reason she wanted to take the vows that would allow her to minister to the ills created by greedy men but never suffer them again.

No. It was Luke that had made such a horrifying thought surface. She loved the peace and order of the days spent with the nuns. She cherished the moments when a smile curved the lips of a child whose hunger was sated. Pride was a sin she was guilty of, but Father Dominick told her she would overcome pride, for she had been blessed with compassion for the sick and the dying. Every week when he came to say mass at the mission and hear confession, he told her this.

She knew where the compassion to sit with the sick and dying had come from; she had discovered it watching her mother die. Watched and knew that all the medicines Sister Benedict made, all the good food and clean linens had come too late to save her. She had promised God she would devote her life to those who needed her most. Luke only wanted her body, he did not need her.

She repeated the words to herself as she recovered the blanket. Shaking it free of the pine needles, she realized her mistake too late. Her hairpins were lost to the forest floor. She hurried to fold, then roll the blanket tight. Setting it down at her feet, she made short work of finger-combing her hair into a single braid. The only tie she had was the ribbon of her chemise.

*Please, Lord, forgive my weakness, and don't let*

*him touch me again.* The words became her litany as she quickly opened his shirt and her gown.

She had just finished tying her hair when he came back leading the saddled horses.

"You ready?"

"You forgot your blanket," she said, walking to where dark, sleek shadows revealed him and the two horses.

"You're wrong again. I never forget anything that's mine."

She heard the warning and chose to ignore it. Domini handed over the rolled blanket and took the reins from his hand. She snatched her hand away from even his brief touch.

"Where are the gloves I gave you?"

"The gloves?"

"Yeah. Gloves. The one's you're supposed to wear to protect your hands."

She struggled to remember the last time she had seen them. Not here, and not when they had stopped for the second rest he'd called. This morning then, when they had eaten.

"You left them behind in the woods when you went off for your bit of privacy, didn't you?"

She listened for accusation. There was none. Nor did she hear disgust over losing his gloves after he had just claimed that he never forgot anything that belonged to him. That sensual shiver of awareness that never quite left her came again. She couldn't stop it, or the thought that he would value and care for the woman he claimed the same way. .

It puzzled her that he wasn't angry over the loss of his gloves. Luke's pay as a hired hand could not be more than the *vaqueros* who worked the *hidalgo* ranches.

"Luke, I'm sorry. I'll find a way to replace them. Truly, I didn't mean to leave them, but I was—"

"Scared and sorry you'd taken off with a man you didn't know," he finished for her.

"Yes. That's true enough."

"Guess this isn't one of the times you're lying."

"I'm not lying. I wasn't lying about what I said before. I don't ever lie about things that matter to me."

"Don't you?" He dropped the blanket.

The question was meant to taunt her. He suddenly crowded her and she fell back against the mare. The horse sidestepped, tossing her head, but he ordered Devil to stand to block the mare on the other side.

He had meant the taunt. He'd never meant to put his hands on her. But he was taking her by the shoulders and hauling her up against him. His legs were spread, and he braced for her struggle. All he felt through the thick cloth beneath his hands was her trembling body.

"Gonna pull that knife on me now? Do you even want to?"

"Let me go, Luke."

"No way, honey. There's one lie I want to discover for myself."

Domini closed her eyes. She didn't want to hurt him. But she had to prove to him that with or without a knife she wasn't helpless.

He lowered his head to cover her mouth with his, and Domini brought her knee up. Fast as she was, Luke was quicker. He wedged his leg between her thighs and rendered the move useless. His hand slid from her shoulder and caught hold of her braid, his grip tight enough to force her head back.

"There's a lesson for you, Domini: I'm stronger and faster than you. If I had wanted to take that knife away from you, I would have. And if I wanted to take you, you couldn't stop me. It's as easy as this."

With a sudden shove he freed and spun her to face away from him. Freedom lasted the time it took to draw a breath. He locked one arm over her chest so she could not lift her arms, and the other went around her hips. One booted foot pried her legs apart, once more wedging a space between her legs for his thigh. In seconds he had hauled her captive against him once more.

She brought her head back to slam his face, and he tightened his hold over her chest until her lungs screamed for air.

"Stop fighting me and I'll stop hurting you."

Panting like an animal left in the sun too long without water, Domini hung her head. She couldn't even nod, much less speak. There wasn't a part of her that remained unaware of the hard press of his body.

She had thought herself safe from the terror that had stalked her nights. Luke had tried to pry open the lid of the coffin she had buried in her mind, the coffin where every ugly, evil terror was hidden. His proving that she wasn't safe at all wrenched open the coffin's lid.

She had been seven when her father left, and in the years following when her mother had become too ill to work, she had taken to the street to beg. For almost a year until she turned twelve, she had managed to keep herself safe from serious harm.

How many times had she been warned not to beg near the cantinas? But there was one, where an old *puta* named Consuela plied her trade, that she felt safe at. Consuela bore the same name as her mother. Perhaps that was why Consuela looked after her, chasing the drunken *vaqueros* upstairs if they leered too close. Sometimes Consuela would point out a man who won at gambling and would be generous when Domini begged.

With her voice coarse from the little black cigarettes she liked to smoke and too much *aguardiente,* Consuela would laugh, then warn her that she was growing ripe and could no longer pass for a child.

Domini didn't need her warning. She knew the *camisa* was too small to cover her rapidly developing breasts. Its cotton was thin from the poundings on rocks in the stream where the village washed their clothes and themselves. She had no other to wear. She had grown taller, too. Her skirt hem barely touched her calves, and the *rebozo* she wrapped around her head and upper body hid so much and no more.

She had learned to run very fast. Barefoot, skirt flying, she'd escape down the back alleys from hands that pawed or offers to sell herself.

But in the darkness one night she had been chased and caught. The *vaquero* young and strong, holding her until she could not breathe. His voice slurred and reeking. *"I fought the others for you, niña. Now you pleasure me."*

She had learned the futileness of pleading, the despair of being too small, too weak from hunger to fight him for long.

She had been forced to swallow her bile and the taste of sour wine coating his tongue. And she had been praying to the Virgin, who had not been listening to her prayers of late, that she would die before he raped her, when he used his knife to slice through the only clothes she owned.

She opened her mouth to scream, scream as she had that night, but no sound came from her lips.

"Domini?" Luke repeated her name, as he had for the past few minutes. His hold on her had already eased, and he did not understand why she continued panting as if still fighting a battle. Her heart raced beneath his hand, and even with the layers of clothing separating their bodies, he felt the icy chill of her skin.

"Domini, talk to me. Tell me what's wrong."

He knew he wouldn't see her eyes when he slowly turned her to face him, but now he didn't need to. Her body was rigid. Her eyes would be glazed with some terror only she could see.

His lesson had triggered some nightmare for her.

He knew the signs of terror. He'd been awakened by them too many times to count.

There were two bottles of whiskey stashed in his saddlebags. He thought of the times he'd used liquor to ease the icy fear until his mind blurred enough so he could sleep again.

And he remembered all the times he had wished there was someone who cared enough to hold him until the fear retreated.

With a gentleness that he wasn't aware he had been capable of, Luke drew her into his arms, slowly rocking her body against his.

Her head was tucked beneath his chin, and he rubbed against the black silk of her hair. With easy, circling motions he caressed her rigid spine, willing her to lean against him, willing himself to find the words that would lead her out of the darkness that still held her in its grip.

Cursing himself was a waste. He couldn't find anything vile enough to call himself for having done this to her.

*But you didn't know.*

There was no comfort in the excuse his mind supplied, because he should have known. The moment she had pulled that knife on him and he had seen her eyes, he should have known.

He wished she would cry or yell, do something, anything to break the terror holding her. He held her a little closer, sweeping his big hands up and down her slender back, rocking her harder against him.

*I only lie a little . . . they learned to leave me alone . . . the nuns were my refuge . . .* The fragments came rushing from his mind as he heard them battering at the walls he had built around himself.

But no matter how guilty he felt, Luke knew he would never allow anyone to get close to him again.

Not even a woman who made him ache with wanting, and feel deep remorse for sending her fleeing into her own dark corner.

He held her and stroked her. He repeatedly called her name and made the same soothing noises he used to calm any wild creature he found caught in a trap, and freed. He never touched the traps set to fill a man's belly with food or to gain fur to keep from freezing. But he freed animals caught to line some man's pockets with gold.

He had had enough of man's greed to last a lifetime. One man especially. The man he was going to deliver this vulnerable woman to.

Domini warmed to the slow strokes of his hands. She sank against his heat and strength, envying them, wanting and needing them for her own. Her breathing grew more even, the racing beat of her heart slowed, and the terror began to recede.

It made no sense that she should feel safe in Luke's arms, not when he so easily and quickly had sent her spinning into the past. But safe and warm was exactly what she felt.

The rough sound of his voice murmuring her name, and the same meaningless sounds she used when a child needed comfort, told her more than any apology he could make. She couldn't blame him. He didn't know.

*You didn't tell him.*

No, she did not tell him, and she had no intention of telling him.

"Luke, you can let me go. I'll be all right now."

He heard her, but still held her, unwilling to let her go. Then the very soft, calm tone of her voice hit him. He stilled and slowly lifted his head, wondering if she had a steel core that kept her back rigid.

"Tell me—"

"You said we had to get away from here. We'd better mount up and ride."

Calm and cold. Her slight step back forced him to drop his arms to his sides. "Just like that? You're not going to tell me, are you?"

"I'm tired, Luke. And I hurt. You caught me off guard. It's a mistake that won't happen again."

"Damn right it won't! I'm the one who held you while your mind ran off to who knows where. I don't need your silence to punish—"

"I'm not trying to punish you, Luke. That's not my place to do." With a long sigh Domini turned away. "It was no more than a bad memory. You didn't know, so you have nothing to be punished for. End of the matter."

"Then you'd better mount up, honey, 'cause we've got a hell of a long, hard ride before I get shed of you."

She couldn't deal with his hostility now. She shrugged, although he couldn't see her, and scooped up the fallen reins of the mare. She was strong. It had taken her a long time to understand that. She had survived more than Luke could ever imagine, more than she could at times believe.

She looped the reins over the mare's head, smoothing the leather alongside her neck. Holding the knot with her left hand, she grabbed hold of the saddle horn. Her body wanted nothing more than to sink to the ground where she stood, but she forced her right hand up to grip the cantle.

"Give me your foot," Luke ordered. He thought she would refuse, but she lifted her left foot from the ground to where his cupped hands caught it. "Let go of the cantle and horn. Hold my shoulder for balance."

Her hesitation was enough to tell him that she was afraid to touch him. Not that he blamed her. Just as he was about to remind her that she was one who pushed for them to leave, he felt her hand grip his shoulder. With a small heave she rose high enough to swing her right leg over the saddle and sit. He fixed her foot in the stirrup, then handed her the reins.

She waited until he was mounted before she called him. "I just wanted to thank you for holding me."

"Anytime, honey. The pleasure, as they say, was all mine."

As she neck-reined the mare to follow Devil, she couldn't rid herself of the feeling that she had hurt him. Hurt him terribly. For she kept repeating what he said, but her mind kept replacing pleasure with pain.

What kind of pain could her terror bring to a man like Luke?

She looked up ahead to where the darkness hid him. And she knew. It wasn't her pain at all. It was his.

It didn't help her to feel certain she was right. Just as she had no intent of telling Luke about her past, she knew he would never share his.

He was a stranger who had offered to take her to meet Toma Colfax. She shouldn't be feeling a terrible sense of loss. But it was there, sharp enough so that she could not ignore it.

She wondered if he would have listened. If he

would have understood the terror of a twelve-year-old child about to be raped. Would Luke know the kind of desperation that had driven her suddenly to lie still and not listen to the drunken laughter accompanying the bites that had remained with her for weeks?

Would he think she had threatened him lightly with her knife if he knew how it came to be in her possession?

Domini didn't think so. She didn't believe Luke would still look at her with desire burning hot in his black eyes if he knew any of the truth.

She had paid dearly. Within two weeks her mother had died. No matter how many times she had been told that penitence had to be made, that sometimes God took retribution even on the children He loved most, for what He alone could foresee, Domini didn't understand why her mother had to pay for her sin.

She was the one who had killed a man. No, he had not been a man, but an animal who preyed on those he thought weak.

It was not the words of a prayer that she sought comfort from, but a few lines from a poem that Sister Ignatius had taught her. *Whatever my darkness is, 'Tis not, O Lord, of Thee: The light is Thine alone; The shadows, all my own.*

As she eased back in the saddle to allow the mare to follow Luke's horse up a steep climb, Domini thought she had the right measure of him. Luke was a man, not an animal. But what darkness he hid, and what shadows that he claimed, were not going to be hers to discover.

Secrets she had learned were a double-edged knife. You bled a little each time you kept one; someone else bled when you told.

The very devil of a dilemma. But then, Luke said he was taking her to meet the devil's own.

# Chapter Seven

❧

The trail grew steep, then steeper as Domini followed him in a climb down gullies and up their banks across open meadows into forest.

She decided that the forest here did not merely cover the land, it overwhelmed the earth. They had left the lodgepole pines behind and rode through dense spruce growth.

The heavy boughs closed out the moonlight, but in places she could make out wind-fallen tree trunks at least three or four feet wide that barricaded the forest floor and forced them to ride around.

She sensed an agelessness about the trees, growing undisturbed for hundreds of years, and at the same time she felt their similar impatience for intruders as Luke displayed when she trespassed his boundaries.

The mare's breathing was less labored than her own.

Domini was beyond exhaustion, mentally refusing the admission of pain. She tried to remember to move with the mare and not against her.

As the hours wore on, the first hint that night was retiring brought the hope that Luke would find a place to stop. Soon. Very soon.

A fine mist filled air too thin to fill starving lungs. As layer after layer of moisture collected and soaked her hair, skin, and clothes, she felt as though she had been wrapped in wet bed sheets and left forgotten.

This wasn't the ghostly fog that rolled in off the ocean, yet a feeling persisted that the gauzy mist drifting over the land had a haunting presence all its own.

The crick in her neck warned her to stop craning for a look upward through green darkness to see daybreak. She was sure it would come soon. The night could not last forever.

It was minutes before she realized they halted a way back in the wood that broke to a meadow before them. Like a long-held breath slowly released a gray light filled the open space. Morning was creeping in as if uncertain of its welcome.

A memory rose of herself padding barefoot on unsteady legs down the hall to her parents' bedroom, seeking the warm comfort she knew she would find, yet unsure of what place there was for her amid soft murmurs and even softer laughter. She need not have worried. Despite the long pauses and deep sighs, the murmurs and laughter went on as she was nestled between them in a bed filled with love.

Then Toma Colfax had come. Days later, her father had left him. It was the last time she ever saw him.

With a rough shake of her head Domini dismissed the questions she knew would follow. She simply couldn't deal with them now.

She pressed the balls of her feet against the hard wood stirrup and slowly—both not to alarm the mare and not to cause cramped muscles one second more of agony than necessary—she lifted herself from the saddle until she could stretch her body straight up. She bit her lower lip, then clenched her teeth, but she wouldn't cry out when Luke went as still as the trees surrounding them.

It was uncanny the way he remained motionless, as if he had taken root in one place, he and the horse he rode as though carved from the same rock.

She stood a few seconds more, then gingerly sat. "A hot bath . . ."

She hadn't realized she had spoken out loud until Luke's murmur floated back to her.

"I can't promise hot, but if you're game for another hour in the saddle, I'll take you to a waterfall-fed lake. Sun'll be up by then. Should warm the water to about freezing."

"Just freezing, Luke?"

"It's spring, not summer, honey. An' you're lucky to find it that warm in these mountains.

Two years ago we had snow higher up right into July."

He didn't sound angry but rather proud of the fact. Domini found herself substituting *my* for *these*, for there was pride of ownership in his voice. And none of the hostility as when he'd last spoken to her.

The thought of a bath, any kind of bath, was tempting. Not only for cleanliness, but she knew they would have to stop long enough to rest the horses. She was about ready to do anything to get out of this saddle before it grew attached to her sore bottom.

"All right, Luke. I'm game."

"You and me both. Gettin' to where I don't want to stand downwind of myself."

Domini responded with laughter. Luke teasing her lightened her mood. It seemed that dawn's coming had done more than chase the night, it had lifted the dark shadows of the spirit as well.

If Luke wanted to pretend the night had never happened, she was more than willing to do the same. But the thought lingered that she had done more, much more than merely stand downwind of him. She had learned how arousing his scent was when he had held her against him.

Game? Domini shook her head. She didn't think so. Not unless Luke had been referring not to his scent at all, but to another game . . . the one played out between hunter and prey.

Thoughtful now, she watched him lead the way

around the meadow. He might have teased her, indicating a lighter mood, but he still held an animal-like wariness as he kept them well within the cover of the trees.

She groaned at the idea of another hour in the saddle. It wasn't her buttocks that bothered her, but the thoughts running through her mind.

Where the hell was Luke? Seated at the opposite end of the long dining table from his father, Matt Colfax barely managed to refrain from asking the question out loud.

He drummed impatient fingers on the table. It was Monday morning, and Meta was serving breakfast. Not that he acknowledged the girl. She was as plain as a brown wren, a near twin for her older sister, Lucy, working within the house because Toma didn't want to lose their father. Kip Lozier was more than a blacksmith, although with a ranch the enormous size of the Gold Bar C there was plenty of work for him. The man's greater value came from his hobby. Kip was adept at repairing guns. With Toma employing an army of men to work cattle, horses, and mines, their guns were as important as the horses they rode. Those, too, were Gold Bar C stock, most of them coming from the wild horses that Luke had hunted and broken for them.

He wondered if Toma would lose his interest in the paper if he mentioned that Caully and Ramsey were out looking for Luke. Damn arro-

gant bastard. And for a moment Matt wasn't sure
if he meant Toma, Luke, or both.

At the girl's approach with the gleaming silver
coffeepot, Matt nodded for her to pour. The rou-
tine never varied. He and Toma breakfasted in
silence until the *Statesman* had been read, and
then Toma would discuss his orders for the week.

His mother, Amanda Clarice Colbere Colfax,
never joined them before supper demanded her
presence. Actually, it was Toma who had made
the demand, and it was one of the few she gave
in to. She ran his house, so he had no cause for
complaint, but she kept to her own suite of rooms
on the other side of the house.

Restless, Matt stared around the gracious home
that his mother had created to remind herself of
where she had been born and bred, a home only
Toma's wealth had made possible.

The sideboard beneath the four velvet-draped
windows was crowded with ornate silver serving
pieces from the finest silversmiths in Boston and
New York. Pieces nearly a hundred years old from
Paul Revere, John Coney, and Daniel Van Voorhis
were displayed with Towle silver.

A wall cabinet of cherry wood, the height of a
man, with its doors of small glass panes set in
thin strips of gleaming wood, dominated the wall
behind Toma. Arrayed on its shelves was delicate
bone china thickly rimmed with gold, made to
Toma's specifications by the English Worcester
Royal Porcelain Company to bear the addition of

a scrolled C crossed by a miner's pick on the service for twenty-four.

The linens gracing the table had been imported from Ireland, soft and silky as the finest silk, the cutwork heavy-edged with handmade lace.

The room choked him, and he stared down with distaste at his plate. If he had had control of the fortune, he wouldn't have wasted money to bring the rich offerings of Europe and the East to this godforsaken mountain.

*But you don't have control. You'll never have control as long as Toma lives.*

Matt rose abruptly and tossed his napkin down. The carpet muffled his leaving.

Toma finished reading the Washington Territory paper. As he took the time to carefully fold it, knowing that it would be passed from hand to hand until it fell apart, he realized that his son was gone.

"Meta, where'd that shiftless stallion take himself off to?"

"I don't know, Mr. Colfax. Mr. Matt, he don't say much to me."

"Just as well, girl. The only talkin' he'll do is to get under your skirts. That boy's useless as a four-card flush. An' you remember that."

"Yes, Mr. Colfax. Only how come you still call Mr. Matt a boy?"

"Cuts himself a fine figure with his fancy duds that catches your eye, does he? Ain't necessary to answer, girl. I see the truth of that myself. Your pa'd be the first to tell you there's more to a man than the right hangin' of bones an' flesh an' what's coverin' 'em." Tapping his temple, where streaks of gray did not diminish but added to the hard cast of craggy features, he added, "It's how a man thinks that tells he'd growed up. Matt's got more growin' to do. A hell of a lot more. Pour me some coffee, Meta, then fetch Madison for me."

When she was gone, Toma glanced around the room, muttering to himself. "Damn devil's pass it comes to when a man's got to ask his hired hand what his own flesh and blood is up to."

But he knew he would have his answers from Madison Grady. He was the straw boss of the Gold Bar C, and a rawhide Texan so tough few men would dare cross him. Matt sure as hell wouldn't. Toma had never deluded himself about the strengths and weaknesses of his son. He left that to his wife.

He didn't want to think about who not only dared to cross Madison once but repeatedly. And lived to tell about it.

Against his will, the name came to mind. Luke. A son of a bitch as wild as the horses he caught, who'd grown to a man before he'd had half a chance to be a boy.

"You sent for me, Mr. Colfax?"

Toma eyed Madison Grady's deceptive rawbone frame. A number of men had been fooled by Grady's leanness. Toma met a gaze of glacial blue and a wolfish smile that matched his own.

"Set yourself down, Grady. This is what I want you to do."

Twenty minutes later, Grady exited the dining room. He didn't linger in the hallway. The big, silent house made him uncomfortable. And he had a job to do.

Flattened against the wall between the corner and the grandfather clock, Amanda Colfax waited until he was gone before she stepped from her hiding place near the dining room. A cold rage settled over her. *That bastard was going to ruin everything.* And with this, as so many other times in her life, she was helpless to do anything about it.

*Damn you to hell and beyond, Toma!*

The curse was as silent as her retreat to her own suite of rooms.

The day stretched before her. Toma had told Grady to hurry. The man would push himself and his horse to get back from Florence before nightfall.

*Chapter Eight*

# *Chapter Eight*

⤳

Domini swore she would crawl before she climbed up into a saddle again. She waited within the shelter of the massive trees for Luke to return.

The place where she waited was a crease in the land that rose ahead to the spot where Luke had disappeared. He'd ridden off with the warning that she was to remain here until he came for her.

The sorrel was as edgy as she was. The mare's ears were pricked forward, alert to any noise above the moan of the wind. Her muscles beneath Domini's hand were boiled. Her long tail nervously lashed from side to side. Domini trusted her instincts to warn of danger.

Very little sunlight filtered down through the lofty pillars that had to be at least a hundred feet overhead. The smell of the earth was rich with decay and damp loam.

Layer upon layer the lace-like patterns of fallen

pine needles had taken years to become the rich,
dark loam. Luke was like that, rich and dark,
shielded by layers. The loam was fertile planting
soil, resting and waiting for a seed to find its nur-
turing richness. Domini sensed no peace in Luke,
only a restlessness that would have him gone before the tiniest seed could find its way past his
guard.

It saddened her to think that he might never
find whatever it was that he searched for alone.
She warned herself that she was spending too
much time thinking about Luke.

Beneath her moccasins a green carpet of moss
drew her eyes. She had become accustomed to
the warblers and jays, listening to them and other
bird calls. Her tension eased as they continued to
flit overhead from branch to branch.

Once more she watched the place where Luke
had disappeared. It was so cool in the green shadows. She still wore his wool shirt despite the
added chill of the damp cloth.

The mare suddenly stilled, her ears swiveled to
the side. Domini followed the mare's move to turn
her head.

For a moment she couldn't see what had drawn
the mare's attention. With bated breath she sent
a searching gaze over the massive tree trunks,
quickly skimming the area, forcing herself not to
panic as she made a complete turn. She began
again, taking her time, probing the dark shadows

beneath the thick, sweeping boughs of the fragrant pines.

The sorrel swung her head and lipped her arm. Domini wasn't so quick to react to the mare's signal that there was no danger. But seconds later she saw the flash of two white fluffy tails between the trees.

"Deer! I swear, girl, I'm getting as wary as Luke. Not that it's a bad thing to be." She lifted her hand to rub the mare's muzzle. The hair on the back of her neck rose in alarm.

She would never forget the feeling of helplessness that had overcome her when Luke grabbed her from behind.

Domini rubbed the sorrel's muzzle with the hand that held the reins. Moving slowly and murmuring, she bent as if to examine the mare's foreleg. All she heard was the mare's breathing and her own.

She ducked beneath the mare's head, spinning around to see what alarmed her before she pulled her knife.

"Luke!"

"You were expecting someone else?"

"Don't joke. You creep about so silently it's a pure wonder my heart didn't stop." When he didn't answer, she understood. Moving like a shadow over the land was so ingrained that he wasn't even aware of it. She was bothered by the thought that he never relaxed his guard for a moment, not even with her.

"Did you really believe I'd leave you where someone else wandering around could find you?"

"No. But I watched for you." Domini waved behind her, in the direction he had left, then walked around the front of the mare.

"I'd never go and come the same way. That kind of predictability can get a man killed."

"Another lesson for me to remember."

The underlying edge in her voice made him take a closer look at her. He tilted back the brim of his hat, his gaze slowly studying her drawn features. He'd pushed her damn hard. She was as finely strung as any wild mare cut from the herd for the first time.

It couldn't be helped. The more wary she was, the better her chance of surviving Toma. And his wife. But he found himself disturbed that she referred to what had happened last night.

"You did good just now. No panic, just nice easy moves that put the mare between you and whatever was coming. If I was another man, I wouldn't have had the chance to catch you unaware." *Unless I wasn't alone.*

His softly voiced approval brought a tentative smile to her lips. Domini glanced down at his outstretched hand.

"It's all right? We can go up to the meadow?"

The eagerness in her voice and the hunger in her eyes as she threw a quick look over her shoulder at the rise, then back at him again, made him wonder what she hungered for the most. He didn't need to ask himself. Even standing motionless next to her, he could feel the hot, heavy running of his blood.

"It's safe enough. That's why I was gone so long."

"Safe enough?" The way he avoided her gaze made her think he wasn't going to answer. "Is something wrong? Did you find—"

"A wild herd's been through. I figure they grazed and watered sometime late yesterday afternoon before they ran off."

"Ran off or were chased off, Luke?" She caught hold of his extended hand. "Tell me."

"A band of Indian ponies ran them off." The feel of her fingers tightening their hold around his own made him add, "They were moving hard and fast. It's not likely they'll be back this way."

"What makes you so sure? And how could you know if they were Indian ponies and not another herd of wild horses?"

"You can tell if a man's riding any horse by the cut of the hoof print left behind. One of the first things you learn to read when tracking is who's riding the horse. A skilled tracker can tell if it's a man, woman, or child. An expert tracker will tell you more than that. You'll know a man's height, weight, if he walks straight or with a limp, what he's packing, if he's right- or left-handed—"

"Luke! I don't think you're lying to me, but I find that hard to believe."

"Then I'll show you. Leave the mare. She'll stay

as long as Devil is near." Dropping the reins, he gave her hand a tug and walked back a ways into the woods, and stopped.

"Look down and tell me what you see."

Amusement lit her eyes. "Moss and the decay of hundreds of years of falling pine needles."

"You're right. On the surface." He hunkered down, and was pleased to see that she did want to know, for she followed his move. He pointed at the spot.

"What I see is that two horses stopped. One full of the devil because he scented water and grass and maybe wild kin close by."

"No fair, Luke. You know there's water and a meadow up ahead."

A devilish smile curled his lips. "True. But then, I wouldn't be much of a tracker if I didn't know the land. There's watersheds all over the mountains. It's spring, bound to be runoffs close by. But there's more. The horse was excited by something he scented. His front hooves tore the earth with pawing, like he wanted to run and his rider held him back. If he was frightened by bear or cougar, the horse would have reared or tried to, and the pivoting would have deeply dug his back hooves into the earth.

"That tells me the rider is skilled, the horse ain't a green-broke bronc but one whose been ridden long and trusts his rider. It also tells me that the man is cautious. He waited here before he moved on."

Domini remembered that Luke had done just that. And she recalled the soft, teasing murmur of his voice soothing Devil's impatience. She watched him poke the leaves, so aware of his closeness that she had trouble breathing without his scent being a part of the air she drew inside. Coils of warmth uncurled. She had to force herself not to look at him. She wasn't afraid of what she would see in his eyes, but what her own might reveal. Desire, she was fast learning, threw caution to the wind.

"Tell me why you keep saying it's a man."

"Big horse. Takes a big man to control that kind of power. His weight cuts the prints deep in the earth. Measure the span of the forelegs, then the distance from the front hooves to the back ones. I'd estimate a horse sixteen or seventeen hands."

"How does Devil measure?"

"Seventeen hands." Pivoting, he pointed to another spot, trying to ignore her voice, which poured like hot honey over him. "The print is lighter there. Mare most likely. Smaller hoof, lighter rider's weight. The man never dismounted, but this rider did. Now, if I was tracking them, I'd study the ground a little longer."

"Why, Luke? You said the horse didn't sense any danger. Odds are the man rode on."

"And a woman waited behind."

"Woman? You want me to believe you could tell it was me?"

"I didn't say that. But I'd guess it was a woman.

The puzzle is that the horse is shod, but there's no boot heel print. Something else ripped up the moss over there. I'd figure, myself, the man. Cautious, remember? If I was riding with a woman, I'd leave her behind while I scouted ahead."

Enthralled by both his knowledge and the fact that he was sharing something of himself in the telling, Domini looked at him. In the green shadows that defined and enhanced his rugged handsomeness, she thought again of fallen angels. He compelled her with the hidden fire burning in his dark eyes.

Compelled her with temptation to taste the forbidden passion that waited. She caught herself leaning toward him and pulled back. It took an effort to look away from him and back to where he pointed.

"Moccasins ripped up the moss," he murmured, very aware that she was backing away, not physically but from the same small claws of need that were sinking deeper inside him.

"Trouble is, they're not worn by any Indians I've had to track. Whoever wore these moccasins didn't know that every minute standing in one spot left its mark. I'd guess the wait was close to an hour. Now, I'll go with instinct and say it was a woman. She's about five foot six—"

"Eight. I'm five feet eight inches tall."

"Yeah, right." The warm, gentle weight of her fingers entwined with his stirred his memory. She was tall enough and built with the sleek curves to drive a man to distraction. From the first time he'd seen her, he'd been wondering if she'd take the strength and hardness of his body with ease. He had to curb his anger at the way he ached just being near her. It was her scent and that haunting voice of hers that made lust rise in a violent rush.

He stood up abruptly, pulling her to her feet. "Enough tracking lessons. As for what I found near the lake bank, it was most likely a hunting party heading back to camp."

She smiled at him with a trust that almost made him tell her to run and never trust him. Especially since he didn't trust himself. But he didn't say it. He dropped her hand.

"Let's go get the horses."

She followed his lead, missing the warmth of his hand holding hers, and wondering what she had done to make him raise his guard again.

"I set a snare, but there's plenty of game hereabouts so you won't go hungry."

"I wasn't worried, Luke. You may take your skills for granted, but I admire them. But I admit, it will be nice to have a fire. I remember something my father said once. It was something about hard beans and jerky tasting sweet when hunger prowls in your belly. After eating jerky I would argue the—" Domini stopped. She couldn't argue with her father about that or anything else. He was dead. And the reason why she had come here.

It was impossible to walk alongside him as the

thick growth of the massive trunks seemed to close in on them. She did notice that Luke was not leading the way over the rise; nor was he heading back the way he had returned. He was going deeper into the woods.

The thought of a hot fire kept her plodding along behind him. "I don't know what I'm more hungry for, a fire, food, or sunlight."

"Sunlight?"

"Yes. Don't laugh."

"Wasn't going to. Just never heard of anyone hungry for the sun."

*Not if you're a man who has always lived in shadows.* She wouldn't say it to him, but she couldn't stop herself from thinking about it.

"I don't know if I could describe how bright the sun in California is. If you look up, you'll hurt your eyes. The earth's been baked with its heat. It was wonderful to be able to escape into the cool adobe brick rooms of the mission in the afternoon. Everywhere you walked, it felt as if hot coals burned right up through the soles of your feet."

"You wear those moccasins there, too?"

Domini paused and glanced down, then continued. "I ran barefoot for so long that the nuns despaired of my ever wearing shoes. These were a compromise."

There was laughter in her voice. No whining that she didn't have shoes to wear. Though he tried to fight it, an image came to mind of Domini running wild, her black hair streaming out behind her. Luke shook his head as if he could rid himself of thinking about her. But he thought about what she said. She'd come from a land of heat. And he wanted nothing more than to capture the fire inside her and see how hot it could burn.

"Luke?"

"What?"

The edge in his voice should have warned her to back off. She had been enjoying their talk and didn't want it to end. All this worrying and wondering was taking its toll on her. Surely he wasn't upset because she wore moccasins and not shoes. Or was he?

"Does it bother you that I wear moccasins?"

*Hell, yes! Everything about you bothers me!* "Suit yourself, I've got a pair, too."

Lord, was this all he was going to give her—talk about footwear? She was not going to let him retreat again. Luke had become more than a means to learn more about her father.

"How do your moccasins hold up in the snow? You do have lots of snow here, don't you?"

"Yeah." *And I could use some right now to cool off.*

"I've never seen snow, Luke. What is it like?"

"White and wet."

"Always?"

"Always. You've come to a land that's been buried in cold so long I don't think there's enough sunlight to thaw it out." Luke shot a quick look upward at the towering canopy of green. "Maybe that ain't true. If they keep on logging the forests the way they do on the lower slopes, none of this might be here in a hundred years. Greed tends to destroy land. Every time a new trail is cut to make mining easier, game disappears. The trees that are cut change the flow of water.

"No water, no trees, no game. Greed and destruction go hand in hand. The Nez Perce have lived in peace, but their way of life is being destroyed. They'll fight to keep what they believe is a sacred trust. Ah, hell, I didn't mean to run on."

"But I want to hear more. I like listening to you, Luke."

The wind moaned through the upper boughs as Domini forced herself up the sharpening slope of land. When he said nothing else, she knew he wasn't going to be pushed into talking. But Luke had revealed a little more about himself, adding to the curiosity that burned in her. Domini was sure he had been talking as much about the land as he had about himself.

Why did he believe that change brought destruction? Had someone tried to destroy him to make him change? She found it hard to believe that there was anyone who could make Luke do something against his will.

Or was this all part of his secrets?

Lost in thought, Domini didn't notice the lighter dappling of shadows as they neared the forest's edge. What caught her attention was the rumbling sound of water.

And Luke. She would always hear his voice.

"Come see why the Indians call *E-dah-hoe*, land with light on the mountains."

Domini walked out of the shadows and into the sunlight to feel the radiant warmth coming not only from the sun, but from Luke.

He watched her, his gaze unwavering and direct. Domini felt something stir in the deepest center of her soul. She had believed that Luke was so guarded, not even the tiniest seed could find a place to lodge itself and find nuturing to grow. She began to realize she was wrong, so very wrong. His handsome, hard-edged features reflected a love for the land.

Her breathing quickened. If Luke could love the land, how much more would he love someone who could love him back?

# *Chapter Nine*

She felt the mare's nose at the small of her back, nudging her forward.

Luke, already stripping the gear from Devil, was watching her. "The meadow's filled with elk thistle, and your sorrel's anxious to get at it."

Domini dropped the reins and walked out into meadow grasses that topped her knees. Jagged mountains demanded her attention. They appeared like beast's teeth ready to chew up the sky. Impassable rock walls, scraped bare, stately and time-stained, enclosed the meadow. From a deep cut ahead, a small series of waterfalls spilled bead-like foam to tumble in crystal chaos into a lake.

Her gaze drank in the sight of the sun's splendor touching an arc of glittering color that changed quicker than thought, half enveloped in its own rising mist, and then the wind carried it away, only to have the arc reform with deeper hues.

Ever changing, breathtaking, Domini saw that a passion for beauty had created part of this wild place, but anger made it whole.

A giant hand had speared the earth with granite and rust slabs that rose with mighty splendor. They challenged the sky and the water. She sensed that nothing but those eternal rocks could withstand the rumbling flow of water that dashed in a torrential rush through its cuts and crevices.

Drawn forward, Domini was unaware that Luke moved to strip the saddle from her sorrel, or that he still watched her discover the spirea and wild hollyhock drooping in a waterfall of flowers over the boulders that formed part of the lake bank.

He was arrested by the overpowering sense that Domini belonged here—wild, free, upsoiled by any man's hand. The mist added luster to the sun's sheen, which turned her hair to the blue-black of a night sky. The end of her long, single braid touched the rising tips of the grasses and wildflowers like a kiss as she raised her face to the sun. She lifted her arms and spread them wide as if to embrace a lover.

He wanted to know if that soft, silky, golden skin that graced her face and neck was the same all over—her breasts, her belly, her thighs, between her legs. Hunger filled him in a violent rush. Were her nipples the same lush, dusky color as her generously shaped lips?

His hands tightened on the saddle he held, and a low, rough sound rumbled in his throat. He looked at her and let out a long breath of cynical acceptance. This was the one place he could never forget that she was Jim Kirkland's daughter.

She had refused him once. He would not go begging. It was one of the first harsh lessons he'd learned—you couldn't beg for someone to care about you.

Domini turned toward him, shading her eyes with one hand. "It's so beautiful here, Luke. How do you ever leave it?"

"Easily," he called out, turning away.

She didn't believe him, and was disappointed that his guard was firmly in place again. She was touched by this place, touched deeply, and had to share her feelings whether he wanted to hear it or share it with her.

"This is one of God's Edens. Timeless and graced with beauty. It's almost too much to take it in all at once, Luke, but I feel a strange sadness here, too. You'll think me foolish, but I feel as if there were lost souls haunting this place." She rubbed her upper arms against a sudden chill and moved to follow him. Casting a last look at the beckoning water, she knew it would wait, as it had always waited. This time she would show him that she was not a burden.

The horses were ground-tied, the reins trailing down as they foraged through the thick grasses. Domini knew then just how safe it was, for Luke would never let them free. He headed back toward the woods, and she hurried to catch up to him.

"The mountains seem so powerful, almost frightening, Luke."

He stopped then and half turned toward her. The longing to talk was in her voice, in those eyes that searched his face. He gripped the saddle horns tighter, not daring to set them down. It was the only way he'd keep his hands off her.

"Maybe the mountains were meant to frighten. They give their own truths to a man. Their height makes you feel small, but their being there offers a challenge, too. A man can't really conquer them, but he's got to look inside himself to find his strength and weakness, as well as facing his fears. He'll find out what, if any, hope he harbors. Survive them and you'll understand your own measure of a man."

"Or a woman, Luke."

His eyes narrowed as he banked his desire. "Or a woman." He couldn't forget that she had faced her own terrors and survived. But there was one terror that he had buried in his mind, and he wondered now if he was never meant to remember it. Perhaps his mind was protecting him from the memory that surfaced in nightmares, only to fade when he woke. Maybe he wouldn't survive remembering what it was.

"Com' on, we'll make camp, then you can have your bath. And you were right about the lost souls. No one knows how many men have lost their lives in these mountains. I remember old Mulekey—"

"Mulekey?"

"He's so old, even he ain't sure of his age. But he taught me all he knew about horses, which ain't as much as he's likely forgotten. He's a fine one for storytelling, though. Nights 'round a campfire he tells tales he learned from the Nez Perce or the Shoshone. Story goes that an Indian brave lost his way and encountered seven demons before he found his way back to his tribe. They named the Seven Devils mountains after he returned.

"The Shoshone call the Salmon *Tom-Agit-Pah*, big fish river, after the salmon that run its waters. Most white men call it the river of no return."

"Why, Luke? Everything has a beginning and an end. Even those mountains." She gestured behind her. "They begin in the sky and end somewhere in the earth below."

Domini saw him hesitate before he entered an almost perfect circle of trees. She had a feeling that Luke had camped here many times, and strangely, she thought it had been a long time since he'd been here. She shook her head as if to rid herself of the feeling that he was facing a few old ghosts before he slung the saddles down near one of the trunks. He went directly to the center of the small clearing and lifted deadfall. Hunkering down, he began scooping out a faint depression in the earth to reveal a ring of stones.

The sounds of the water were muted here, insulated by the thick trunks with their sweeping boughs. Even the bird calls seemed distant. Domini watched his hands take the last scoop of partially decayed matter out of the shallow pit. She saw not the strength of his hands holding her captive, but their gentleness when he held her.

Without his asking, she began to gather deadfall as he began building a fire with dry needles and smaller twigs.

"Tell me about the river, Luke."

"Sure. It's a white fury. Almost looks like it boils with rage against anyone daring to think they could ride it down. It's a fighting river with nearly eighty miles of tortuous waters studded with hugh boulders, jagged sawtooth rocks, small chutes and cascades that appear suddenly to fool you after a stretch of calm water and deep, easy flowing pools. A man could attempt to swim across in a few low spots, but he takes his life in his hands to try. Even the ferry raft depends on the season to make its crossings. Mostly in winter."

Domini lowered the armful of dried branches she had gathered to his side. "When I first looked out, I had this strange thought that despite how beautiful it is, anger played a part in creating this country."

He looked up at her. "Maybe that's why I feel at home here. But not all of it looks like it was ripped from the earth and left to fall where it would. There's hidden valleys, meadows, and lakes like this one. The Selway takes its name from a Nez Perce word, *selwah*, meaning smooth water.

If it was all created in anger there wouldn't be enough food to substain an ant, much less a man."

"Food?"

He lowered his head and hid his smile. Like a child she was licking her lips and rubbing her belly. He struck a match to the kindling, watched it catch, and fed it slowly.

"I did promise to feed you, didn't I?"

"I'll get the bacon and—"

"No. I'll show you what I meant. Just give me a few minutes to make sure this fire won't go out. Then I'll go foraging for a feast."

"Then we'll need a basket." She stripped off his wool shirt and spread it open on one of the low-hanging limbs. She unwrapped her shawl and quickly tied its ends to form a pouch. Slinging the knotted end over her arm, she turned around. "There's your empty basket."

Catching her lighter mood, he tossed his hat near the saddles. "Your supper awaits. But walk behind me, Domini—"

"You did know my father, didn't you? You had to. He was the only one who ever called me that."

"It's a name that suits you. Are you going to ask questions or come with me?"

Unwilling to have the hostility he was so capable of come back, Domini shook her head. "Coming with you. But I don't understand why I need to walk behind you. How will I know what to look for if I can't see what you do?"

"I'll show you. You walk behind for two reasons. One, you'll crush new shoots without ever knowing that you killed off some animal's food. Second, there's cougar and bear up here. Not to mention that hunting party or ten more—"

"All right. You made your point. I will walk behind you."

"I'll give you a choice of supper. Fish or grouse?"

"Both."

"Both? You're a greedy woman."

"Just a very hungry one, Luke."

Domini started walking, remembered what he said, and waited for him to go first. When he didn't immediately join her, she looked back to find him standing near the fire. Her gaze clashed with the full power of his dark, intense stare.

"Food, Luke. That's all I'm hungry for."

"Pity." The corner of his mouth curled up, the smile cynical. Her gaze was wide, wary, vulnerable. His smile faded and left him with a vague, disturbed, itchy sense of having violated some imagined line. "Let's go."

He showed her how to find bitterroot, an elegantly shaped pink flower without any leaves that grew low to the ground. With his knife he dug up the root, a white, thin fiber about the size of a sliver of wood. Cleaning one off on his shirt, he offered Domini a bite.

When she took it from his hand, Luke was struck anew with the gift of her trust. He watched her bite off and chew a small piece, laughing at the face she made.

"It's like a raw turnip, bitter, but not unpleasant. But I wouldn't want to live on it."

"Just as well you won't have to. Com'on, we'll have a stew pot if I've caught grouse in my snare."

He filled her shawl with wild onions and parsley, the starchy root of elk thistle to be roasted, the bulb of the mariposa lily, which the Indians considered a great delicacy.

In the forest again, Luke showed her how to find a large, fleshy mushroom. When Domini did as he asked and lifted it to her nose, there was a faint but exquisite scent of apricots coming from the bright orange fungus.

"Chanterelles," he said when she asked what they were. "Some French trapper showed me them. Makes even the toughest game taste good."

"I'll take your word for it." Domini followed him to the edge of the woods, where he walked until they were halfway around the lake. This time she didn't need Luke to point out what they could pick. Huckleberries were just starting to ripen.

She ate the first handful she picked, licking the tart juice from her lips. "I want to pick more, Luke, but they'll get crushed in my shawl."

He stripped off his shirt and made another cloth sling. "Here, pick to your heart's content. I've got a yen for something sweeter."

She eyed the knotted shirt he slid over her

shoulder. If she turned around . . . but she wasn't going to look at him.

"Rabbit," he leaned close to whisper in her ear.

"Wonderful idea, Luke. We'll add it to the stew pot."

"That wasn't what I meant and you know it." He toyed with the end of her braid. "Where did the ribbon come from, Domini?"

"It's just a ribbon."

"Don't get so tightly laced. It was just a question. Anyhow, I know where it came from." He ran one finger up her rigid spine, from her waist to the bare skin of her neck. "Such a scared little rabbit. You can't even look at me. And the only thing that's stewing around here is my—"

"Luke, truce. Please." He was so wrong, but she was not going to admit it. The past hour of being with him was teaching her more about hunger that had nothing to do with the wild foodstuffs they had gathered. He had told her the lake would be near freezing. Domini knew she would welcome the cold. Something had to relieve the heat that stirred inside. Every word that he spoke was a brush over her skin. Hunger. She could name its levels, and it was more than she wanted to know.

"To have a truce we need to come to terms. What are you offering?"

Domini glanced down at the shirt she held. "I'll wash your clothes with mine."

"Not good enough."

She felt the light caress of his finger tracing the

length of her spine again. This time she couldn't stop him from feeling the tremor that rose to her skin.

"What do you want from me, Luke?"

"You. I want you."

She shied away from him. "That's not good enough." Her sleeve caught on a bramble and Domini pulled it free, only to stumble back against a hollow tree trunk. Two birds flew up, their feathers a beautiful powdery blue in the sunlight.

He watched the quick way she shaded her eyes to keep the small birds in sight and knew, before she could ask, that she'd want to know what they were. His body was whispering other things he could teach her, things that would stop the need that raked his skin like steel spurs.

"They're mountain bluebirds."

"Do the Indians have a legend about them, too?"

"About all the birds and how they got their colors."

Domini watched the birds until they were out of sight. There was nothing but the soft clouds to look at in the bright blue sky. Luke wasn't going to say any more until she looked at him.

Reluctantly she did. There was no softness or comfort in his dark eyes. But when she opened her mouth to speak, Luke placed two fingers against her lips.

"I'll tell you the legend if you promise to stop shying away from me. Deal?"

Domini nodded, wishing he would take his fingers from her lips before she gave in to the temptation to taste his skin. Her gaze fell to the pulse beating in the hollow of his throat, then lower to his broad shoulders. A blue neckerchief had replaced her bandage on his upper arm.

Seeing the direction of her gaze, Luke lifted his fingers from her mouth after he traced the bottom curve of her lip. "I changed it last night. It's healing just fine. Don't worry about it. And since we have a deal, I'll tell you while we pick the berries."

She worked beside him as he talked, trying hard not to shy away every time their hands reached for the same ripe berries, or the bare skin of his arm brushed against her sleeve. She had made a promise and was finding it a most difficult one to keep. Tension coiled around her. She couldn't stop thinking about the dark mat of hair that formed a diamond-shaped wedge on his chest. Could it be as soft as it looked? *Don't think about it. This is surely the devil's temptation testing you.*

No matter how many she repeated it, she couldn't dismiss the thought. The devil's snare couldn't catch her unless she was first caught by the devil's bait. No one had warned her that her own feelings would be part of the trap.

"So there you have it, the Great Spirit in despair because the trees lost their colorful leaves each fall. Since there were no birds, he turned the leaves into them. The russet oak leaves became robins, the yellow aspen leaves goldfinches. And so on. But the bluebird had no color."

Holding open the cloth shirt sack for his larger handful of berries, Domini asked, "How could he be called a bluebird without any color?"

"Since I didn't make up the story, I don't know. But the bird was disappointed and flew to heaven to complain. Bits of the blue rubbed off on him when he blundered into the curtain of the sky, and that's how he got his color."

"It's a pretty story. I wish I could fly to heaven and have the color of my skin changed. My skin, my hair . . . how silly of me to go on."

"Why?"

She looked up, startled. "You can see for yourself that I'm too dark. Whites take me for a half-breed because of my eyes, and in a way it's true. My father was Irish and my mother *mestizo*. The meld of French, Spanish, and Indian was so tangled in her family that no one knew its lines for sure."

He had at first thought her a breed. But it hadn't mattered then and didn't now. He reached out to cup the back of her head, intending to show her how much her golden skin and black silk hair pleased him. The seductive curve of her lips sent a shaft of hunger through him that was almost painful. It wasn't the sudden wariness in her eyes that stopped him, but his own unruly reaction to her. Luke dropped his hand.

"Take these back to camp." He picked up her

filled shawl, handed it over, then looked out toward the open meadow. "Make sure you stay close to the edge of the woods."

"Why? Aren't you coming back with me?"

"Is that what you want, Domini?"

Her breath caught. He was asking for more than accompanying her back to camp. She sensed it, just as she sensed the sudden tension riding him.

"Luke, please—"

"I'd like to, honey. You just keep saying the wrong words. Get back to camp, Domini."

His voice held the cutting edge of a chilling wind. Domini withdrew at the sudden change in him.

"Are you going deaf? Get back to camp *now,* or there'll be blazing hell to pay."

He waited until she was draped in shadow and sunlight at the edge of the woods. "Domini, if you'd come to me asking to change anything about you, I'd refuse."

She stilled, wary as a spooked fawn, and turned to him. Luke rubbed the back of his neck, wondering why the hell he didn't just let her go. But he might as well finish it.

"Maybe one thing. Yeah, there's one I'd change."

"Only one?" she asked in a husky, breathless voice.

"Yeah. Just one. I'd make sure you forgot how to say no."

# *Chapter Ten*

❦

Luke stayed away as long as he could. The sound of her humming drew him back, for he heard her voice in the rush of the water, the sweet sighing wind, even the quiet that lay over this small corner of wild land. He couldn't explain the feeling, even to himself, or maybe he didn't want to examine it too closely, but Domini made him feel the same emotions he'd had the first time he had found this haven.

*But you weren't alone . . .*

*And I ain't alone now.* He stepped into the clearing, holding a piece of honeycomb where she could see it.

"I was getting worried. You were gone so long." She came to her feet slowly, studying his face, unsure of his mood. Spying the treat he held, she hurried to him.

"Honey? Did you get stung?"

"A little. I've already packed mud on them. But

we've got something to sweeten those tart berries."

He stood for her touching the places where the mud had already caked and dried on his forearm. His breath hissed in as though he'd been burned.

"Stop, Domini. Stop worrying. The hive is older than me. Those bees should be used to having me steal their honey."

"You want them to be grateful that you stole from them?"

"When the thievin' doesn't hurt anyone, sure."

As far as she could see to satisfy herself, there weren't any stingers left. But she couldn't stop touching the raised welts.

"I once saw a man die from bee stings. His face and arm nearly doubled in size and he couldn't breathe—"

"There's nothing wrong with my breathing. Leastways there wasn't until you started touching me."

She whipped her hand down to her side, clutching her gown as if she'd been the one stung. Domini had to back off. She wasn't foolish enough to provoke him when that cutting edge clipped every word. She glanced over her shoulder at where she had been working.

"I found that flat slab of rock to use for a table. There's no water left in the canteens. I used every bit to wash the roots and berries. You told me not to leave camp—"

"So I did. And I promised you a bath, too."

"Yes. You did." She made herself look up at him. "It's still all right, isn't it?"

"Tear off a piece of bark from that big deadfall so I can set this comb down." He walked closer to the fire and saw her things neatly laid out on top of her carpet bag to one side. He grinned seeing the bar of soap and cloth.

"Little thief. You took those from the hotel."

Ripping off the bark, Domini handed it over to him. "You just stole honey. Isn't that the pot calling the kettle black?"

"I've always had the choice of buyin' or takin' what I want, Domini. Don't matter much which way it goes. But you, stealing's got to matter unless those vows you intended to take were lies. Bet you prayed for forgiveness, didn't you?"

She turned away, frightened that he could read her so well.

"Makes a man wonder what kind a nun you'll make. Liar and thief—"

"I'll make a very good one, Luke. I will have the compassion not to condemn a hungry child for stealing."

Luke grinned, but it never reached his eyes, which raked her from head to toe and made a slower perusal back to her face.

"You're not a child anymore, Domini. And soap ain't food."

He saw the shudder that went through her, and once more he wondered how much came from fear and how much from the wild, hidden sensuality that was awake and growing. He shifted his stance to ease rapidly hardening flesh, but the move was useless. He wasn't going to get rid of this ache alone.

Luke set aside the bark and lifted his hand to his lips to lick the honey that had dripped from the comb to his skin.

Domini's lips parted, her breath caught, held, then rushed out.

He looked down at the golden drops. His own breathing matched her quickened cadance. Luke could no more help it than he could stop watching her staring at his hand. His gaze lay in wait to snare hers when she finally looked up at him.

A knowing smile curled his lips. Fire licked his loins just as his tongue licked up the first drop. "Sweeter than I've ever tasted it. Warm, too." *Like her skin, like her lips*. He thought of tastes that were sweeter, hotter, and smooth as silk to his tongue. *Tastes soft enough to ease a man's pain*.

He dismissed the thought as he had the first time the generous shape of her mouth brought it forth. Just as he dismissed the nagging question of why he had wanted to kiss her.

Kissing was an intimacy that he had never offered another woman.

He caught up another drop, savoring the small burst of sweetness, cool in the heat of his mouth. And he savored her unconscious move to moisten the center of her bottom lip with the tip of her tongue. Shadows played over the strong, striking features of her face. Features that he knew he would never tire of watching. Her eyes widened with sensual awareness. He couldn't look away from them as he sought one more taste of honey.

But he wanted to. He wanted to know what changes were happening to her body hidden beneath her clothes. If she stopped staring at his mouth and dropped her gaze, Domini would know exactly what he was thinking, what he was feeling.

He was hard as a whetstone, fighting need sharp as a blade honed on its edge.

A woman's arousal was hidden beyond the flush tinting her skin and the slight flare of her nostrils that mimicked his own. And he had to look. Had to know.

His gaze slid down the lifted curve of her chin past the graceful length of her neck. He could see the pulse beat in the hollow, beat as wildly as his own, and measured the quick rise and fall of her breasts. He looked lower to find nipples beaded tight beneath the thin cloth. In the silence of his mind he cursed the arousal that notched up to a level near pain.

As slowly as he began, his gaze returned to target her eyes again. He held out his hand to her.

"Want some? Don't bother to deny it. I can see the hunger in you. I'm not a selfish man, Domini. I'm all for sharing anything you want, anyway you want it."

"Luke, please . . ."

"I'm tryin' like hell's on fire, honey. Just tell me what you want."

Domini closed her eyes. It was the only way she could think to hide from the blazing intensity of his. A wild spiral rose inside her, as shocking and dizzying as the first time she had felt it. Emotions tangled, crashing and separating only to collide again. Each sensation was sharp and exquisite and painful. Devil's snare. Devil's bait. A test of will, of conviction. Her hands curled so tightly around the cloth of her gown that she could feel them go numb.

He had called her a thief. Luke was right. She had stolen in the past. But what he asked her for now was a thievery of her soul. He didn't love her. He wanted her. Like the sweet honey he had licked from his hand, she would satisfy a momentary craving.

*And you? Won't you satisfy the same?*

*Se rindió.* Give in.

*Válgame Dios!* Heaven help me, I want to.

"Domini, a man'll wait so long."

"Stop it," she whispered in a broken voice. "Stop tempting me and taunting and—"

". . . teasing till you can't think of anything else. A wild ride down the river of no return, Domini. That's how it'll be. And I *know*. When you're ready to stop lying to yourself, you'll know, too. Get your things. I'll walk you down to the lake."

Her shoulders sagged under the burden he'd placed on her. But it had to be her choice. He scooped up the piece of bark with the honey and set it in a high crook of a tree.

Clutching her things, Domini's puzzled gaze went no farther than his hand lowering to his side.

"It might keep a bear from prowling too close and stealing my honey. Like I told you, I'm real possessive about what I claim as mine." He stepped over to the saddles and slid his rifle from the scabbard.

"I thought you set a snare for supper."

"I did. All nicely baited, too. I should catch something to satisfy my hunger. After you bathe, I'll go fishing."

"With a gun? Isn't the one you wear as if it were welded to your hip and thigh enough?"

Holding aloft the rifle with his right hand, Luke looked at her. "You don't call this a gun. It's a rifle. A .44 Winchester. This," he added, sliding his left hand down the smooth wooden butt and leather that indeed felt as if it were part of him, "is what you call a gun."

She hadn't wanted to follow the movement of his hand. She did and regretted it the same moment. Luke's waistband dipped below the narrow wedge of dark hair that centered his chest, revealing lighter skin that had not been touched by the sun. A little devil teased her with the thought that the sun was the only thing that hadn't touched his skin. She hated the image of a woman's hands caressing . . . No! She wasn't going to allow the image of cool hands—her hands—sliding open the horn buttons to discover flesh hard enough to strain glove-soft cloth.

Prayer wasn't helping to remove wicked thoughts. Domini knew how foolish she was to hope it could. Wickedness stood temptingly arrayed before her. As Luke said, a snare nicely baited. But nicely was wrong. Too weak a description.

Domini tore her gaze away and asked him again why he need both weapons.

"Walk out with me and I'll show you."

Holding her clean clothes, soap, and cloth in a death grip against her chest, she walked as quickly as her legs would move out into the sunlight blanketing the meadow. Despite the return of screaming muscles, she would have kept walking, but Luke's hand coming to rest on her shoulder stopped her.

"See that slab of rock above the second fall?"

Following the rifle barrel he pointed, she saw the tilted granite slab that rose in a spray of diamond mist.

"I see it. But I still don't understand." A tremor underscored her voice, the same tremor that rippled from the skin beneath his hand to tighten her breasts.

"I'll be sitting up there. It's a good vantage point to watch the woods around the lake."

"I thought you said we were safe here." Domini forced herself to speak. All she could think about was an invisible line from where he would be sitting to the sparkling surface of the lake. Now, now matter how much she wanted her bath, she wished she had never mentioned it. She had assumed that he would remain in camp to give her some privacy.

Luke felt the tension gripping her body. "You could always change your mind."

"Change my mind?" Not again. Dear God, not again. I can't refuse . . . I will. I must.

"About the bath. What the hell else did you think I meant? Never mind. I know, don't I? Like I said, the choice is yours. You want a cold water bath, it's all yours. But I could give you one that's warmer."

She saw his tongue gently licking up the honey and trembled where she stood.

"Who are you more worried about, Domini? Me or yourself?"

She wished she didn't understand what he meant, but she did. God forgive, she did too well.

"This isn't fear that makes you quiver like a sapling in the wind. It's me touching you, isn't it?"

"You know exactly what it is, Luke. Why ask? Why torment me? And yes, I want a cold water bath." *I need time and space away from you.*

His fingers trailed up the side of her neck. He caught the lobe of her ear between the tips of his thumb and forefinger. Very gently he applied enough pressure so she wouldn't pull away, and rubbed the fleshy, soft skin.

"Listen to me." He leaned close to whisper in her ear. "I'm not climbing that rock to start an itch I can't scratch. Just watching you react to me is enough to do that. But I'm a man, Domini, not a boy who can't or won't control himself.

"And we've already proven that if I wanted you stripped, naked, and flat on your back, there isn't much you can do to stop me. Right?"

Color deepened on her cheeks, and she jerked her head to one side. Looking at him with eyes the dark green of the forest, flashing with temper, she spat out a string of curses.

"Well, you got that part right, honey. Bastard is my middle name. As for the rest of that *mestizo* mess you're spitting at me, there wasn't a prayer in a word. And I'm not greedy, Domini. Remember? I offered to share. But if you'd think a minute, you'd realize that I don't have a choice, either.

"I can't see worth a damn from camp to the lake. You flounder in that water with a cramp an' you'd drown before I heard you. If any other kind of trouble comes sniffing 'round that lake, we both know just how much you can and can't handle alone.

"Go on, have your bath." He gave her a slight push. "Head for the right. There's a rock shelf there where you can put your things and reach them easily."

She didn't answer him. She walked away at an angle from where he strode to the falls. Domini didn't fight the compelling need to look after him. Bathed in full sunlight, he moved with the easy grace of the wind through the meadow. Muscles rippled across his back. Muscles covered by skin that was crisscrossed with thin white scars.

She opened her mouth to call out. Her lips and teeth closed over the cloth she raised to hide her cry. Someone had beaten Luke. No, not beaten but whipped him.

Her mind struggled with the thought that anyone could hold him down . . . No!

One man couldn't hold down Luke and whip him at the same time. Not unless Luke had been unconscious.

Or very young. Too young to fight back.

*Secrets, Domini. Just like you keep yours hidden, Luke hides his.*

He had to know that she saw him. But he gave no indication that he knew or cared. Before she reached the boulders spilling in a curved arc from the falls, Luke had already climbed high. The water beckoned, and she heeded its call. The cold would leech the shimmering heat he called forth from a body still shaken with this last encounter.

She ignored him by turning her back toward him.

Luke settled himself on the granite slab. He sat in perfect silence and perfect stillness, the rifle across his knees. This was a gift. A gift of stillness. From the time he had begun to ride, he had found he could will his body reactions down, animal-

like, stiller than death. From the biting wind and
the spray a coldness seeped through his pants and
boots. The cold worked its way through his skin
and chilled fevered blood, settling in the marrow
of his bones. His arm throbbed. He refused to
acknowledge the ache.

He deliberately blanked his mind from thoughts
of Domini sliding into the water, as sleek and dark
as an otter. He was one with the land.

The peace he sought wasn't there. The land had
never cared enough about him to be concerned
that a few bee stings welted his flesh.

Domini had cared. Every time she had looked
at the wound she inflicted on his arm, remorse
had filled her eyes.

But he wasn't going to think about her, wasn't
going to turn his head to see her strong strokes
carry her back and forth in front of the rock shelf
with nary a ripple on the lake's surface.

It was ridiculous to think that he could hear
the slide of cloth against flesh that had never been
touched by the sun beneath the rumble of the
water.

It was only the moan of the wind filling his
ears, not sighs of pleasure from her lips.

Ruthlessly, as if chased by a demon, Luke
ripped aside layer upon layer to climb into the
one inviolate place in his mind. Nothing could
follow him there. Nothing ever had.

He would be as he'd always been—alone.

Her image followed him.

He dug deeper to escape her.

*Domini*.

Face raised to the sun. Water cascading down heavy black, satin hair. Tendrils curled, clinging and stealing blue from the sky.

Luke dug deeper, fighting to erase her.

Image upon image flowed, one into another, pursuing him.

Droplets of captured sunlight splintered into shards, all falling, running together, soaking cloth thin as the mist rising at his back.

*Domini*.

Black eyes gleaming, licking sweet water from dusky lips. A child's joy. A woman's pleasure.

Luke's mouth went dry. He was every bit as hard as the rock he sat on. All he could see was softness and velvet shadows.

No. There was strength in her sleek, graceful body. She wasn't all soft heat. Dusky flesh, tightly beaded from cold, offered a sultry invitation to his parched lips.

Luke felt the force of his grip on smooth, dark walnut and blue-black metal that wouldn't break. But all he saw was lushly rounded golden skin that would bruise easily with the strength of his hands.

His breath caught, held, then rushed out with the wild desperation seizing him. He couldn't easily rid himself of blood that sizzled with need.

*Domini*.

Once his promise. But death made mockery of Jim's someday promises to him.

Honey-hot whispers that pierced his skin, flaying him alive. Husky laughter caught in memory to torment.

How many times had his hands shaped her slender waist? And let her go? Let go, when he wanted to slide them down to rounded hips and nestle his aching flesh in womanly secrets veiled by black silk that was hotter than the sun and sweeter than rain?

Luke's muscles clenched in agony. In his mind he ran faster. But he couldn't escape.

*Domini.*

Needing to be held from the shocking truth of her frail defense. Rocking against him. Fitting him perfectly from mouth to mouth, breast to hip, thigh to knee.

His heart pounded with a force that nearly suffocated him.

She was temper and passion, fire and fury. Soft enough to take away a man's pain.

*She doesn't know.*

*I can't tell her.*

*You won't.*

*I won't tell her about a nightmare I never fully remember.*

Eyes alight with sensual curiosity. Asking. Begging. Unaware. Arousing a storm of violent emotions when her lovely mouth whispered denial.

Luke had the scent of her filling him. Eyes closed or open didn't matter now.

He saw her standing before him, naked, veiled in sunlight, lushly scented.

*Domini.*

Jim Kirkland's daughter.

Flame bright to rival the sun.

Hot enough to scorch a man.

"Luke? L-Luke."

He opened his eyes and wiped the sweat beading his brow.

"Luke, what's wrong?"

She stood below him, hand shading her eyes against the glare of the sun.

He'd never denied himself anything he really wanted.

*What did Toma want with her?*

If you really wanted . . . never denied . . .

"Answer me, Luke. What's wrong?"

He looked down at her with eyes forged in hell.

# Chapter Eleven

❧

Domini pressed one hand against the damp cloth covering her chest. Luke looked wild. An angry god, all dark, pagan beauty where he sat above her, still as the mountains. His silence, that absolute silence, unnerved her. She started backing away and stopped. She couldn't draw her gaze away from him.

Although he appeared carved from the same stone that challenged air and time to diminish it, she sensed the heat of raging conflict pouring out of him.

"Luke, what have I done?"

His eyes seemed to bore down into her. She retreated. An explosive darkness surrounded him. She shook her head, but the image persisted. What had happened? The whole time she had bathed, she had watched his back.

"Get your things together. We're leaving. It's time for you to pay the devil his due."

"I don't understand, Luke. What about supper?"

"Lost my appetite."

"And the snare you set? You're not going to leave some poor creature to die."

"Trap's sprung. Came up empty."

*What's wrong!* She didn't know this cold, even-voiced stranger. He rose to his feet. Domini flung her head back to look at him. The wet weight of her braid strained the arch of her throat. She stared at the rocky ledge and the man, assaulted by the raw, predatory power that locked his gaze with hers.

Domini didn't know how long she stood there, watching him, just as he watched her. She knew he was right, that they had to leave here. She'd been alone too long with him. Too long with the confusion he created.

It was Luke who broke the silence stretched taut between them. His high, shrill whistle brought Devil trotting across the meadow. After a few moments the sorrel followed.

She didn't wait for him to climb down the rocks. Domini ran for the clothing she had spread to dry. By the time she turned around, Luke was already leading the horses back to camp.

What caused that chilling, detached sense of violence that came so easily upon him? She wasn't sure she wanted to know. Domini followed the path he had left through the tall meadow grass. She was lying to herself. She did want to know—

wanted an answer with a need as compelling as
Luke himself.

By the time she reached the clearing, instinct
alerted her that whatever danger Luke had presented minutes before had passed.

The shirt he wore was as wrinkled as the damp,
patched gown she had hurried to put on after
bathing. He worked with a quick economy of motion that she tried to duplicate, just as she dupli-
cated his continued silence.

He had saddled the sorrel first, then Devil before he went back to fill the canteens. Domini
was mounted and waiting by the time he returned.
When he slung both the canteen straps over his
saddle horn, she understood that he didn't want
to come near her. Didn't want to touch her, talk
to her. His gaze avoided her, and she didn't sense
but knew how badly he wanted her gone from
sight.

She thought back to what she had said to him.
Had seeing her dark olive skin brought home to
him what mixed blood she had? Until her bath he
had wanted her. She hadn't been mistaken about
the blaze that gleamed in his eyes, rode his voice,
hardened his body.

*You should be rejoicing that danger is past.*

The fact that she wasn't bewildered her.

She turned for a last look at the clearing. The
fire had been smothered, then covered over. Even
the flat slab of rock she had struggled to move
close to the fire pit was back in place as if she

had never touched it. She lifted her gaze, and it caught on the honeycomb in the crook of the tree.

Luke hadn't touched that. Ants and flies were already attacking the forgotten treat. She must never forget for a moment this was a land of prey and predator. Survival depended on skill and cunning.

But when Domini looked ahead at Luke, maintaining an easy pace across the meadow, she knew this time prey had escaped through no effort of its own. Luke was as cold, hard, and wary as any predator, far more skilled and cunning at baiting devil's snares than she.

Luke wasn't what she needed to worry about. As he had reminded her, it was time for her to pay the devil his due.

What Luke didn't know, and she wouldn't tell him, was that the opposite was true. Toma Colfax would be the one who paid. And she didn't care if it was to God or the devil.

These past few days spent in such close company with Luke had made her lose sight of the reasons she had come here. She had to fight the lure of passion's promise. It was only a momentary satisfaction. At least that is what she had been told, what she believed.

Love endured. Luke offered one without the other. Following him out of a narrow neck of woods into a steep-sided pass, Domini wondered if Luke even knew what love was.

She warned herself to be more guarded, for no

matter how carefully she wove her reasons against Luke, she was far too aware that he had only to look at her for passion to stir and stretch, rending her weavings useless.

Late afternoon sun turned the peaks a rich scarlet. They continued to ride in silence, and Domini grew tired of gazing at rock like the bare, brownish hillside that they were climbing. The footing was treacherous for the horses on the talus slope. Masses of ice-chipped rock fragments covered the earth. On either side stunted trees gave way farther down to majestic evergreens. The long, straight trunks were a rich orange, the branches a bright emerald green. Once more they plunged down into a fragrant spruce forest, following a wide stream where the water appeared green from the reflection of the trees. The sun dropped behind the spruces and the air turned chilly.

And Luke's growing tension communicated to her that they were nearing Colfax land. This, too, was a puzzle she wanted to solve, but he had not once turned to look at her. Lost in thought, she nearly rode past Luke, unaware that he had stopped to wait for her to catch up with him.

His arm shot out and caught hold of the sorrel's rein. Startled, Domini rocked off balance for a few moments.

"Past this stretch of woods is the pass into a valley," Luke said, biting off each word. He hid his annoyance that she avoided looking directly at him.

"We're here, then?"

"You've been on Colfax land the moment we rode into that meadow."

"I see." She bit her lip, fighting not to look at him, fighting not to ask him why, if they had been this close, he had stopped there.

"Don't think you do, but it's of no matter now. I'm giving you a last choice. Once we ride into that pass there's no way out."

"There's always a way, Luke."

"Not here. This is the devil's caldron, honey. His pot, his stakes, his game. Toma don't like losing. He'll bottom deal or up the ante for your soul if it gets him what he wants. Better men, a hell of a lot more skilled than you, have come away dazed to find themselves owned."

She looked at him then. His hat brim was canted low, adding shadows to the black stubble covering his lower face. Outlaw. The word aptly described him. Yet despite his threatening appearance, tendrils of sensual tension coiled between them. The sorrel danced in place, bringing her knee against Luke's. If touching with cloth between them could send a flare of heat streaking up her leg, what would it be like if skin rubbed against skin?

"Did you hear me, honey?"

"Stop calling me that, Luke. I'm not your honey. I'm not your anything."

"Don't be too sure about that. Right now you're rock hard and mule thick not to listen to what I'm saying."

"I listened. I heard. I don't have a choice. Lead on, Luke."

Domini was proud that her voice didn't waver. Her gaze fell to his smile. The three-day growth of black stubble made the curve of his lips savage. Her gaze slid down to his bare, tanned throat and the half-buttoned shirt that revealed black curling hair and the glitter of sweat caught there. She didn't know she had touched her tongue to her lips until he swore at her.

Like his smile, the curses were savage.

"Everything you've told me about Toma Colfax tells me that you've clashed with him, even if you've worked for the man. Did he get you into a game where you lost your soul to him, Luke? Or have you the skills to walk away the winner?"

"You're about to find out, honey. Smile pretty and say hello to Ramsey and Caully. You remember them, don't you?" he asked, never turning around to watch the two men coming up the slope toward them. "These generous men were willing to share you around."

Domini remembered too well the night she had stood ready to face them alone. Her gaze barely skimmed the two men, but went instead to the barely noticeable bandage beneath Luke's wrinkled shirt. She wasn't likely to forget the result of that night or her first taste of a man's hungry passion.

"Christ, Luke!" Ramsey said, reaching them first. "Where the hell have you been? Matt's had us huntin' your tail for three days."

"Nice of him to be concerned."

"Yeah, well, you know him, Luke." He shot a quick look at the woman, eased his hat brim back, and then gazed at her again. "Well, well, if it ain't that little green-eyed breed." And to Caully, who joined them, he said, "Don't need to ask what's kept Luke away. The old man ain't gonna like you bringing her here." He took in the long, hasily made braid, her wrinkled pale blue gown, tracking the line of tiny buttons that rose from her slender waist to her throat.

The knowing look he exchanged with Caully sent a shudder of repugnance through Domini. Luke was still holding the sorrel's rein's, keeping her beside him. She was thankful that he was between her and the two men. Even so, their gazes felt like hands crawling over her skin.

Caully, randy as any bull, ignored Luke's narrowed gaze. "Was she worth it?" He all but licked his lips.

"She musta been. Luke ain't never taken up with no woman an' brought her here," Ramsey answered before Luke did.

"Remember that while you ride ahead an' tell Matt you found me. And the old man. Tell him, too."

Domini looked from the two men to Luke. He had spoken softly, in a hair-raising whisper, but they merely nodded, circled around them, and walked their horses off through the trees.

"Why did you let them think I'm someone you brought along for your amusement?"

"That what I did, honey? Didn't sound that way to me."

"You know what you implied," Domini accused, trying to pull the leather free from his hand.

"Sure as hell wasn't that you *amuse* me. You haven't yet. Now if you said I'd made it plain as your gown being a size too small to be decent, honey, that I'd bedded you till neither one of us wanted to move for the past three nights an' still had a itch that wants scratching, you'd be closer to the truth."

Domini didn't bother to look at the cloth pulled tightly across her breasts. Thinking they had another night to sleep in the open, she had chosen another of her old gowns to wear. She didn't need to look down to see her nipples clearly revealed by thin layers of cloth. She had felt the tightening the moment Luke's knee brushed against hers.

"Does it give you pleasure to know you make me feel like a *puta* you bought? You're a cold-blooded bastard, Luke."

"Told you before, bastard's my middle name." He eased deeper in the saddle, leaning back to stop himself from grabbing hold of her and hauling her up into his lap.

"The kind of pleasure I want from you is steeped in sin. All the sweeter for it, but fickle as a disappearing vein of gold." He released her reins and Devil pivoted on his hocks. Luke looked back at her. "But you can't accuse me of being cold-blooded, honey. Not around you. You keep my blood pitched hot enough to burn down the mountains.

"An' if you want anyone to believe that I'm-holier-than-the-vows-I'm-about-to-take nun act, don't curse. After all, you've only got your word that you're who you claim to be."

"You accepted it quick enough. I wasn't lying then, and I'm not lying now, Luke. James Kirkland is my father."

"Was, honey. He's dead, remember?"

If her gaze was a loaded gun, Luke's back would have been riddled with holes. *I remember, Luke. I can't forget.*

Domini found herself adding his warning to the others he had given her. Just as Luke's wariness increased, she found herself digging deep inside to bring forth the same finely honed edge of wariness that had helped her survive. Hard as Luke's razor-like coldness was to swallow, she remained quiet and followed him. But she still wondered if Luke had lost his soul or come out a winner in a game with Toma Colfax.

Not more than ten minutes later, Domini rode out to where Luke waited and looked upon a valley that stole her breath.

"Beautiful, isn't it?"

Domini could only nod in response to Luke's question. The setting sun spread scarlet fire over granite walls rising like sentinels protecting the verdant bowl of the valley floor. Gem-like ribbons of water dotted the lush meadows, and a lake shimmered in a cupped depression.

With each sweeping look Domini added details. The snake-back rail fences that divided one side of the valley revealed, upon closer inspection, small herds of horses and cattle. Riders appeared in twos and threes, all heading toward the corrals near log buildings shaded orange and gold as the sun dipped lower behind the snow-capped mountains.

The last dying rays cast blood-red shadows on a sprawling house built of native stone. A few towering pines shaded one side. Her gaze swept over that house time and again, barely touching upon the smaller sheds and barns.

She was staring down at a man's empire, an empire bought with gold. She fully understood now, as she had not before, the immense power and wealth she was about to confront. Alone. She glanced at Luke. He leaned forward with forearms resting on the saddle horn, watching as she watched the tiny stick figures moving around.

"You ready to go down?"

Was she? Domini wasn't sure. But she had come this far, and the choice had never been hers alone.

"Lead on, Luke." She cast one last look below and told herself the shiver rippling over her was from the chill in the air. It had nothing to do with the dark stone walls that enfolded the valley. It was only the reddened light of the sun that made her think of the fires of hell. That, and Luke's constant reminder that Toma Colfax's home was the devil's caldron.

She looked up and tracked the lone flight of an eagle. In watching the massive bird of prey's gliding flight on air currents, Domini spotted a small log cabin nestled against the towering pines on a rock shelf above them. She could only imagine the spectacular view it afforded whoever lived up there.

Luke noted her interest but said nothing. They were drawing closer to the stone fortress where Toma ruled. The clang of the supper bell rang from the bunkhouse porch. Riders kept at a distance as they rode to heed its call. He wondered if Three Fingers Moran was still cooking for the hands.

He shifted in the saddle, trying to ease the tension that tightened every muscle. Closer they rode, and from a nearby pasture a muscular appaloosa stallion, distinctively marked on the rump and back with black spots, trumpeted a challenge and galloped toward the fence with his sweeping black tail raised like a banner.

Devil tossed his head to whinny a greeting, but the sorrel flicked her ears uneasily, dancing in a nervous side step despite Domini's effort to hold her to a walk.

"Let out the rein an' give her her head," Luke ordered. "She knows he's caught her scent, an' the lady ain't anxious to be mounted. She'll settle once we're passed."

He made sure Domini obeyed him, ready to take control of the mare if she didn't settle down.

"Since I brought you into the valley through the hind end, you'll have to ride a ways to come around front of the house."

"I'll have to ride . . . alone?" Domini couldn't look at him. She couldn't fault Luke's knowledge about horses, for the mare had stopped fighting her even though the stallion trumpeted another call from the end of his pasture fence.

"Didn't figure you'd like the idea." He neck-reined Devil to veer off the beaten dirt track, heading for the trees that sheltered one side of the massive, sprawling house.

Luke, in the lead, saw the welcome party waiting on the front porch. His tension increased and communicated itself to Devil. Snorting, the horse made an attempt to rear, chewing the bit resentfully until Luke regained control of himself and his horse. Snugging his hat brim lower, he he steeled himself. Matt Colfax wasn't alone. Coming down the wide stone steps was the old man himself, with the wrath of the devil gleaming from eyes black as his own.

## Chapter Twelve

~

"**W**here the hell have you been? I got to hear from hands that you were in Florence. Sent Grady to look for you, an' come to find out that Matt already had Caully and Ramsey trying to find you."

"Hello to you, too, old man. It's been a while. Not long enough, but who's countin'." It was just like Toma to forget their last fight, when the old man ordered him to leave because he thought the only way to do anything was his way.

"What's this you got with you, Luke?"

"It's a woman. Or have you gone blind since I've been gone?"

"I ain't blind. Can see for myself that you're bringing your trash with you."

Domini felt the heat that colored her face. She sat up straighter and reined her sorrel a little closer to Luke. She didn't understand why he was plainly reluctant to introduce her and insisted on goading a man who could only be Toma Colfax. She sensed someone standing well back in the shadows of the porch, but couldn't take her gaze from the man who called her trash.

He was as tall as Luke and as straight as a lodgepole pine. Gray peppered his thick hair, two almost white streaks springing from his temples. She gave him back stare for stare, refusing to let the powerful cast of craggy features intimidate her. He wore his wealth in gleaming black leather boots, finely tailored pants, and a ruffled white shirt beneath a supple black leather vest. A rich sheen of gold relieved the black vest in the watch chain strung between pockets. On his left hand he wore a pinky ring with a blood red stone set in gold.

Despite his wealthy trappings, Domini formed a decision based on years of sizing up those she could beg from—Toma wasn't one. As her gaze returned to clash with his beneath hooded brows, she knew this was a man who had no charity in his soul. Why then had he paid to have her taken in by the mission? Why had he sent her money to come here?

She couldn't wait for Luke. She had to tell him who she was.

But Luke spoke before she marshaled herself.

"Actually, old man, she ain't mine. Think of me as your personal freight deliverer."

"What in God's name are you talkin' about, Luke?"

"I'm talkin' about the fact that I picked up your ordered package an' delivered her safe and sound to you."

"My ordered—" Toma looked from Luke to the bold young woman who watched him with eyes older than his own years. "Who the hell is she?"

"Toma Colfax, meet Jim Kirkland's daughter."

"Daughter?"

Domini didn't miss the choking sound of that word or the way Toma quickly hid his shock. She glanced at Luke, thoroughly confused.

"I swear I didn't lie to you. He did send for me."

"Send for you? Like hell I did! Didn't know where in tarnation you were." Toma started down the step, then changed his mind.

"Com'on, old man, you ain't forgot Dominica. Jim used to talk about her all the time."

"You believe this cock an' bull story?"

"Look at her eyes, old man. Or are you blind? She's got Jim's green eyes. What you should be askin' is who sent for her if you didn't." Luke set his blunted spurs to Devil's side, and the big horse backed away. "I've done my part. I know you'll excuse me so you can get on with this touching reunion." He flipped his right hand at his hat brim. "Nice to see you again, Matt. I was real touched that you were concerned about me. Only the next time you send Caully after me, I'm comin' after you."

"Stay where the hell you are, you bastard!" Toma ordred, coming down the steps to grab hold of Devil's reins. "You're not dumping this on my step and riding off again." Aware that they were attracting attention, Toma released the reins to motion away his curious hands.

"Let's go inside and sort this out." Turning to Domini, he added, "If you are who you claim, I'll get to the bottom of this. In the meantime you're welcome into my home."

"Gracious old bastard, ain't he?"

Domini didn't answer Luke. She saw that he did dismount, but she remained on the sorrel. The vicious undercurrents that she sensed made her waver. *But you've come so far and waited so long.*

Truth that could not be denied. Yet fear touched her, too. If Toma wasn't lying, then who had sent for her? And why?

She broke off her thoughts. Toma was already inside. Luke had his back toward her, tying off his horse. There was no sign of the man Luke had addressed as Matt.

"Luke, what's going on here?"

"Beats me. But you heard him. Welcome to his home. He won't shoot you. Toma's become too civilized to settle his problems with a bullet."

He saw her give in for a moment to fear. Then with a rough shake of her head, she contained it. He admired that in her.

"Climb down, honey. I don't want to put my hands on you."

"I trust you, Luke."

"Yeah. I know. Hell of a burden to put on a man who doesn't trust himself."

Motionless, Luke waited and watched her with a hunter's patience. He was discovering that sensual teasing mixed with honesty worked with a young woman as passionate as Domini.

The flashes of passion she had revealed were a lure greater than the gleam of midnight hair and a body that sweetly curved to the fit of his. And the passion in her called to him as restlessly as the wind whispering promises.

He thought of Matt, waiting inside, and knew she would never know the rough edge of his tongue—Matt would whisper loving lies, smooth and skilled, using the manners of a gentleman while he unfastened her grip on virtue to plunder soft heat.

"Luke? It's all right? I won't put any more burdens on you." She slid down and clung to the saddle, the slight trembling of her hands belying her words. Right now she wanted him to hold her. Hearing the savage hiss of his breath, Domini sheltered her eyes beneath a thick fringe of lashes, fighting to regain control of herself.

She should be thinking about the confrontation to come with Toma. She should be sorting out the lies Toma had spoken. All she could think about was Luke. *A wild ride on a river's fury, that's how it'll be.* And she could feel desire's siren call flowing through her, weakening her resolve. She wanted to laugh and release the tension coiling her insides. . . . Luke hadn't even touched her to make her feel this way. *What would it be like if he did?*

"Better go on in, Domini. No sense kicking up his temper before you've said your piece."

Domini took a deep, steadying breath, released it, and looked away before she was ready to move. She started to untie her carpet bag when Luke stopped her for a moment.

"Leave it. O'Malley'll come for your bag."

"No. I don't want anyone else touching it." She managed the tie and lowered the bag to the ground.

"You let me carry it, Domini. What difference—"

"I told you I trust you, Luke. Curse all you want, but it's the truth. There's something I have to show him in this bag." She looked over to where he stood. "You will come with me, won't you?"

His answer was to stare at the house.

"Luke, Toma invited us both inside his home. He said we'd be welcome there."

"Maybe for you, honey. There ain't no welcome within those walls for me."

She picked up her bag, clutching it tight, and walked to his side. She didn't understand what spurred Luke to a barely hidden savagery, but she wanted him with her.

"Please, Luke?" she asked, touching his rigid forearm.

Luke released his breath in a soundless rush of air. Her touch increased the intensity of his desire. But one look into those wide green eyes and he saw her worry. He could no more refuse her than he could refuse his next breath.

He lifted his hand, fingers trailing beneath the curve of her jaw, lifting her face. "You don't know what you're askin' of me, Domini. But I'll stay with you for a while. Just until you get this sorted out. The thing is, I want something for my trouble."

She gazed into his eyes, staring at the tiny splinters of gold lighting the black like fires burning. "Since you know I don't have any money, you'll be wanting something from me."

"Nothing I haven't had before. And not now. Later. I'll claim my payment later."

She couldn't go back on her word that she trusted him. Her need for his support outweighed whatever Luke wanted from her. As much as she tried to ignore and deny it, Domini knew she stood at a crossroads that would change her life.

Taking her hand from his arm, she nodded. "I agree, but no more than what you've already had."

In his mind he'd already had her seven ways to Sunday, and he grinned. "Just remember your terms, Domini. And if I'm not mistaken, O'Malley's standin' just inside the door takin' this bargain in, an' about ready to remind us that Mr. Colfax's waitin'."

"Right you are," Mr. O'Malley said, stepping

out onto the porch. "Mr. Colfax is not known for his patience, miss. Best come along."

Domini climbed the steps with head high and back straight, wishing again that she had had time to change. The stone floor of the porch gave way to gleaming wood floors once she had crossed the threshold. Crystal prisms shimmered with rainbow colors from the two tall lamps lit to dispel the evening gloom.

"I'll take your bag, miss."

"No. This stays with me until after I've spoken to Mr. Colfax."

"Just lead the way, O'Malley," Luke said, taking hold of Domini's arm. And to her, he whispered, "The old man will be in his office. Plenty of power an' intimidation waiting there."

Domini hung back a little as Mr. O'Malley started down the hallway. "Have you ever been intimidated, Luke? By him or anyone?"

"When I was too young to fight back." He shot her a look, then slid his hand from her elbow to entwine his fingers with hers. With a gentle squeeze he added, "Don't worry. I won't let him or Matt hurt you."

The gentle touch was at odds with the underlying savagery in his voice. Domini wondered if he was even aware of it. Seeing that Mr. O'Malley had paused near a doorway up ahead, Domini quickened her pace.

The bandy-legged man stood aside to let her

and Luke pass inside, then closed the door behind them.

Domini didn't need Luke to confirm that his guess had been right. This was a man's room, with all the trappings of power prominently displayed. Toma stood by the fireplace, not a hint of his thoughts revealed on his face. Seated in a leather chair so that only his profile could be seen was another man, younger, far more handsome than Toma, and she knew this had to be Matt. The one that Luke had warned he'd go after. It was too much to sort out now. Her curiosity rose that Luke could talk to Toma's son that way without a word to stop him.

"I suppose you feel you have a vested interest in this, Luke."

"Yeah, Matt. You could say that." Luke eyed the glass held in long fingers that would never know a callus from work. "You still drinking that fancy stuff?"

"Brandy is a gentleman's drink."

"An' the old man still drinks his rotgut. Right?" Luke asked, glancing at Toma.

"Some things a man keeps to remind him where he's been an' where he's standin' now."

"Ah, those humble beginnings." Luke turned to Domini. "Matt drinks and talks like a gentleman, but he's got the manners of a pig. Would you like something to drink? O'Malley should be along with coffee, but if you'd like something stronger . . ."

"No. Thank you, Luke, but no."

"Then grab yourself a seat, but don't sit close to the old man. He likes standing and staring down at people. Makes him feel real big and you mighty small."

"Still the same son of a bitch on the prod, Luke."

Domini never expected Luke to laugh, but he did. And she had her first good look at Matt when he leaned forward and turned toward her.

If Luke was an angel of darkness, Matt was surely an angel of light. He appeared as tall as Toma, with the same lean, rangy build. From the low-burning fire and the lamps lighting the room, his light brown hair seemed glided and bronzed. Whereas Luke's hair was as black and straight as her own, and long enough to cover his shirt collar, Matt's curled slightly to tumble over his broad forehead. His sideburns and back were neatly clipped.

Luke was the disreputable outlaw, black stubble covering his lower face, fairer-skinned Matt freshly shaven. Faster and faster the contrasts came to her, unaware that the three men were watching her, too.

Matt's boots were the same rich brown as the leather wing chair he sat on. Like Toma, his pants were finely tailored, and the woven cloth of his cream linen shirt had a sheen to it. His neckerchief was the same silky light blue of his eyes, tied around a tanned throat, and it drew her gaze up to his face. Luke called him a gentleman. Domini agreed that on the surface it was the right judgment. But his lips were thinned with displeasure, and his eyes, fringed with thick lashes a woman might envy, appeared more cunning and calculated.

She suddenly realized that she had been staring for some time. And what she saw within Matt's eyes did not fill her with the same sweet fire as when Luke looked at her.

She was the one who turned away. A quick look showed her that no matter where she chose to sit, Toma would command center stage. She decided to remain standing.

Luke tossed off a drink, then poured himself another one. He opened the door to O'Malley's knock, grinned at Domini when the man entered carrying a tray of china cups and a silver coffee-pot. They were all silent until the man had set the tray on a small table beside Matt, asked if he should pour and when refused, left them.

"Would you care for coffee?" Matt asked.

"No. I want to know why you would lie about sending for me, Mr. Colfax."

"The last man that called me a liar to my face is pushing up grass from the underside."

"If you didn't send for me, then who did?"

"Show me proof," Toma demanded.

"I can't. Both the letter requesting me to come and the money I had left were stolen after I purchased my stage ticket."

"Rather convenient," Matt remarked, sipping his drink.

Domini didn't look at him, but she had to answer him. "You still think I'm lying about who I am? I'm not. Jim Kirkland was my father. My mother's name was Consuela. And you," she said, pointing at Toma, "came to our home two days after my seventh birthday to take my father with you. It was the last time I saw him."

"That's nothing more than anyone could have found out."

"Then you're not denying it happened."

"Never said I didn't know Kirkland."

"Stop denying that I'm his daughter. You were more than acquaintances. He was your friend. I remember him speaking about you. Someone has sent money to the sisters at the mission to pay for my care all these years."

"The hell you say, young woman!" Toma tossed down his drink and held out the glass. "Get me another one, Matt."

While Matt rose to walk over to the sideboard, where crystal decanters reflected the light and their contents shone like polished amber, Luke sauntered to where Domini stood.

"Honey, the first rule of warfare is not to go on the defensive with an old warhorse like Toma."

"You believed me, Luke. Why won't he?"

" 'Cause havin' you show up might muddy the claims he filed on. Ain't that right, old man?"

Luke's goading tone sent a deep flush stealing

over Toma's craggy features. Domini didn't understand why Luke could get away with this, too. When Toma finally spoke, the rebuke came without much heat.

"Matt's right. You're still a bastard on the prod." Toma slugged down half the drink that Matt handed over before resuming his seat and sipping from his own glass.

"You didn't really figure that five months away was going to change me?"

"Nothing will ever change you, Luke. You're a wild card fillin' in a hand on your own whim."

"Stop this! I came here," Domini stated, fighting for calm, "because I sent for. I didn't want to come. Not at first. But Sister Benedict said I had to. And then I realized that I wanted to know about my father. I needed to talk to the man who was with him when he died."

Toma met her gaze head-on. For a moment Domini had the strange feeling that she was seeing Luke's eyes, so black and piercing that she had to force herself to stand her place.

"You got that all wrong. I wasn't with Jim the night he died."

"That's right," Matt said. "My father wasn't there." His gaze shifted from Domini to Luke before he looked at the fire.

Domini caught his look, but she didn't turn to see Luke's reaction. She had been sure that Toma was with her father the night that he died. She wasn't even aware where that had come from, the thought was simply there.

"What else did this Sister Benedict tell you?" Toma asked, setting his glass on the mantel.

"My mother was ill. We had lost our home when she couldn't work. My mother told Sister Benedict about you before she died. I didn't know anything about this until a few months ago. Sister had written you, or someone," she amended when his brows knitted across eyes in a chilling stare.

"Go on. I'm still listenin'."

"But you don't believe anything I'm telling you, Mr. Colfax. Suit yourself. As I said, someone wrote Sister back with instructions that I was to remain at the mission under their care. Money came every three months for nearly ten years."

"Letters were going back and forth all this time?"

Domini looked at Matt. "No. Not until Sister did as she was first instructed. If I wished to marry, she was to write."

"So it's money you've come for?"

Domini met Toma's sneer with all the pride she could summon. "You're wrong again. I didn't want to come at all. The letter that was stolen demanded that I come here before I could take my vows. There was a written promise that if I came, the money would not stop. The mission is poor, the money goes far to help the children."

"Anyone who knows me will tell you I'm not a

charitable man. I never sent any money to keep you at some damn mission. And not for ten years."

"Someone did. Someone who used your name."

"Stop tweakin' the devil's tail, Domini. Show him your proof. Show the old man that you are Kirkland's daughter." Luke raised his glass in silent salute when she rounded on him. "Go on. Open up your carpet bag and show him."

# Chapter Thirteen

*⌒*

"Y ou knew?" The words were a mere thread of sound coming from Domini.

"Honey, you said yourself I'm a bastard through an' through. An' I'm no fool for a pretty woman. Yeah, I knew you could prove who you are." With a nod of his head toward Toma and Matt, he added, "Now, show them."

Domini didn't know why she was surprised that he had gone through her bag. But she was. Dropping to one knee, she opened the carpet bag and reached down past her clothes to the small book at the bottom.

She lifted it out, smoothing the thin, cracked leather cover, before she rose.

"This is my mother's prayer book." She opened the cover and gazed at the faded writing, then walked until she stood in front of Toma. "Not just anyone could have this."

Toma eyed the small ragged book as if

a snake about to bite him. Domini didn't move, didn't insist, and in the end he took it from her hand. The ink was faded, not so much from age but as if someone had rubbed the words over and over. Or cried on them. He tilted the book up toward the light from the lamp behind him.

"Read it out loud. Matt wants to hear, too."

Matt didn't deny Luke's claim. He sat forward, shoulders hunched, elbows at rest on his knees, turning the glass he held around and around between his spread legs as if he found the play of fire on amber liquid more fascinating.

Toma cleared his throat. He glanced up quickly to find Domini's penetrating green eyes watching him. Luke was right. They were Jim's eyes. And when he looked again at the handwriting, he knew Jim had written the words.

"Married this third day of March, in the year eighteen fifty-eight, James Thomas Kirkland to Consuela Teresa de Zurdo y Picaro. Church of the Holy Virgin, San Miguel, California." Angling the book again, Toma continued, "Born to me this nineteenth day of September in the same year, a daughter, Dominica."

"He was so sure that your mother carried his child that he married her?"

"Shut up, Matt." Soft but deadly, Luke's order worked. Matt sat back and tossed down his drink.

Domini didn't turn to acknowledge Luke's coming to her defense. The room was overpowering her with its death trophies closing in no matter where she looked. The fire spread its heat and made breathing difficult after all the fresh air she'd had these past few days. The tension from Toma's continued silence held her still.

She didn't know how badly she wanted another human's touch until she felt Luke's hand slide up her back to cup the base of her neck. His thumb rubbed small circles beneath her braid and eased a little of the tension.

Like Domini, Luke had his eyes on Toma. When Toma looked up, his gaze went right to Luke.

"Did you put her up to this? You the one scheming behind my back all these years, sendin' her money?"

"Old man, if I'd known where she was, I wouldn't have hidden a damn thing from you. Why don't you ask Matt what he knows?"

"That will not be necessary."

Luke didn't turn, but Domini did. Her quick turn brought Luke's hand down as she faced the woman who stood in the open doorway.

"What the hell are you doin' in here, Amanda?"

"Toma, you'll have Dominica believe that a wife isn't welcome to visit her husband."

"You never have before." His gaze shifted between his wife and the young woman who stood poised to flee. "Dominica, is it? Then you're the one who's raised hell by bringing her here."

Amanda smiled. Eyes the blue of a snow-capped mountain's shadows, just as cold and hard, targeted Toma. "Oh, yes, Toma. At first I merely wanted her safe. But then so many delicious ideas came to me. And I so wanted you to meet her again, Toma. I want you to return to her what you stole. Her father, her childhood, money, too."

"Return? To her? Or to you, Amanda?"

Domini glanced from Toma to his wife. Amanda's smile never faltered but became malicious, and she did not answer. Quaking inside, Domini could only admire the woman's utter calm. The rose silk long-sleeved gown revealed a willowy, petite figure. Domini wondered if it was a trick of the lamp light reflecting the rose shade of her gown that added the tint to alabaster skin. Not one feature that Domini studied was flawed. Even Amanda's white-blond hair was smooth perfection pulled back from her high forehead into a coil at the back of her head.

It was hard for Domini to believe she was Matt's mother, Toma's wife. She looked far too young. But the hardened glare in her eyes as she stared at her husband in a silent battle of wills left no doubt that Amanda was indeed Mrs. Colfax.

Her benefactor. Her lying benefactor. Why?

Bewildered by the hatred surrounding her, Domini turned to Luke. He was the only one not looking at Amanda, the only one she felt she could trust.

"Luke?" His eyes meeting hers were as black as midnight water on a moonless night. He had been guarded with her before this, but now she couldn't begin to fathom what his thoughts were. Domini knew her every thought, every confused feeling, was revealed to him. She no longer had the will or the strength to hide them.

"If you don't want your bait puddling down to useless before you spring your trap, you'd better get her out of here. She's past exhaustion."

"No thanks to you," Matt snapped, rising from his chair.

"No thanks to any of you," Amanda clarified, coming away from the door. "I apologize for the lack of manners both Matt and my husband have displayed. It is one thing they both excel at. Despite this, Dominica, we are civilized people. Come," she offered, holding out her hand. "I'll have Lucy show you to your room. After you have had an opportunity to refresh yourself, we will dine, then discuss this matter further."

It wasn't as much an offer as a velvet-clad command. Domini hesitated and looked at Luke again.

"Go on," he said. "You'll be safe enough."

"Will you stay, Luke?"

"He never does, Dominica," Matt answered. He closed the short distance between them and stood at her side. "You won't object to my using your first name, will you? Miss Kirkland seems too formal under the circumstances."

"No, I don't object." Domini still waited for Luke to answer her. When he didn't, she felt exhaustion sweep over her. She was being battered on too many fronts by conflicting emotions. Waiting seemed to be the only choice.

"Luke's right," she finally said. "I am very tired."

"Then come with me, dear child," Amanda coaxed.

Domini kept hoping that Luke would stop her, that he would say he'd take her to her room. She didn't want to be alone with Amanda Colfax. But Luke remained silent.

Domini started forward only to turn. "I want my mother's prayer book back."

"I'll just hang onto this for now," Toma answered. "Don't worry, I'll put it in a safe place."

Luke saw the way Domini's shoulders sagged. The light went from her eyes. She didn't yet understand that with Toma, with any of them, you never showed your weakness. Never allowed them to see what mattered a great deal to you. They would use it like a twisted noose around your neck.

Luke lunged forward, ripping the book from Toma's hand. He topped Toma by a few inches, and his body had been honed into a powerful build that Toma could not match in strength.

"Since Domini kept it safe all these years, Toma, she can do the same here. This way," he said, tossing the book to Domini, "it won't accidentally disappear or get destroyed. Things are real prone to accidents around here, aren't they?" Luke didn't expect an answer, and he didn't get one.

"For sure," he added, "this can't be used to force her into any of your schemes." He turned to Domini. "I warned you, didn't I? Best stay sly as a vixen an' keep your claws sharp as any cougar's, honey. Their games are deep and vicious. If it gets too bad, send word to me by Ellamay. She's the cook."

Domini clutched the book in one hand and reached out with the other to stop Luke as he strode past her.

"Please, Luke, won't you stay for supper? For me?"

"Honey, you need a long spoon to eat with the devil. Mine got broken a long time ago."

"Stop it, Luke." Soft and low, Amanda's voice nevertheless demanded their attention. "You're behaving like an animal with those ridiculous threats and warnings. You are the only uncivilized thing in this room."

"An' whose fault is that, Amanda? My being an animal, that is?"

"Shut up, Luke." Matt took a step toward him, then roughly shook his head as if he was coming to his senses. "Just leave. Every time you—"

"Yes, Luke, just leave. All you are doing is frightening this poor child with your vicious lies. Once more you have overstayed your welcome in this house."

Tight-lipped, Luke stared straight ahead. Only Domini's gasp revealed that anyone had heard and cared what Amanda said to him.

Luke shrugged off Domini's hand and started forward when Amanda's soft, brittle voice flayed him again.

"Despite all efforts, you are an animal. How dare you come into this home—"

"Home, Amanda? You ain't got a clue to what makes a home."

"Keep silent when I am speaking to you, Luke. Or have you forgotten how you learned to be respectful?" Gloating, Amanda swept aside the flaring skirt of her gown. Her blue eyes glittered with hate. "I will hold you fully accountable if you have done anything to hurt Dominica. She is an innocent child and I will have—"

"You'll have what you've always had, Amanda. Nothing. You can't do anything more to hurt me. All of your threats are empty now. An' take a good look at who you're calling a child. Dominica is a woman grown." Scorn rode his voice and his look at Amanda. "But I'll give you right about her innocence, and her honesty. Two things you never had, and never will."

"Get out, Luke! You're not wanted here."

"Never have been."

"Luke!" Toma ordered. "That's enough. Remember who you're talking to."

Domini couldn't believe the change that had come over Luke. For long moments he appeared the outlaw she had silently named him. Dark. Dangerous. Ready to strike out. Undercurrents of hate and scorn added to the silent battle between

Luke and Amanda. From one breath to the next, Domini saw that Luke wrapped his seething emotions securely; even the light in his eyes was banked.

She was unaware that she had covered her mouth with one hand not to cry out until she felt Luke's fingers gently take hold of her and lower it.

"Please, Luke, I'm asking you again. Don't go."

"Not even for you can I stay here. And stay out of this."

Domini had no choice but to do as he asked when he rounded on Toma.

"Old man, I'm holding you personally responsible for her welfare. Anything happens to her and I'll come after you."

"Damn you, boy!"

"I'm not a boy anymore, Toma."

"I'll skin your hide and—"

"*She* already tried that. Remember?"

"Luke," Matt interjected, coming closer to him. "Let it be. Every time you come back—"

"This'll be the last time. I've come to take my horses. I won't ever be back again."

"Now, just hold on, Luke. You owe me."

"Owe you, old man? I've paid your devil's due more times than I can count."

"By your reckonin', not mine. There's sixty head that you promised to break. Sixty days or thirty if you're of a mind to kill yourself. You're already three weeks behind on our deal. I've contracted those horses to the army. Now that they're intending to chase the Indians to hell and beyond, they want them delivered. Those were the terms we agreed on for my care and feeding of your horses till you came back."

Domini didn't understand the smug tone of Toma's voice. Or why Toma goaded Luke with a challenging glare that almost dared Luke to deny their agreement. The strange thought crossed her mind that Toma wanted Luke to stay despite all that had been said here. In the next moment Domini changed her mind. That simply did not make any sense.

Luke clenched his hands at his sides, barely able to hold himself in check. Domini whispered his name very softly. He inhaled sharply, and she thought she heard his breath tremble as he released it. But when he looked at her for a few seconds, she caught the icy glint in his eyes. Then he stared at Toma.

"That was the deal. I suppose you've taken my stock and hidden it away to make sure you get yours first."

"You don't expect me to admit that, do you, Luke?"

"Why not? Figure a little honesty might curl and shrivel up your tongue? No matter. But old man, don't ever think you won anything else from me. I'll break your horses, then I'm leaving."

Toma lifted his glass in silent salute before he tossed down the last of the liquor.

Domini wanted to stop Luke from leaving her

alone. She sensed that he had built a cage around
his emotions, one that would break at any time.
Perhaps it was because she had done that same
thing to her emotions. The only thing that gave
her comfort was that Luke would be close by
breaking Toma's horses. Sixty days or thirty if he
wanted to kill himself.

The brush of his fingertips against her cheek
startled her.

"Remember what I told you, Domini," Luke
leaned close to whisper.

The second the door closed behind him,
Amanda slid her arm around Domini's shoulders.
"I cannot apologize enough for you having to wit-
ness this. Please, Dominica, you must not be
frightened, or believe any of Luke's horrid lies. No
one here means you any harm, child. Luke is wild
and unprincipled and—"

"That's enough, Amanda," Toma ordered. "Luke
is what he is. Like it or not, we all contributed to
it. Let Matt show her to a room. You've got some
answerin' of your own to do to me."

"All in good time, Toma."

"No. Now, Amanda."

"Very well. Dominica, this is not the welcome
I had planned for you. I had hoped—"

"Why did you bring me here?"

"For nothing sinister, I can assure you. This
display is best forgotten. We will begin anew."

Domini found herself reluctant to agree. Even
if she had wanted to believe Amanda, what she

had seen and sensed for herself could not be ignored. She had to fight the powerful temptation to shrug off Amanda's surprisingly strong arm around her shoulders and run after Luke. Running would not gain the answers she had hoped to find. Only staying here in this house, with these people, would give her what she needed.

"Dominica?"

"Yes, Amanda. We'll begin again."

Domini bent to pick up her carpet bag, the move forcing Amanda to release her, but her fingers brushed the back of Matt's hand as he lifted her bag.

"Allow me, Dominica. And let me add to my mother's apology. It's unfortunate that we didn't receive word that you have arrived. I would have considered coming down to Florence to fetch you my pleasure. Luke is too wild for his own good. We'll all make sure that he stays away from you."

Hemmed in on either side by Amanda and Matt, Domini decided not to answer him. There was a warning beneath Matt's soft, cultured voice. Until she knew more, she could not defend Luke.

Domini swayed where she stood, overcome by the heat in the room, the heavy musk-rose scent that Amanda wore, and the subtle aroma of bay rum from Matt's skin.

"Go on an' get that girl settled, Matt. Your mother has plenty to answer for."

If Domini had not looked up, she would have missed the look exchanged by Matt and his

mother. Amanda's minuscule nod brought Matt's
free hand to cup her elbow.

"Go along with Matt, dear. Lucy has already set
a fire and has a bath waiting for you. The blue
room, Matt." Amanda stepped back and eyed Domini's clothing. "Tell Lucy to find a gown suitable
for dinner."

"I have a gown to wear, Amanda."

"I'm sure that the good sisters provided you
with the best that they could, dear. It was not
meant as an insult, only that you should feel comfortable. We will have all these little matters settled before the evening is over."

"Damn right we will," Toma added.

Domini was ready to bolt from the room. She
had no desire to be dragged into the thick undercurrents between Toma and Amanda. Any fool
could see that Toma was furious with his wife.
And she needed time alone to sort out the conflicting stories she had been told.

Matt escorted her from the room, and as she
walked beside him, Domini turned once. Amanda
stood in the doorway of Toma's room, watching
them. A chilling shiver crawled up Domini's spine.
There was something about Amanda . . .

"Here we are," Matt said, opening the last door
in the long hallway. He crossed the deep blue and
ivory floral-patterned carpet to set her bag down
on the bench fronting the four-poster bed.

"I'm sure you'll be comfortable here, Dominica.
Lucy or her sister, Meta, will be in to help you

unpack." He glanced with satisfaction at the newly laid fire that was just beginning to warm the room. Seeing that she was still hesitating by the door, he motioned her inside.

When he repeated his urging, Domini stepped over the threshold. The lightest shade of blue in the carpet was used in the drapery that hung in swags across two windows on her left, where they framed a rough stone fireplace. A settee covered in the same blue color fabric was placed in front of the fire in invitation to enjoy the warmth.

A marble table stood at one end, a silver tray holding a crystal decanter and two glasses resting on top. On the mantel were a pair of silver candlesticks and a delicate statue. Everywhere Domini looked, she saw riches that could have fed the mission's children for more than a year. She did not belong here. The room did not welcome her, it made her feel smothered.

She hadn't realized that Matt had come to stand beside her until he took her hand in his. "If you need anything, just pull the cord near the bed. I'll come and get you to escort you to dinner at eight. Will two hours give you enough time?"

"Yes." Domini couldn't imagine anyone needing two hours to bathe and dress. She had certainly never taken that long. Tugging her hand free of Matt's hold, she stepped away from him. "I'll manage. And if you'd—"

"Leave?" he finished for her, then smiled.

"Yes."

"Luke was right. Your honesty is refreshing. I'm sure you're overwhelmed by all that you heard, just so long as you keep an open mind, Dominica. Your sudden arrival was a shock to my father, and to me. But a most pleasant one." He ignored Domini's attempt to evade his reaching for her hand again and raising it to his lips.

"A personal welcome from me to you. I hope you and I shall become friends, Dominica. For a start, that is."

"I don't know if that is possible, Matt." She saw the way his gaze sparked dangerously, only to be quickly banked. The second after his cool lips had touched her skin, she snatched her hand away.

"I think you'd better go." Domini was hard put to keep the panicked edge from her voice. She was overwhelmed and needed to be alone.

"All right."

She watched the door close behind him with a feeling of relief, only to start when it opened immediately.

"I'm Lucy," a young woman announced. "Miz Colfax said I should fetch your gown to be pressed and see if there was anything else you'd be needing."

*Peace. To be left alone. The truth.* But the words remained Domini's silent thoughts. She merely nodded and indicated her bag, uncomfortable with having someone come to help her. And all she could think about was why Amanda had insisted that she come here.

# *Chapter Fourteen*

~

Dinner passed in a haze for Domini. The candlelight gleamed on the linen, china, crystal, and silver gracing the table, all constant reminders that reinforced her feeling that she didn't belong here.

Amanda, gowned in black silk, sat at the head of the table opposite Toma. She, like Domini, ate very little of the food set before her. Matt attempted to keep conversation flowing, and Domini tried to answer his questions, but the tension that seemed to come from Toma and Amanda made him give up.

Domini watched Matt carefully as he sat across from her, for the array of silverware confused her. It was with a great deal of relief she heard Toma order Meta to bring them coffee in the front parlor.

This time Domini waited for Matt to come around the table. She resented behaving as if she was helpless to rise from the chair by herself, but the sharp reprimand Amanda had delivered earlier, that a lady waited for a gentleman, had made a lasting impression. If Domini had had any doubts that she didn't belong here, Amanda's stinging rebuke removed them.

Toma offered his wife his arm and led the way from the dining room. Like Matt, he wore a white starched shirt, string tie, and a black suit made from some material that was as soft as kitten fur to her hand. Matt favored a heavily embroidered vest, while Toma's was as somber as his expression. Domini couldn't help but wish she had been a fly on the wall in his office when he had spoken to Amanda.

But as they entered the large front parlor, where lamps scattered about on tables lent a soft glow to the massive wood furniture, Domini had a feeling that her waiting was at an end. Toma poured small crystal glasses full of a dark reddish liquor, and Matt brought one to his mother, who sat on a lady's chair placed near the fire. Domini, choosing to stand, remained opposite Amanda near the curved-back sofa.

"A toast," Toma said, "to make amends for the past between us."

Domini barely touched her lips to the edge of the glass. It disturbed her that Matt stood behind her.

"Dominica," Toma began, "your sudden arrival and the manner in which it was accomplished have left me with a serious problem. I want to make it clear to you that my wife had no right to sneak money all these years for your upkeep while keeping it secret from me.

"However, she did it. I want you to understand that I'll do right by you."

"Right by me, Toma? I don't understand."

"You will." He moved to stand behind his wife's chair, his move possessive and warning as he laid his hand on his wife's pale bare shoulder. "And you agree with me, don't you, Amanda? My way will make everything right?"

Even where Domini stood she could see the press of Toma's fingers against Amanda's skin. For a moment the woman glazed at Domini, then looked down at the drink she held.

"Yes, Toma. Your way will make everything right."

"You see, Dominica, my wife is a very practical woman. She understands the value of compromise and barter."

"Your wife may understand, Toma, but I don't." Domini set her glass down. She clasped her hands together, then looked up at Toma. "Nothing you can do will give me back my father. You certainly can't repay me for the agony my mother suffered until she died. And you understand this, Toma," she stated with anger edging every word, "there is nothing you could give me—"

"Don't make rash, foolish statements, Dominica! Not that I'd expect a woman to follow a logical path."

"And you think you can buy anyone with your money," Domini returned, feeling anger for this arrogant man give way to the rage she had carefully caged.

"Just listen to him, Dominica," Matt urged from behind her.

Domini turned on him. "I will when he says something worth hearing. Like how my father died. And why it took so long for someone to write to my mother. And why your mother made my coming her a condition for the mission to keep receiving the funds she's sent." Closing her eyes briefly, Domini took several harsh breaths, fighting to regain her control. Screaming at them wouldn't get her what she wanted.

She faced Toma again with a semblance of control.

"You finished actin' like a half-wild filly?" Toma asked, his gaze hard.

"I'll listen to what you have to say."

"Good enough," he said with a curt nod. "An' just to keep things clear, I never said anything about buying you. Money'll come. But that wasn't what I was proposin'."

It was the gloating tone of Toma's voice that made Domini tense. Suddenly she didn't want to hear what he had to say. She didn't even want to remain in this room, this house, for another minute. Matt moved closer behind her, and she felt as if he would cut off any attempt at escape. She didn't turn to look at him. Toma's speculative look held her in place. That and the glitter of satisfaction in Amanda's eyes.

"As usual, Toma," Amanda said, "you have no finesse. Why not sit down, Dominica? No? Ah, child, there is nothing to be gained by treating us as if we are your enemies. That simply is not true. Toma did not mean to frighten you. His manner is rough, but in this instance he means well. We all do.

"I know you are upset because we discussed the matter of what is to be done with you. Wait," Amanda said, lifting an elegant hand so that the lamplight caught and held on the gleaming pearl ring and bracelet she wore. "Please have the courtesy to listen to me, Dominica."

"Will you just get on with it, Amanda?" Toma's suggestion sounded more like a demand, but his wife heeded the warning squeeze he gave her shoulder.

"You have had no one to guide you, Dominica, beyond the good sisters. When Sister Benedict wrote, she mentioned that she feared your choice to take the veil did not come from a true desire to serve the church, but as an escape. Was she telling the truth? Is that the reason why you wanted to take vows?"

Domini couldn't look at either Toma or Amanda. She glanced toward the partially draped French doors that led out to the surrounding porch. The doubts about her desire to take the vows that would allow her a life of peace resurfaced. From the moment she had agreed with Sister Benedict that she had no choice but to come here and discover the truth, those doubts had begun. The time she had spent with Luke had reinforced those doubts.

"I want an answer to that myself, girl."

"Please, Dominica," Amanda said, "the very fact that you cannot immediately give us an answer should be an answer to you. Do you truly wish to bury yourself behind convent walls, devoting yourself to prayer and the service of others, before you have had a chance to enjoy the advantages we can provide for you?"

Domini closed her eyes and prayed for guidance. But honesty forced her to admit her doubts. She simply was not sure. Opening her eyes, she blinked, thinking it was a trick of the light that made her believe she saw a shadow moving out on the porch.

Coming to stand beside her, Matt gently touched her cheek, then let his hand fall to his side. "Dominica?" he queried softly. "What's wrong? Why won't you answer?"

"It's a difficult question to answer, Matt. I thought that's what I wanted to do, to be honest, I'm no longer sure."

"Damn right!" Toma said. "All a bunch of nonsense. No man would want that for his daughter. An' the offer I've got for you is ten times better."

Domini looked at Toma. She felt as if she had been carefully cornered, but couldn't sense where the danger came from. The only thing she was sure of was that she was threatened.

Despite his rough manner Toma appeared supremely confident. And why shouldn't he? Domini thought. He owns everything and everyone. *Including you?* a little voice asked. She knew it wasn't true now, but then Toma hadn't yet offered her what she wanted. No matter how well anyone thought of his ideals and motives, Domini did understand that given the right price, she, too, might sell her soul to the devil. The need for the truth burned inside her.

"I'll take your silence for a fact that you're finally willing to listen to me. Right?" Toma waited for Domini's nod, and when she gave it, he smiled at her. "You're smart. Now, what I'm proposing is that you get hitched."

"Hitched? As in married, Toma?"

"You're hearin's fine enough. That's what I said."

"If that's your solution, the answer is no."

"Well, young woman, it ain't like I'm givin' you the choice."

Domini felt anger flush across her cheeks. She took a few steps toward Toma, then stopped herself. Shaking her head, she added verbal denial. "I won't marry on your orders. You don't own me. I came here of my own free will. I'll leave the same way."

"And who the hell do you think is going to take you, girl?" Sliding his thumbs into his vest pockets, Toma rocked back on his heels, watching Domini. "Ah, that caught your attention, didn't it? I own the land as far as your eye can see and beyond. There's not a man on this place that'll risk his job or his life to help you."

"Luke would," Domini countered.

Toma threw back his head and laughter rocked the room. As suddenly as it started, it stopped. "Luke ain't gonna help you. He ain't gonna lift a finger in your direction, girl. Now be still," he ordered. "Matt, set her down an' keep her there till I'm finished."

Domini shrugged off Matt's hand and had started for the door when Amanda spoke and stopped her.

"Think, Dominica, think before you act too hastily. If your father had lived, he would have wanted marriage for you."

"How would you know that, Amanda?" Domini rounded on her, shooting a look full of the betrayal she felt where the woman sat, serene and inviolate.

Amanda lowered her head, softly saying, "I know. Leave it at that, Dominica."

Domini swayed where she stood, remembering Luke's last warning. *"Best stay sly as a vixen an' keep your claws sharp as any cougar's, honey. Their games are deep and vicious."* But she reminded herself that you couldn't play any game unless you knew the players and the rules.

"Come and sit, Dominica," Matt said, his voice, like his hands on her shoulders, brooking no argument.

She went with him only to give herself a few more minutes. But she wished that Matt had not chosen to sit beside her on the arm of the sofa. Her every indrawn breath was filled with his scent. Domini couldn't stop herself from adding another wish—that Luke was in his place. She didn't want to believe Toma, couldn't believe that Luke wouldn't help her if she wanted to leave here.

"Amanda, is this the true reason you brought me here, to marry your son?"

"There is no need to sound so accusing, Dominica. I paid for your care because of your father. Later, as Toma pressured Matt to find a wife, I began to think that when you were old enough, you would be a perfect choice. Every mother wants her son to have a good wife. I also wanted you to have what should have been rightfully yours. When you—"

"But why did you hide what you were doing from Toma?"

"My dear child, you must stop delving into matters that simply do not concern you. Now, as I began to say—"

"I'm sorry, Amanda. I feel uncomfortable talking about this now."

"If you are concerned about Matt, do not be. My son will do whatever is best. Whatever will please me. Rid yourself of any fear that he does not want this marriage. Now, I will finish what I have tried to say. When you have the opportunity to fully understand the advantages such a marriage will bring you, Dominica, you will agree that it is the perfect solution."

"I don't want your perfect solution, Amanda." Matt prevented her from standing, but Amanda no longer had Toma holding her. Domini watched her graceful rise from the chair, the precise way she set her glass down on the small side table and saw the chilling appearance of her features as she moved closer.

"Obedience is the one lesson I expected you to have learned at the mission, Dominica. I told you that I wanted my husband to give you what is rightfully yours. Half of the Gold Bar mine belongs to you. Toma is not about to sign that over to you. The only way you will have what your father owned before his death is to marry a Colfax. Do I make myself clear?" Her patience was near an end. Once Matt married, he would inherit everything from Toma, but only if Toma approved of his wife.

"Yes, Amanda," Domini answered moments later. "You have made yourself quite clear. But you're assuming that I want money. All of you are. And it isn't true. I'm—"

"Manners seem to have been another lesson the

good nuns neglected to teach you. Stop being rude," Amanda snapped, seeing in a flash the ruin of her plan because of this young woman's stubbornness. Marriage equaled inheritance equaled an unfortunate accident for Toma, and she would be free. Nothing was going to stand in her way.

"Toma has told you this is the best offer you will receive and I agree. Matthew, I have already explained, believes you will make him a suitable wife. He does find you attractive."

"But only if I'm made over in your image, Amanda?" Domini clenched her hands. She should have been sorry for the cutting remark, but at the moment Domini couldn't summon guilt for the way Amanda gasped, then paled. She had to keep remembering Luke's warning and use whatever weapons at hand to fight them.

Matt snagged her chin with his hand, forcing her to turn toward him. "Your remark was uncalled for. Now apologize to my mother, Dominica."

There was the promise of violence in his eyes, and Domini tried to jerk her head free. His grip only tightened. A shudder of fear swept up her body. She fought to contain it, knowing she could not show him how afraid he made her.

"Will you apologize now?" Matt asked very softly, his thumb pressing her bottom lip. The moment she nodded, the darkness left his gaze and he released her.

"I'm sorry, Amanda," Domini mumbled. She

saw the woman retreat to her chair, and looked up at Matt. He was smiling at her, a smile full of approval. And he went on talking as if the incident had never happened.

"I do find you attractive, Dominica. I know we'll get on well together. Say you will give me a chance."

With every moment that she remained silent, Matt's mouth thinned with displeasure. "Dominica, let me reinforce what my father told you. You don't have a choice. No one on the Gold Bar C will help you. These are troubled times with the Indians taking up arms to fight. Accidents happen. Often fatal ones," he leaned closer to whisper.

Domini pressed against the sofa. She closed her eyes against the penetrating strength of his. Confusion reigned. Matt's threat made no sense. If they wanted to kill her, why didn't they? There was no need to go through the farce of a marriage. There had to be something more. But what?

Matt straightened in his perch on the sofa's arm. He trailed his fingers from Domini's shoulder down to her hand, then raised his hand to cup her cheek.

"Marriage is truly the best solution, Dominica. Say yes."

"Is this a private proposal or can anyone get in on the action?"

Luke. Domini felt relief flood through her. But she noticed that Matt was tense and very still before he lowered his hand and slowly turned to where Luke stepped into the room from the open French doors.

Domini wanted to run to him, but as he stepped into the lamplight she saw his forbidding expression as his gaze swept over each one of them in turn. She didn't bother to look and see what Toma, Amanda, or even Matt thought of his sudden appearance.

She noticed that he seemed different, but it was more than the change of clothes and his shaving the thick growth of stubble. Luke's hair was tied back, and an open-throated soft blue shirt set off the lean, hard planes of his face. A black leather vest hung open, revealing the gleaming of a fancy silver buckle on his belt. Domini's gaze slid down to the gun he wore as he came into the center of the room.

"This has nothing to do with you, Luke." Matt rose and stood with his hands curled into fists at his side.

"Doesn't it?" Soft, Luke's voice was nonetheless taunting.

"Toma." Amanda demanded her husband's attention. When he didn't answer her, she looked up at him. "Tell him to leave. Matt is right. This has nothing to do with Luke."

But Toma was smiling. "Luke is right. Pour yourself a drink. Hell, boy, pour me a man's drink, too. I've had enough of this fancy swill."

Amanda rose. "I will not stay—"

"Sit down. You'll stay until I say you can go.

Luke has every right to be here. Matter of fact," Toma said, grinning at his wife's discomfort as he took the drink Luke handed him, "I'm gonna up the ante."

With drawing horror Amanda stared first at Toma, then turned to look at Matt. "No. Do something. You cannot allow—"

"Matt's got no more say than you do, Amanda."

"Of all the cruel, inexcusable acts I have had to suffer through over the years, Toma, what you are going to propose—"

"Keep quiet, woman. This, my dear, deceitful wife, is the play you began with your secrets and your lies. I'm just adding another player." He would never admit to her what had prompted his decision. Luke wasn't going to back down about his decision to leave for good this time. Maybe Toma was getting old, or maybe all his sins were coming home, but he was going to seize this opportunity to make things right with Luke. He had allowed Amanda her way in most things, even when his guilt made him turn away from her cruelty over the years.

"Please, Toma. Please do not do this. Dominica certainly does not deserve—"

"You should have thought of that before you brought her here," he returned in a chilling voice.

"Stop it!" Domini bolted from the sofa and repeated her demand in a louder voice. "Stop tormenting her, and stop tormenting me. I won't be a player in your game."

Matt came to stand beside Domini. "Damn you, Toma! Haven't you punished my mother enough? Why insist that Luke stay? He's made his feelings about you and everything that that bears the Colfax name plain through the years. He doesn't want any of it!"

"But you do, Matt. You and your mother have schemed to that end. You think I don't know? More the fool you, boy. You'd like nothing better than for me to turn it all over to you. And I still might. But Luke gets his chance with the little filly and what I've built."

Matt took a threatening step forward, then stopped himself. "Why the hell shouldn't I want it all? I'm the one who's has to live here and put up with your impossible demands, trying to measure up to your idea of a man. And nothing I did was good enough, was it? You always compared and found me wanting no matter how hard I tried to please you. No one can fill your damn boots, Toma, not without getting crushed by you in the process."

"You don't get yourself settled down, boy, I'll use these boots to do that an' more."

Matt shot a wild look at Luke. "You put him up to this, didn't you? I should have known better than to believe you were really quitting and pulling out this time. There's only one reason you'd be here, Luke. So what the hell did the old bastard offer you?"

Domini had to look at Luke then, for she

ed to see him when he answered Matt. But
wouldn't or couldn't meet her direct gaze. He
tossed back his drink, and she watched the strong,
tanned column of his throat as he swallowed, then
wiped the back of his hand across his mouth.
Both his gaze and smile were taunting as he stared
at Matt.

"Answer me! What the hell did he offer you,
Luke?"

"Guess about the same as he was offerin' you.
Puttin' up the Colfax holdin's for grabs. Winner
takes all." He didn't look away from Matt, but
his question was put to Toma. "Ain't that right,
old man?"

"You don't need me to answer. You're doin' just
fine, boy."

Hearing Toma's prideful tone, Domini shot him
a look, but Luke spoke and she glanced back at
him.

"It's this way, Matt. He's figured out the perfect
solution to get what he wants. A salve for his conscience. Pardon," Luke said, followed by a short
mocking laugh. "He doesn't have a conscience, no
more than his wife does. She brought Domini
here to use as a knife to twist in the old man's
gut. Why the hell he's willing to let her is something you'll have to find out from him."

"Luke?"

He heard the tremble in Domini's voice, but he
couldn't look at her. Wouldn't. Not until he saw
that once more she stared at Toma. He knew that

Toma's smile confused her—it wasn't just the frown creasing her brow, or the pleading way her hand rose, then fell to her side. He could feel it. And he knew it was because confusion over why he was here was in his own mind.

"You're all forgetting one thing," Domini said softly into the tense silence. "I don't want to marry anyone."

Luke ignored her. "What the old man wants, Matt, is for you and me to fight it out. Take her for a wife, and you gain everything that carries a Colfax brand."

"Over my dead body."

Luke's hand spread over his holster. "Any time, Matt. Just tell me when."

Domini flung herself at Luke. "Stop this. You can't threaten to kill someone." She grabbed the edges of his vest, demanding, "Look at me! How can you be a part of this? How can—"

Luke took hold of her shoulders in a punishing grip until she released her hold. He spun her around and held her in place. Over her head he stared at Toma.

"Tell her."

"Luke's got every right. He's a Colfax, too."

"Colfax?" Domini whispered.

"My younger son. Mine and Amanda's."

# Chapter Fifteen

Secrets. She'd known Luke had them. It made no sense that she was shocked. But Domini twisted away from him, then evaded Matt until she stood shrinking against a wall, pressing both hands against her chest. Her heart pounded until her whole body felt buffeted by the rhythm of its beat. Chills tingled over her skin. She wondered if any of them could see that she was shaking.

He'd lied to her. Domini didn't realize she had whispered her accusation out loud until Luke loomed in front of her.

"Never. You asked if I worked for him. I do."

"You lied by omission, Luke. Never once did you tell me who you really—"

"I'm me. Luke. Period. I gave up cashing in on the Colfax name a long time ago."

"And you are the sole judge of what lies and secrets are innocent and which ones are harmful?" Domini wrapped her arms around her waist—she was chilled to the bone. Had she been blinded? How could he have fooled her? Why hadn't she seen the resemblance that was so plain now? Toma's son!

"Leave me alone, Luke." Her voice wavered and cracked.

Luke muttered profanity that had her turn her head away from him and close her eyes.

"Get away from her," Matt ordered, shoving his brother aside.

"Touch her an' you'll find it's the last time you use that hand." Crowding Matt aside, Luke leaned close to Domini. He cradled her chin with one hand and reached for her shoulder to turn her toward him, but Domini jerked away.

Smugness rode Matt's voice. "Now, will you leave her alone? She's made it plain that she doesn't want your hands on her." His face suddenly looked older, harder, almost threatening.

"Call him off, Toma, or the deal's done right now."

"Matt, come away. I'm sure you'll have plenty of opportunity to state your case to Dominica." Toma moved to refill his glass. "Matthew." His order was harsh with command that expected instant obedience.

Domini heard their voices, but they all sounded far away. Luke had lied to her. Luke was Toma's son, a Colfax. He had . . . No! She couldn't think about any more now.

"Step aside, both of you," Amanda ordered. She

shot Luke a glaring look of warning when he stood firm. "Toma, if you want a bride alive, get rid of him, too."

"What I want is for everyone to stop mollycoddlin' that girl so she gives me an answer."

Amanda reached for Domini, but she shrank away from her touch. Luke spun Amanda around, ignored her yelp, and with a gentle shove sent her toward Matt. To keep his mother from falling, Matt held onto her. With both hands braced on the wall, Luke used his body to cage Domini where she stood and protect her from the others.

"Listen to me," he leaned close to whisper. "I haven't changed any. Forget that my name's Colfax. I'm all you've got between you and them, Domini." He swore viciously when she lifted bruised, bewildered eyes to his.

"That's it. I'm taking you out of here." He swung her up into his arms, his look so forbidding that both Amanda and Matt stood aside for him. He was thankful that Domini wasn't fighting him as he reached for the brass-work handle on the door. Before Luke managed to get it open, a sharp knock made him step aside as Madison Grady burst into the room.

"Toma, we got trouble. Big trouble. The Nez Perce killed thirty-four soldiers up in White Bird Canyon last week. There's gonna be hell to pay with them running loose in these mountains. The army's got—"

"Amanda, leave us," Toma said, moving quickly

to pour a drink for Grady. "Luke, you take that girl to her room an' come back here. You tossed your hat in the ring. That means you need to know what's going on."

Luke nodded. He had done just that. Involved himself when all he wanted was to get away to where no one had ever heard of Colfax land, Colfax money. His hold on Domini tightened a bit when he saw that Grady was looking at her. Toma saw it, too.

"Never mind the girl, Grady. She's none of your concern. Drink up. Soon as Luke comes back—"

It was all Luke heard as he strode out into the hall. There was no sign of Amanda. He'd been afraid she would be lying in wait. He rubbed the side of his cheek against Domini's hair as his quick steps took them down the hallway to her room.

Once inside, Luke set her down on the settee. The wood box, he saw, had been replenished, and the fire built up to last the night. When he rose and looked at Domini, he found himself pained to see her pale. She sat with her arms crossed over her chest, rubbing her upper arms as though chilled. And maybe she was, he admitted, but only from the past hour's company.

He wondered if he should attempt an explanation. The thought was dismissed in the next few moments. Luke doubted she would listen to anything he had to say. But there was a need in him to tell her why he had become a part of Toma's scheme.

She looked up, right through him, her eyes glazed as she began rocking back and forth. Luke couldn't walk away from her.

"Domini?" He came to hunker by the side of the settee and tried to take one of her hands within his. His mouth tightened just as her fingers did on her arm. "All right, I won't touch you, but—"

"Go away." Weak and soft, it was all she could say. Tears burned her eyes. She refused to cry. If she cried, she would let the pain free.

Luke reached up to her braided coil of hair and began plucking out the pins. She jerked her head back, but he caught her around the neck with his free hand until he was done. Tucking the hairpins in his vest pocket, he rocked back on his heels.

Domini refused to acknowledge his continued presence. *Their games are deep and vicious.* Luke's words. Luke's warning. But he had never included himself. And his was the deeper, far more vicious game.

She was suddenly so lightheaded she thought she would faint. Domini squeezed her eyes shut on hot tears. Determinedly she blinked them back. She couldn't give in to the need to cry. Shaking her head in denial, she tried to remember that Luke would hone in on weakness the way a predator honed in on prey.

"Honey, I'm a patient man when I want to be.

I can stay here all night until you're ready to talk to me." He gazed at her, his mouth gentling as he reached out to touch her cheek. Her flesh was cold. His eyes were thoughtful when she finally lifted her head to look at him.

"Why?" Domini cleared her throat and tried again. "Why did you do it? You don't want to marry me."

"I had my reasons."

"More secrets, Luke?"

It was the pleading that reached him. "Would you believe me if I said I did it to protect you?"

She studied him for several minutes, somewhat surprised that he stayed still and waited. "Do you consider me a child as Amanda—I mean, your mother—"

"Don't ever call her that!" There was a blaze of anger in his eyes as he hauled her to her feet. "She never wanted me. And never once—ah, hell, forget it. Finish what you were gonna say."

Her fingers trembled as she lifted her hand to cup his cheek. "I want to believe you. I want to trust you."

"But?"

She looked away from his intense gaze. Her hand slid down and she pushed against his chest. "Let me go, Luke. I'm confused. I need time alone to sort this out."

"Toma," he said, giving her a rough little shake, "isn't gonna give you much time. And if you've got any thoughts of leaving, forget them. What

Grady said in there," he grated from between clenched teeth, nodding toward the door, "means that no one but no one will leave the ranch now."

"Not even you."

"Not even me." He gazed at her bowed head, and desire—that strong possessive force that made him want to rip Matt apart for touching her—rose until he could feel himself shake.

"Domini?" The moment she looked up at him, his mouth descended on hers. He was thorough, and not particularly gentle. But then, he wasn't feeling any gentle, tender emotions. All the antagonism raised by his coming back, raised by Toma's grand scheme and what was between him and Domini, was there in that kiss, but it was charged and explosive with more. Much more than he wanted to name.

When Luke released her, Domini, flushed and breathless, took a step backward, leaning against the settee. Her legs were trembling so much she was in danger of collapsing on the floor.

"Don't ever—"

"No more, Luke."

His hand rose and brushed against her breast. "Matt will never make your heart pound like that."

Mutely she stared up at him, seeing the mockery fade suddenly from his eyes, watching them grow curiously intent as his hand moved with new purpose on the swell of her breast, his fingers seeking the tumescent nipple through the thin cloth of her bodice. She shivered with awakened desire.

Luke dropped his hands to his sides. "Don't expect me to apologize. Just remember what I told you. Toma's a bastard, Amanda's a bitch, and Matt's their son. I wouldn't take bets on a nest of rattlers surviving the three of them."

"Then I will need to pray very hard for strength, Luke."

"If it gives you comfort, go ahead. Lock the door."

Domini nodded and heard him cross to the door. She almost called out to him, but bit her lip.

Domini didn't rise to lock the door; she couldn't move from where she huddled at one end of the settee. Watching the fire, she finally admitted to herself that the Indian troubles made her a virtual prisoner on the ranch.

It did little good to berate herself for not making a firm declaration that taking vows was her true vocation. The convent and the life it offered had always been there, security, protection. Now, by her admission she had lost it. Innate honesty forced her to acknowledge that she had told them the truth. And to herself now, she added that the time she had spent with Luke had influenced her. She couldn't seem to put aside as easily the desire she felt.

But desire had not prompted Luke's offer. He didn't want to marry her. Could he have told her the truth, that he had offered to protect her? Was she in danger from Toma, Amanda, and Matt?

Rubbing her head, feeling the tension that made it pound, she stared into the brightly burning fire. Amanda had planned to use her all these years. She was the foolish child the woman had called her, but no one could force her to marry. She had to cling to that. Toma could threaten all he wanted, yet there was no way he could force her to repeat wedding vows to either of his sons.

Could he?

Domini woke with a crick in her neck from the awkward position she had slept in on the settee. A knock at the door roused her as she blinked at the sunlight flooding the room. The fire had been reduced to ash, she saw, stretching the aches from cramped limbs.

Hearing Lucy call out and knock again, Domini rose and went to the door. Lucy waited with her arms full of clean, pressed laundry.

"Miz Colfax would like you to join her for breakfast soon as you're dressed."

Domini watched the efficient, tall young woman make her way to the dresser. "Did she say why, Lucy?"

"No. She wouldn't be saying much to me."

"But you know, don't you?" When Lucy hesitated, then looked at Domini, her plain features almost without expression, Domini knew she was right. "I imagine there are few secrets kept from you and the other members of the household."

"I don't gossip."

"I didn't ask you to, Lucy. I simply wanted to know—"

"She sent for you. That's all the reason she needs."

"I see."

"Soon as I fetch hot water, I'll help you get dressed."

"That won't be necessary. I'm not comfortable having someone wait on me." Domini walked to the window, and found that it faced the back of the house. She could make out the corrals and the crowd of men around one of them. She thought of Luke's deal to break horses. And with that reminder came the memory of the scars on his back. And last night . . .

Toma saying, "*I'll skin your hide,*" and Luke's reply, "*She already tried that.*"

She bit down on her hand to keep from crying out. Dear Lord, what had Luke lived with in this house? How could anyone survive such hate? How could a woman hate a child she had given birth to? What hold did Amanda have on Toma that he would have allowed her to whip his son?

Secrets.

Domini found herself rubbing her arms against the inner chill that rose inside her despite the warmth of the streaming sunlight.

"I'll come back and take you to Miz Colfax," Lucy said.

Delving into questions would serve her no purpose now, so Domini turned away from the window. Lucy had filled the washbasin behind the screen with hot water. Spread on the bed that Domini had not slept in was her clean chemise and petticoats. A pair of ladies high-button shoes rested on the floor. Next to the stockings on the bed, Lucy had put out a two-piece printed calico polonaise. It was the only other presentable gown that Domini had to wear. Eyeing the shoes again, she was surprised that Amanda had not commented on her moccasins.

Foolishness! Yes, but she needed to concentrate on such foolish items or the pain would be back in full force. She needed her mind clear to deal with Amanda.

Hurrying to strip off her wrinkled gown, Domini refused to dwell on the reason for Amanda's summons. Nor could she form a plan of action. The image of Luke's back kept coming to mind. Domini felt anger swell into rage against Amanda as she washed and dressed.

She ignored the shoes and laced her moccasins on. The long, ruffle-trimmed skirt hid them. She buttoned the bodice that extended past her hips, its drapery looped back to form the polonaise. She wasn't vain about her appearance—vanity was not indulged at the mission—but she did take the time to inspect herself while she brushed out her hair. The gray background of the cloth was enlivened by tiny yellow flower sprigs. She found the matching yellow ribbon and used it to tie her braid. Luke had kept the hairpins he had taken from her last night. She was disappointed to find herself appearing a young schoolgirl, when she wished to meet Amanda as an equal. Squaring her shoulders, Domini heard Lucy at the door. She followed the maid not to the dining room, as she had expected, but to Amanda's suite.

The drawing room Lucy led her to was opposite the front parlor. Gold drapes were pulled across the front windows, but it was light enough to see that everything in the room was gold and white. Gilt furniture, the lines delicate, was covered in a variety of white embroidered materials. White on white. Domini thought it strange. It was not a room that welcomed anyone to sit and be comfortable. But then, she reminded herself, Amanda wasn't a woman who made one feel welcome and comfortable.

Tabletops were crowded with porcelain figurines, crystal, and glassware. Domini had the impression that Amanda had invested a great deal of effort to remind anyone entering this room of the Colfax wealth.

Lucy opened a door at the end of the room where she waited. Domini hurried forward. This was a smaller sitting room, again furnished in white and gold. A round table was set for two in the middle of the room. There was no sign of

Amanda, and when she turned, it was to see Lucy close the door behind her.

Domini was drawn to the gilt-framed portrait above the fireplace. It was Amanda, a much younger Amanda, hair flowing free over a white gown. Pink roses were scattered around the gown's hem, but it was the face, more precisely Amanda's eyes, that captured Domini's attention. There was a hint of a smile on Amanda's lips, but the eyes sparkled. The artist had caught the first moments of laughter.

The more she stared up at the painting, the more saddened Domini felt. What had happened to make Amanda such a bitter, vicious-tempered woman?

"I was seventeen when that was painted."

"And happy," Domini said, turning around to find Amanda, dressed in a blue silk morning gown, lifting the silver covers off the serving pieces.

"Yes. I was very happy that day. My father had accepted a proposal of marriage from someone I loved. Come join me. I am sure you will find that Ellamay is an excellent cook."

Domini took the place across from her, hands folded in her lap while Amanda served poached eggs over steaming biscuits.

"So tense, Dominica? There is no need. I invited you to join me for breakfast, not to be the meal."

"Why?" Domini blurted out, realizing that

Amanda was right. She was drawn tight with tension.

Setting aside a delicate china cup, Amanda sat back. "Everything went wrong last night. Toma is not a man who will ever understand subtlety or acquire patience. My hopes were for you and me to have an opportunity to know one another. I also wished for Matt to have a—"

"Amanda, I'm not marrying Matt." Domini gave up any pretense of attempting to eat.

"I am sorry to hear you say that. In the absence of your parents I had hoped that you would be willing to allow my knowledge and experience to guide you. I simply did not want you to make the same mistake I did."

Domini glanced at the painting, then back at Amanda. "Toma wasn't the man who you loved."

A statement, not a question, but Amanda answered her. "No. Toma was not the man I loved. He was a man I lost due some unfortunate debts my father accumulated within months. When my fiancé discovered the extent of debt, he called off our engagement. I was broken-hearted and humiliated. Seventeen is such a dangerous age for young women who believe that they know what is best for them.

"Toma was visiting his cousin. We met, and while he was older, much older than any man I had been attracted to, Toma had one advantage none other could give me. He was leaving for the western territories to try his luck at mining. I decided to go with him."

"You weren't in love with him?"

"No. Love at that time was vastly overrated. A fickle emotion suitable for children to dream about. I was attracted to him. He was handsome, wild enough to be a little dangerous, but very tempting. As I said, Toma's most attractive feature was his intent to take me away from painful memories."

Amanda shrugged and reached out for her china coffee cup. "I admit it was not a good reason for a marriage, but it was one that made perfect sense to me at the time. I refused to listen to my mother's warnings that I could never change him. I was not wise enough to hear her counsel about his temper. I certainly was beyond having respect for my father's opinion.

"You see, Dominica, I blamed my father for losing my love with all the foolish blindness that the young are capable of doing."

"Why are you telling me this?" She watched Amanda take a delicate, cat-like sip of her coffee.

"I see within you the same spirit I once had. If you choose the wrong man, Dominica, it will be snuffed like an unwanted, unneeded candle."

"Last night you said that you knew what my father wanted for me. How could you? Weren't he and Toma alone in these mountains looking for gold?"

"Is that what they told your mother?" Amanda's

short laugh was bitter. "No, they were not here alone. Toma had built a small cabin on the very spot where this house now stands. We were living here when he returned with your father.

"I know how angry you are, Dominica, how betrayed you feel. Did it ever occur to you why your father left you and your mother behind in California? Left you both alone to fend for yourselves while he chased after a dream of finding gold? Toma dragged me from one mining site to another for almost fifteen years—"

"You and your sons?"

Amanda's fingers tightened around the cup until her knuckles showed white. Very carefully, as if she was afraid she would break it, she set the cup down on its plate. Her gaze was chilling as she stared at Domini.

"Yes. He dragged me and my son with him. I am trying to help you avoid my mistakes. What has—"

"Amanda! Stop denying Luke! He's—"

"Never, do you hear me, Dominica, never dare to raise what has passed between Luke and myself as a subject of conversation again. Toma Colfax claims him as his. I will not speak about this again. Do you understand?"

"Perfectly." But Domini didn't. Amanda's voice was shaken. Last night Luke refused to have her named his mother. Secrets. She was beginning to hate the twists and turns of the Colfaxes.

But Domini couldn't shake off the feeling that

this was something she needed to know to understand Luke. He wouldn't tell her, and now Amanda refused to discuss it. What could have happened to make her hate her own son?

Looking up to find Amanda thoughtfully studying her, Domini pushed the matter aside. There had been so much more that Amanda revealed. The question of why her father had left them behind begged an answer.

"Amanda, how well did you know my father?"

"He lived with us for eighteen months."

"I see." Fussing with the placement of her silverware, Domini tried very hard not to read into that answer more than Amanda stated. But she thought of her mother's tears, the loneliness she had suffered, the poverty they had both endured, and found that she was not blessed with the gentle goodness that Sister Benedict claimed she had.

"Dominica, I doubt that you fully understand. Your father was very different from Toma. James was a kind man, a most compassionate one. He loved to read. We shared many enjoyable hours with the few books I managed to keep. All those months learning to laugh again made me realize that the marriage I thought myself reconciled to was a failure. I grew bitter with Toma's verbal abuse, with his women—oh, yes, there were women, Dominica. And then there was his drinking."

Domini closed her eyes briefly, praying for some

guidance. A few moments of silence passed, then she opened her eyes and stared at Amanda.

"What are you telling me?"

"Exactly what you came here to find out."

# *Chapter Sixteen*

〰️

Domini denied Amanda's words. Eighteen months? If her father had lived with them that long, then Luke had known him very well. Yet she recalled that while Luke admitted knowing who her father was, he had given the impression that it was a casual acquaintance. The deeper she probed into the past, the more secrets turned up to confuse her.

She rubbed her head, feeling tension return to begin the pounding behind her eyes and at the base of her neck. Had Luke actually lied to her? Dear Lord, she couldn't remember.

"Dominica, did you hear me? That is why you readily agreed to come? To find out about your father's life and his death?" Amanda nodded and sat back when she saw that she once more had Domini's attention.

"Yes," Domini whispered. "Damn you, yes!" She rose and threw her damask napkin down. Bracing both hands on the edge of the table, she leaned forward. "Yes, Amanda, I do want to know the truth. I had to watch my mother die! Do you know what that does to a child? To be made to feel helpless? To know that there was no one to turn to?

"No, how could you know? You've been safe and secure here, wrapped in your Colfax money, playing with my life." Shuddering, Domini closed her eyes, struggling to regain some control. She had been screaming. When she looked across at Amanda, hate rose in a terrifying force. The woman remain unmoved, not a hint of emotion in her eyes.

"Are you finished?"

Domini couldn't answer her. She was afraid of what she would say or do.

"It is likely that you have a great deal more to say. But please, Dominica, let me answer a few of your questions. Toma did not kill your father. I did not kill him. As for the rest, no, I do not know what it is like to watch a parent die. But I pray that you never experience death of self."

Amanda rose. "We will speak again. I do believe you are too upset—"

"Bitch." The moment the word escaped, Domini clamped one hand over her mouth. But when Amanda offered a curt nod and a cold smile, then turned away, Domini realized that she had meant it. The woman was a bitch just as Luke called her. How could she remain unmoved? How could she just walk away?

At the door to her bedroom Amanda turned. "Dry your eyes before you leave, Dominica. There is no point in allowing the servants to have more gossip to spread."

It wasn't until the door closed behind Amanda that Domini managed to lift one trembling hand to her face. She was crying.

Her only thought was flight. She ran blindly out to the hall, only to see through her tears that Matt was coming toward her. Domini bolted for the front door just as Mr. O'Malley came out of the parlor.

"Allow me, miss," he said, reaching the door before Domini.

Shooting one last look over her shoulder, Domini ran. She didn't want to see Matt. Didn't want to talk to any of the Colfaxes. Darting around to the side of the house, she kept running until she was out back. The shouts and laughter from the far corrals sent her fleeing in the opposite direction. Matt shouted her name, but Domini ran faster, heading for a small cluster of trees. It was cool and shadowed beneath the thick-leaved branches, but Domini couldn't find a place to hide. There were no low-growing shrubs to conceal her. The sound of Matt's voice was coming closer just as Domini stepped out of the trees. Warm sunlight did little to take away the cold encompassing her. She made a frantic search of the land before her, seeing nothing that offered respite.

Not until she looked up and spied a small cabin. She ran for the woods at the base of the mountain. There had to be a path leading upward.

Matt stopped short when he saw where she was heading. He wasn't going to make a fool of himself by running after her. With an angry gaze he watched the last of her disappear into the woods. Raking his hands through his hair, he turned back to the house, but not before he cursed the man who had drawn every free ranch hand to the corrals. Luke didn't want the ranch or the mines. But Matt had seen how his brother looked at Dominica. He might spurn the Colfax wealth, but Luke wanted her. Only this time Luke wasn't winning. No matter what he had to do.

Matt wasn't sure what made him glance again toward the corrals. He was sorry he did. The crowd had parted and he saw his father slapping Luke on the back. Even from where he stood, Matt felt the pride Toma had for Luke. Pride never once shown to him. He had thought he had learned to cope with it, but this time Toma had made the stakes too high. And with the escalating Indian troubles came deaths. Smoothing his hair, Matt returned to the house. His mother had a great deal to answer for.

Spotting Matt heading back to the house, Luke shrugged off Toma's hand. He had been up before dawn working alone and quietly with the first of the horses he had to break. With the back of his hand he wiped the sweat off his brow and took his hat from one of the hands. He hadn't missed Domini fleeing as if the devils from hell were after her. Nor had he missed where she was headed.

"Com'on up to the house with me, boy," Toma said, once more attempting to sling his arm around Luke's shoulders. "After a workout like this you need to eat. 'Sides, I want to hear where you've been an' what you've done."

"Later, Toma. There's something I need to do now." Luke walked away without a backward glance. Toma refused to understand that it was too late for them. Luke already regretted his actions last night. Enough that he had tossed and turned trying to figure out what had possessed him to compete with Matt for Domini. His brother would never back off. And he knew how dirty Matt could fight. He had been forced to live with the results of it until he was old enough to begin fighting back.

His long strides brought him quickly across the open land and into the woods. The path to the cabin twisted up a rock-strewn trail. White yarrow bloomed in clear spaces, and huckleberries ripened along one side. Luke ignored them, his eyes pinned to the top of the path, his thoughts solely on the woman who waited above him.

Domini huddled near the side of the log cabin, clutching her side. Her breathing was harsh from running, but she felt safe for the first time since

Luke had brought her here. Sunlight filtered through the trees that stood sentinel around the small cabin, blocking it from view. The logs and chinking showed age. The front had an overhang where split logs were piled high to season before use.

As her mind cleared, she wondered who lived here. Amanda had said that the original cabin had been built down below where the house now stood. Unless she had lied . . . Domini touched the golden log wall. Could this have belonged to her father?

"Domini?"

She spun around, bracing one hand against the wall to keep her balance as Luke came out of the shadows. "I didn't hear you. I—"

"Why were you runnin'?"

He stood waiting for an answer, and Domini found herself seeing him as she had the first time, when she had turned at the stage depot and found him behind her. He hadn't made a sound then, as now, and the impact on her senses was heightened to a frightening degree. His gray shirt bore the damp spots of sweat from his labor with the horses. Dark stubble covered his cheeks and jaw, that rigid jaw silently communicating anger to her. With his hat brim canted down she couldn't see the expression in his eyes. Was he angry with her?

"What did Matt do to you?"

The words were evenly spaced, spoken through gritted teeth. Domini shook her head in denial.

"Nothing. Matt did nothing more than call after me." Her eyes targeted his fists that slowly uncurled. "Why do you hate each other?"

"Who? Me and Toma? Amanda? Matt? You've got a hell of a choice. And why not ask them?"

"I tried, Luke. I asked Amanda about you and why—"

"She wouldn't tell you. None of them will."

She decided to leave it alone. The last thing she needed to deal with was Luke and his smoldering anger. "Who lives here?"

"I do. Have for the last ten years. When I've come back, that is. Mulekey keeps an eye on things for me."

His isolation reached through her own pain. Before Domini thought about it, she went to him. "Will you invite me inside, Luke?"

He stared down at her face, hearing her ask for more than an invitation to his cabin. She had been crying. Her lashes were wet, spiked together above the sheen of her green eyes. He couldn't stop himself from raising his hand to smooth his thumb over her cheek, his gaze holding fast to hers.

He recalled his thought when he had first seen her, that he would pile up grief for himself. But it had already been too late then, as it was now. The sweet, clean scent of her was inhaled on his every breath, and he could feel the faint tremble of her body just from where his thumb rested on her cheek.

"Luke?"

The whisper of his name ran through him. Deep. Dark. Fast. Liquid as hot honey, her voice sizzled his nerve ends. That's was all it took, just the whisper of his name from her lips and he was aching, full and hard, and filled with wanting to bury his flesh in hers. To lose himself in all that was Domini. And she knew. His gaze drifted lower as he heard her ragged inhaled breath as if she scented the danger he presented to her. She didn't know the half of it.

"If I take you inside, Domini, I won't let you go till I've had you."

In an abrupt move he dropped his hand and turned away.

"That's one hell of an invitation, Luke."

"It's the only one I'm giving you."

There was a dangerous stillness about him. Domini thought for a few seconds about what he offered. Regret laced her voice when she answered him.

"I can't accept your invitation, Luke."

"Won't."

"All right, I won't. I want to. I never understood what desire meant until I met you. But there's so much anger inside you. Anger that I sense is directed at me. That I don't understand."

She breathed a sigh of relief when he leaned against the wall. She had been afraid that her refusal would make him leave her alone.

"The anger," he began in a tired voice, "isn't all

for you. Part's for my bringing you here. I swear
I didn't know, never thought that Toma would
demand you marry one of us. Truth is, I guess I
stopped thinking about it along about the time I
kissed you."

His voice had grown husky with the last, and
Domini stared at the hard planes of his profile.
Just the mention of the kisses they had shared
unfurled a coil of warmth inside her. It was too
easy to recall the wildness he had set free, of his
temptingly handsome features that had whispered
of hunger and darker passions. And that simmering promise of danger.

With a mental jerk, she stopped herself from
being drawn into the beckoning well of sensuality
that he spun so effortlessly around her.

"Is that why you're so angry with me, Luke? Is
it because Toma forced—"

"Toma stopped forcing me to do anything the
day I turned fourteen." He looked at her then,
seeing the play of sunlight and shadows over her
face. Bruised shadows of a sleepless night curved
beneath her eyes. Her green eyes were leveled at
him, but his gaze drifted lower, to the curve of
her breasts, the flare of her hips, and he remembered all too well the perfect fit of her body to his.

Meeting her gaze, he said, "The anger is for
what you make me want, Domini. Not just your
body, though I ache to bury my flesh in yours.
There's still love in you, an' mine got all used

up a long time ago. Truth is, there was a time I hated you."

She wrapped her arms around her waist. "Hated me? But why, Luke? You didn't even know me."

"Sure I did. I heard stories about you from your father. I envied you having not one but two parents who loved you. How's that for honesty?"

His voice was calm and soft. Maybe too much so. One of the hardest things Domini ever did was take the first step toward him. She didn't know if he would reject her, leave, or lash out, but she hurt for him. Hurt until tears fell unheeded down her face as she stood before him.

"I don't want your goddamn pity."

"P-pity, Luke? N-no. Never that. You're too strong to be pitied. But are you strong enough to accept love?"

His features darkened with frightening speed. From one second to the next, his lazy, leaning stance shifted to that of an alert predator.

"Is that what you're offering me, Domini? Does love wrap up the gut-deep ache in a prettier package for you?"

"If there's no love, Luke, then it's a mating like animals."

"Honey, man is an animal. The worst kind. The most vicious—"

"The only one capable of love, Luke."

"Think you've got me and everythin' else all figured out, don't you? In case you missed hearing me, I was talking about the past, honey."

"Don't call me that. Not when you make it an insult. And if it was all in the past, Luke, you would let go of the hate."

He reached out for her, his fingers closing one by one in a deliberate manner over her upper arms, and just as slowly, holding her gaze fixed with his, he dragged her up against him between his spread legs. The small rippling tremors of her body acted as a caress to his. Luke was struck again by the strength of her features. She wasn't a soft, fragile, pretty woman, but now he knew his first assessment of her had been right—a man would never tire of looking at her. He never would.

She stared up at him with a vulnerable, uncertain expression and his grip eased slightly. Without thought he began making light caressing motions with his thumbs on her upper arms.

"You're not afraid of me."

Domini didn't have to think. She shook her head.

"You should be."

"You want me to be afraid, Luke. But there's too much good—"

"Haven't you learned anything?" he demanded, his fingers biting into her arms with the rough little shake he gave her. "I'm the bad seed. Bad blood. Bad down to the bone."

"No. You don't believe that. You can't. I don't believe it."

Her eyes implored him to believe her. But Domini didn't know she was trying to fight a dark, angry tide that had built over years of having his badness, and his admission that there was nothing good about him beaten into him. She had been taught that it was wrong to hate. But a tide of overwhelming hate rose inside her for those who had punished him. She wanted to wreak vengeance on Amanda for doing it, Toma for allowing it, and Matt because he was every bit as cruel as his parents.

She struggled to raise her hand between the press of their bodies. He felt her fingers trace the jagged scar on his cheek.

"How did this happen to you?" she asked softly.

He didn't want to answer. Yet the words slipped out. "I was too curious for my own good, too little to understand why Amanda hated me. I snuck into her rooms and she caught me touching one of her china dolls. She scared me and I dropped it. She used her riding crop on me." He closed his eyes against the memory of the blow, wanting to refuse Domini's gentle touch, which seemed to offer healing, and he wanted to refuse her compassion.

He had one weapon against Domini. He used it. Ruthlessly.

"You shouldn't have come up here, Domini. Don't you know what I could do to you? What I want to do to you? Toma declared open hunting season on you. I'll be damned if Matt gets you first."

The tremors grew deeper until she was visibly shaking. Now she was afraid. And he didn't care. He couldn't let himself care about her. *But you do*, a small voice whispered. *You care too much. Else you wouldn't have agreed to Toma's scheme.*

He shut out the voice of conscience, and let the anger that had smoldered flare to life.

"If you're not afraid of me now, you will be before I'm ready to let you go."

His eyes were so black that she wanted to close hers against their heat and fury. "W-will—" she shuddered and forced herself to finish, "hurting me help you?"

Her head was angled back as if in offering. He gazed at her bared throat, then her hips, before he looked into her wide green eyes.

"Are you offering yourself like a lamb for sacrifice?"

"If t-that's what you need, Luke."

"What I need is a woman. Willing or not." With a savage twist of his body he changed places with her, pressing her against the solid wall of his cabin, pressing his body against hers. His mouth claimed the bare length of her throat, his voice rough and hoarse with need.

"I want to be inside you. I want to take you every way a man can have a woman, Domini. And I want that so badly I hurt. But sex won't be enough. I want all of you until there's nothing for you without me."

And he knew as he claimed her trembling

mouth that he had lied. Sex wasn't all he wanted from her. He wanted to believe as she did that Amanda was wrong, that there was still some vestige of good in him. He wanted to believe that as badly as he wanted Domini. He wanted justice for the years she'd been alone and the years he had been denied his rightful place. But he kept these wants silent. He couldn't let go of the painful lessons learned in the past: of giving voice to a desire only to be refused.

"Fight me, damn you," he whispered against her mouth, taking her lips with all the pent-up hunger in him. Christ! She was soft. Soft enough to ease a man's pain. He needed to drown in her softness, in the sweet heat of her giving.

It was the generous giving of herself that defeated his churning anger. He couldn't hurt her. Didn't want to. But her lips met his with an explosive demand that he could not have stopped even if he had found the will to. Their harsh breaths mingled like the rush of the wind in a dizzying force around them. His hips ground against hers and found only the pliant yield of her body.

Domini couldn't have fought him if she had found the will to do so. He had unleashed a storm that battered her emotions until he had his wish. She couldn't think of anything but Luke and the gut-deep need he had set free. He had tempted her from the first to taste the forbidden passion that waited. Passion he offered. Could teach. And satisfy.

But even more enticing was the thought that she could lead Luke out from the shadows that he had lived with for so long. Once she had questioned why Luke believed that change brought about destruction. She had wondered if someone had tried to destroy him to make him change. She had answers. And only wished to bring him ease and comfort. If he would let her . . .

There was goodness in him, just as there was love. And need. It was so strong that she tasted it in his kiss.

He was drowning in her. Luke could barely contain the overpowering need he had to see if that golden skin that graced her face and neck were the same all over. Hunger filled him with a violent rush. He wanted to strip her clothes from her, to see if her nipples were the same lush, dusky color as the generous mouth that answered the thrust of his tongue with a small sensual duel. She made him want everything, all the long ago childhood dreams of having someone to care what happened to him, someone to love him, someone for him to love.

All the wild, hidden sensuality that he wanted to claim was here, held within his arms. He was as hard as a whetstone as he brought her hips against his. He felt how hard and tight her nipples were through the thin cloth. He knew how perfectly she would fit him. Mouth to mouth, her breasts soft, flattening to the muscles of his chest, soft but for the small, hard nipples that burned

him. He rocked his hips against her, desiring to
nestle his aching flesh within soft black silk that
was hotter than the sun beating down on his back,
and sweeter than rain.

Domini whimpered. His mouth bruised hers.
He was all darkness, filled with an explosive rage
that she was not sure she could combat. He
wanted her. But she still sensed that he hated her
for the desire that flared so wildly between them.
The quick, hungry touch of his lips brought her
hands up to hold his cheeks, but the thick black
silk of his hair beckoned and her fingers slid
through its length. She moaned, kissing him back
with all the hunger he brought to life, pressing
closer, then closer still, wanting to be absorbed
into his very flesh. She wanted to be lost in the
heat, and the pleasure and the passion. Every bit
of her skin felt hot, prickly. Her mouth was damp,
bruised, her breasts felt swollen, her entire being
on fire with need. And all the warnings disappeared as Luke lifted her into his arms without
breaking their kiss. Only the cooler, shadowed in-
terior told Domini that he had taken her inside
his cabin.

# *Chapter Seventeen*

~

The moment Luke kicked the door closed, Domini wrenched her lips from his. He was already lowering her to his bed when she cupped his cheeks to stop him from kissing her again.

"Are you sure this is what you need, Luke? Will having me get rid of the demons that haunt you and keep the hate alive?"

He jerked back, his arms falling away from her. Domini no longer had his complete attention. He was still, and then she heard what he was listening to—the crunch of boots outside on the path to the cabin.

Luke moved quietly to the door before the knock came. He opened the door a few inches. "Mulekey."

"Said to fetch you when the next one's ready. Well, she's awaitin' on you, son."

Luke's grip on the edge of the door tightened until his knuckles showed white.

"Christ, Mulekey, not now." He pressed his forehead against the wood. Silently swearing as he struggled to bring his unruly body back from the wild edge where promised satisfaction waited, he tried to avoid looking at Domini sprawled on his bed. He might as well have asked himself to stop breathing.

The taste of her, the need for her, was lodged in him like a bullet in the flesh. Hot. Painful. Damn impossible to forget. She made him restless. Angry. And when he gave in to the need to look at her, it made him snarl. She was every yearning, every foolish dream of childhood that he believed dead.

"Give me a minute, Mulekey."

"Sure thing, son. Was up to me, you could have the rest of the day. But you got to know I ain't the only one what's knowin' you ain't alone up here."

Luke eyed Domini for a long minute. She still had not moved.

"Luke, you know the old man's gonna hold you to your deal. You ain't got time for foolin' with no woman. 'Sides, a woman's trouble, son. Just naturally go together like fleas an' a dog."

"Wait for me," Luke said, closing the door. When he turned back, Domini was no longer on the bed. She stood in a shaft of sunlight before the fireplace and stared at the lone object on the mantel.

Sunlight caught in her hair as she hesitantly reached up to touch the wood figure with her fingertip. Luke braced himself for her accusation of thievery.

"The carving," she began, glancing at him, then once more gazing with joy at the wooden hummingbird. "My father must have loved you very much to have given this to you, Luke."

He should have known that she never did what he expected. Yet he was still afraid to trust. "What makes you think he gave it to me? Maybe I stole it."

"He made this for me. I wanted him to have a present when he left. Something that would make him remember me. I ran to get this from my room and Toma grew impatient, but my father made him wait. He promised me that he would keep it unless he found someone who would treasure the little bird as much as I did." She turned, and her smile came despite the sheen of tears in her eyes.

"Thank you for keeping this."

"Take it. It belongs to you." She overwhelmed him with her goodness. He heard Mulekey whistle. Without another word he spun around and left her. He didn't turn back, didn't say a word as he followed Mulekey down the path.

"Mighta known it was a woman. That's the only thing can make a man look uglier an' meaner than homemade sin." He spat a stream of tobacco juice off to the side.

"You haven't met Domini. When you do, Mulekey—ah, hell, forget it."

"Easy enough for me to do, son. Can you?"

Luke was quiet so long that Mulekey didn't think he would answer him. And when he did, the words were softly spoken, but there was a savage intensity behind them.

"I can't forget her."

Domini remained huddled on Luke's bed, still feeling the trembling desire he had aroused and left unsatisfied. Difficult as it was for her to focus, she forced herself to think of Mulekey's interruption as a blessing in disguise. Too much had happened this morning: first her talk with Amanda, then Luke's revelation about her cruelty.

She didn't have trouble believing that her father would have offered Amanda comfort. He was a loving man. Toma, from her own observations, was not. But had her father been Amanda's lover?

That was what Amanda had implied. And Luke, just how close had he been to her father? Did he know that Amanda . . . Domini stilled. If what Amanda said was true, then Toma and Matt would have known. Matt was older. He had to be aware of whatever had happened with his mother . . . her father.

As much as Domini wanted to avoid thinking, she couldn't deny that Amanda had asked one vital question. Why had her father abandoned them when he came north with Toma? He had to have known then that Toma had his family with him. Why had he left her and her mother? Why?

A tormenting question that begged an answer,

but Domini found that her strength of will was considerably weakened. Tears that she had not shed at other times came far too easily now. Pain formed a cold, hard knot inside. The question of why became a litany drumming with the pounding in her head.

Who could she go to for the truth? Amanda had her own deep game to play. Domini simply didn't trust Matt. On the deepest, instinctive level she knew she couldn't. Toma? His pride was a stone shield she couldn't hope to break. He would never admit that his wife had wanted another man. No, she reminded herself. Not just another man. Her father had been his friend and partner.

As she watched the play of sun and shadow on the bare plank floor, Domini roused herself. Hiding was not going to give her what she wanted. She couldn't remain here, waiting for Luke, for she knew too well how his needs and passion mirrored her own. That admission forced her to move when nothing else had.

The small wood carving of the hummingbird dipping its long beak into an open flower drew her near the fireplace. She traced the shape of the tiny bird and thought of what she had told Luke. Her father had loved him.

It saddened her as she looked around the cabin to realize that this gift from her father was the only treasure that Luke had from his childhood. Cupping her hands gently around the carving, Domini brought it to her lips and kissed it.

"Perhaps," she whispered as she replaced the bird on the mantel, "Luke will see it now with different eyes. Maybe he'll come to understand how easily the gift of love can be given, and what richness it brings to both the giver and the receiver."

Domini closed the door behind her and, once down the path, walked across the meadow. She fought the temptation to join the crowd of men around the corral who shouted encouragement to Luke. She caught glimpses of Luke when the horse he rode bucked high, then the trees around the house blocked her view.

Meta was cleaning her room. She informed Domini that Matt was eating alone in the dining room. Since Domini didn't wish to see Amanda, she chose to join him.

She wasn't sure if her defenses were so battered that Matt's undemanding company was a welcome respite, or she was learning that she could pretend as well as he that last night had never happened. Whatever the reason, Matt went out of his way to make their meal a pleasant time. By its end, Domini felt as if she knew the families that lived close by to form a tight social circle.

She refused his offer to go for a ride, but found herself restless enough to agree to go for a walk with him. Matt chose a path that led away from the corrals, and Domini offered no objection. She didn't want Luke to see them together. Not after the fury of last night and this morning, when he had thought that Matt had done something to her.

Domini stopped beneath the spreading branches of a lone tree. It was quiet here, and she almost forgot Matt's presence until she felt his hands gently touch her shoulders.

"You seem troubled, Dominica. Won't you share your thoughts with me?"

His soft, cultured voice was so at odds with Luke's rough, impatient tone. She made the comparison without conscious thought. Hoping she wasn't being obvious, Domini managed to turn and step away to remove his hands. And it was time for her to be done with pretense.

"Your mother's talk disturbed me. She hinted that she had been more than friends with my father."

"And you believed her?"

"You were here, Matt. Why don't you tell me if it was true?" She moved away, turning to face him. Placing both hands behind her lower back, Domini leaned against the wide trunk of the tree. She felt somewhat protected in this position.

A wry smile creased Matt's lips. "You needn't be afraid of me. I won't hurt you."

She lifted her chin and leveled a direct gaze at him. "You hurt me last night."

"I was angry." He rubbed the back of his neck, his smile more a boyish grin. "I apologize, Dominica. And my anger was for Luke, not you."

She let the lie stand. It had taken her a while

to understand that she would gain no information from him unless he thought she trusted him.

"You haven't answered my question, Matt. Was my father in love with your mother?"

"It's not a simple yes or no. And she is my mother. Whatever her faults, Amanda is my mother. Tell me, why did you run off to Luke this morning?"

"I didn't. I had noticed the cabin the day he brought me here. I was upset and ran. It wasn't until later that I found out it was Luke's cabin. You must admit it's odd to have your brother live on his own when the house is so big."

Domini tensed as Matt looked away toward the house. She released the breath she held when he nodded and turned back to her.

"Luke's always wanted to be alone. From the time he learned to walk he'd run off."

This was getting her nowhere. Leaving her place of safety near the tree, Domini walked to Matt's side. She forced herself to place her hand on his arm, and could only hope that her expression conveyed a plea when she wanted to loose the fury of being told half truths.

"Matt, your mother hates Luke. Why?"

"Why do you want to know?"

"Your father told me to make a choice between you. I can't do that unless I understand what it is that would cause a mother to favor one son and hate the other. What did Luke do to her?"

"Oh, it wasn't Luke," he said, covering her hand

with his. "At least not directly. She nearly died giving birth to me. Toma wanted more sons. He knew he was going to find gold, knew how harsh a toll this land could take. My mother feared that her delicate constitution wouldn't allow her to survive having another child. She denied him her bed, such as it was."

He raised his hand to touch her hair, smoothing it back, then abruptly turned away. He took a few steps and stopped. "This is both painful and a violation of family secrets."

She went to him, this time finding it easier to offer him the compassion that was so much a part of her. "I'm sorry. I truly am, Matt. I don't want to cause anyone pain. I think we have all had our share. I still don't understand why she hates Luke—"

"Don't you? Just think about it a moment, Dominica. Do you believe that Toma offered her the comfort and the true understanding that she would have expected from her husband and a gentleman? I realize you've only been here a short time, but surely you've formed an idea of what Toma is like?"

"Prideful, arrogant, a man who would do anything and use anyone to get what he wanted."

"An excellent summation of my father's character. There is no delicate way to explain that he raped my mother until she became pregnant, and when she lost the child he barely waited until she was healed before he did it again. She conceived

Luke that second time, and she swore that Toma would never use her again."

Domini backed away and stood staring at his rigid back. His voice held no emotion. It was as cold and dry as the words he spoke. Before she could absorb all that he'd said, Matt turned.

"You do understand now, don't you? When Luke was born she couldn't bear to look at him, much less care for him. He represented everything she hated about my father."

"But he was innocent. An innocent babe!"

"No. He was the price Toma demanded from my mother so that she could remain with me. She paid it. We both have paid Toma his due. And now, knowing the past, can you truly blame us for feeling that Luke has no right—"

"Matt, I have no right to judge any of you, I— I'm sorry. Truly sorry." Domini bowed her head. When Matt came and put his arms around her, Domini offered no resistance.

"Dominica, please, find it in your generous heart to give her some compassion. She has suffered. But you must never let her know that I told you. It would grieve her that you knew." Placing his fingertips beneath her chin, he tilted her head back. "Promise me?"

"I promise, Matt."

"Thank you."

She closed her eyes as he leaned closer to brush his lips across hers. Before he could deepen the kiss, Domini slipped free. The cold knot of pain spread until she had to bite her lip to keep from crying out for Luke. She had suffered, too. But not as he had. She had had a core of loving memories to draw upon, but he had been given nothing. Now she understood why he said he had hated her, why he had envied her the love of her parents. Toma may have gotten the second son he wanted, but Matt was right in saying that they had all paid his price.

She shivered from the cold imprisoning her and rubbed her arms.

"I've shocked you," Matt said, sliding his arm around her and drawing her close. "Come back to the house with me. I'll have Ellamay make you some of her soothing herb tea. Both Mother and Mrs. Mayfield swear there's little it won't cure."

As Domini walked back to the house with him, she noticed that the drawing room drapes were parted slightly. Was Amanda watching them? Well, if she was, she should be pleased to see her with Matt.

It wasn't until later, as she rested in her room, that Domini realized Matt had never really answered her question about her father. Sipping the soothing tea that Ellamay had brought to her, Domini spent the remainder of the day piecing together what she did know.

By the time she dressed for dinner, Domini had come to one conclusion. Despite Toma's denials, he was the only one with reason to kill her father.

All she needed to do was prove it. But how?

# Chapter Eighteen

⌒

Domini didn't see Luke until after dinner the next night. She knew he was avoiding her, which was just as well. She hadn't quite come to terms with her growing feelings for him.

Matt had left that morning with four hands to ensure there was no trouble at the mines. Amanda, pleading a headache, had kept to her rooms all day. Domini had been unable to force herself to sit across the table from Toma and share a meal with the man she believed had killed her father. Ellamay seemed to understand and brought a tray to her room.

But the vague, restless unease that had plagued her from the moment she had awakened intensified and sent her fleeing from the house. Domini felt stifled within its walls.

Even to herself she didn't admit that she hoped to find Luke near the corrals. Ellamay told her he often checked the horses he had worked with that day. But he was heading back to his cabin when she drew near the corral. A few horses milled about as she approached the pole fence enclosure.

Domini started when she realized she was not alone. A bowed-legged man with a hint of a pot-belly came closer to where she stood.

"So you're the one."

"Pardon?"

"Name's Mulekey, missy. Luke tole me 'bout you," he announced in a testy voice. "Says you're Kirkland's daughter."

"That's true." Domini's teeth scored her bottom lip. She tried to bite back the question, but it begged to be asked. "Did you know my father?"

"Heard tell that's all you're askin' folks."

"And most of them refuse to give me a straight answer."

"Now, missy, ain't a need to get surly. Most folks don't like nosy critters. I knowed him some. Was doin' some prospectin' in these mountains long before he come up here with Toma."

Domini angled her head to the side, studying the bewhiskered old man. The fading light allowed her to see his thinning hair and the way his right eyelid blinked furiously in a nervous tic. He stood at ease under her assessing gaze.

"I have a strong feeling that you deliberately sought me out to tell me something."

"Could be. Lived long enough to hand out advice. That is, if you're willin' listen to an old geezer who ain't lost his smarts when he lost his hair."

"I have a great respect for the wisdom that comes with age." Domini smiled, then added, "But I can't promise that I'll do more than listen to your advice."

Mulekey rubbed his jaw. "Fair enough. I got to have my say. Been festerin' inside. Luke'll likely raise a hell of a ruckus with me, but you're trouble for him. Tole him so. He's got so he thinks he's a law unto hisself. Jus' like his daddy. But he's never gotten his boots tangled up in a lady's petticoats. Never had much truck with women."

"Then you come along." He settled his thin arms across the middle cross pole and stared at the horses. "Boy's twisted inside out. If he don't keep his mind on breakin' 'em horses for Toma, he's gonna end up hurt. Hurt bad. You do that boy a favor an' stay clear of him."

"Did Luke put you up to this?"

"Missy, listen up. Ain't what I said. I tole Luke you're trouble. Now I'm tellin' you so's to protect him."

Far from taking offense, Domini mulled over his words and found herself stepping closer to the old man. "I'm glad that someone besides Ellamay cares about Luke. Really cares what happens to him."

" 'Course I care." Mulekey snorted and shook his head. "Wouldn't be wastin' time spinnin' words to the wind if I didn't. An' it's wasted time, ain't it?"

"Now it's you who isn't listening, Mulekey. I never said that. I'm standing here and I'm listening to you. I feel guilty enough for what Luke did. I know he wants nothing to do with Toma or the Colfax holdings. I'm not sure why he felt he had to protect me by agreeing with Toma's ridiculous scheme. I don't want to marry anyone."

"Seems to me I smell a lie as well as I smell that horse dung in the corral." Her silence had him shaking his head again. "Missy, you can't be knowin' half the hell that boy's lived with. He was all set to clear out for good after this last trip. Been named a bastard from the day he was born, an' he's been tryin' to live up to the name. Tried to tell him it ain't the way. But Luke's a stubborn cuss at times."

"Just at times? I don't agree. He's always stubborn. But you're wrong when you say I'm trouble for him. I care a great deal about what happens to Luke." The moment she spoke, she knew it was true. She did care. Perhaps too much.

"Care enough to love him? 'Cause if you do, missy, you'll leave him be. All Toma wants is to get a rope 'round Luke. You don't ever listen to that man. Toma's poison mean. He'll use you to get Luke so's he can have that boy comin' an' goin' at his beck an' call. They've come to blows in the past, missy. One of these days Luke or his daddy ain't gonna walk away."

Impulsively, Domini put her hand on his bony arm. "I don't want to see anyone put a rope around Luke. He's like these wild horses, meant to be free. All I wanted was answers about my father's death, Mulekey. I don't know how to convince you that I have no intention of hurting Luke. I know he's been treated brutally here."

"You mean that?"

"Yes, Mulekey, I mean every word. Luke . . . well, I know there's goodness in him. He can be kind and gentle. He sees beauty in a harsh land and . . ." Her voice faded as images of being alone with Luke on the trail came rushing back to her.

"Take a saint, a heap of love, an' maybe a whole lot of the good Lord's blessings to heal that boy. Luke's afraid to want things, or people, too much 'cause that leaves him wide open to a whole new kind of hurtin'. If you're smart, you'll stay away from him. Boy's a heartbreak waitin' to happen."

"Mulekey—"

"Luke don't know what love is, missy. Ain't a woman born with the patience to teach him."

*Love?* Twice Mulekey had mentioned this word. It gave Domini pause. Did she love Luke? The obsession with the past and the answers she wanted had clouded her mind. She knew her feelings had deepened for Luke. But love? She shivered and rubbed her arms.

Domini glanced up the steep climb to where the lonely cabin stood within the sheltering trees. She knew Luke was up there despite the lack of light from the cabin. She closed her eyes, for the warm, sultry breeze seemed to whisper his name with a longing she couldn't deny. The restlessness that had sent her fleeing from the house focused into a need to see Luke, to be with him. And only him.

"You gonna go up there?"

The decision was made. "Yes, I'm going. And nothing you can say will stop me."

"Don't get all lathered up. I's jus' wonderin'. Luke wants tamin' for sure, but you'll be needin' a buggy whip for the job."

"You're wrong, Mulekey. You said it yourself. Luke needs love. He's had enough of whips and people trying to change him."

"You be careful, missy. Luke gets his back to the wall an' he's likely to come out snarlin'. Don't say I didn't warn you."

Domini turned to walk away but stopped. Once more impulse ruled her. She leaned closer and kissed his whiskered cheek. "Thank you, Mulekey."

"What for?" he asked, rubbing the spot where she had kissed him.

"For caring about Luke. For making me understand how much I do, too."

"Well, I'll be . . ." Scratching his left ear, Mulekey squinted in the fading light as he watched her walk across the meadow.

"Here's me, unpleasant as a snappin' turtle with a sour stomach, an' she jus' ups an' kisses me. Thanks me, too, for carin' 'bout that boy. Beats all. You hear that, horse?" He stroked the muzzle of a bay who poked at him through the pole fence. "Maybe I was wrong. Maybe she'll be good for him. Then again, maybe she'll be the death of that boy."

The warm breeze that stirred the tips of the meadow grasses carried the sound of Mulekey's mutterings but not the exact words. She didn't know if it was a mistake to go up to Luke's cabin. She couldn't forget what had happened the last time. . . . When Luke touched her, when he reached out silently with that need and hunger in his kiss, she lost all sense of right and wrong. She lost time and reason.

Need. Hunger. They entwined to whisper through her. Joined they became powerful, sharpening into something else.

Something Domini was afraid to name.

The courage to continue across the meadow came from knowing that Luke felt it, too. Domini looked up once more. She hesitated. Would she find welcome or rejection? Was Mulekey right? Was it possible that she could be Luke's salvation? Or condemn him into Toma's net?

Luke stood at the edge of the cliff's jut. He watched Domini head for the path with a narrow-eyed look. Lifting the whiskey bottle to his lips, he took no more than a sip of the harsh liquor. It wasn't the taste he craved. Whiskey wasn't what he wanted. Liquor only warmed his insides, but it intensified the ache in his loins.

He wanted Domini. Wanted that strong, graceful body beneath his. Open. Welcoming. Passion heating her blood.

He had tasted it. And having tasted passion, her passion, he wanted it as nothing before.

He had stayed away from her. Despite the desire that heated his blood, he had tried. And he had tempted and taunted her by turns. But then, her father had wanted them together.

He should feel guilty for withholding that from her.

Only guilt made a man weak.

He had had guilt beaten into him. All he had learned was that he couldn't afford that flaw. Never could he forget that he was his mother's son, and his father's. From both he had inherited their capacity for cruelty.

Domini couldn't matter to him beyond slaking his need.

He wouldn't let her matter.

Cradling the bottle between his thighs, he pulled out his makings from the shirt pocket and built himself a smoke. By the time he had the cigarette lit, Domini was no longer in sight.

If he had any sense he would be waiting for her at the top of the path, ready to order her to turn around and go back to the house.

It was a safe option.

He wasn't feeling safe. He felt wild, and reckless, and hungry.

Could be, he thought, taking a deep drag of the

cigarette, that the broom-tail mare he'd spent most of the afternoon breaking to ride easy under a man had jarred loose what little sense he had left.

Especially when it came to Domini.

She brought to life all the old, bone-deep hungers that he swore he didn't feel. He'd never wanted more than to collect his small herd of horses, pay off the debt he owed Toma for their care, and end any connection with the Colfax family.

His acute hearing picked up the small rocks that slid beneath Domini's moccasins. She was coming closer. And every step made him aware that he was lying to himself.

He had come back here and stayed because of Domini.

He had been running, as he had always run from the dark, swirling undercurrents of hate that filled his world from the minute he had fully understood what hate was.

Domini drew him with the clean, bright fire of her passion and the deep-seated goodness within her.

She threatened him in ways he couldn't name.

She made him hurt with needs so tangled he couldn't sort them out.

It had taken him years to build a thick, hard shell around his emotions. From the first, Domini had begun destroying that shell.

Seeing her with Matt yesterday had released all

the pent-up vengeance he had stored. Vengeance he thought he needed for the years of torment and lies.

Luke heard her call out to him, but he didn't answer. He crushed the unfinished cigarette beneath his boot heel. Lifting the cover to the rain barrel where he had washed away the dust and grime of labor, he replaced it and set the whiskey bottle on top.

Leaning back against the log cabin wall, he waited for her to come to him.

He could walk away. There was still time.

Usually he could lose himself when working with the horses. There was no past, no future, just him and an animal whose intelligence and strength he respected even as he sought to tame it. He hated calling what he did breaking a horse. Breaking meant destroying the very spirit a man needed to depend upon. Only to himself did he call it gentling. And no one could fault him—no one, that is, but Matt. His brother ridiculed his methods as too slow, too soft. Luke took silent satisfaction that when he was finished with a horse, no man had to fear being thrown or abandoned by his animal.

Domini had stolen his peace with his work today. She had interfered with his thoughts. She had forced him to think about making decisions.

She made him dream again. She made him want to put the past behind him. If he put the past behind him he might bury the pain.

Domini brought back dreams and with them came hope. He admitted it now that her footsteps faltered as she neared. She had him thinking about what life could be if she was a part of his.

The thoughts should have jolted him. He should have been running as far and as fast as he could. Could she bring him what he desperately wanted?

Did he want to give her a chance?

"Luke? Luke, where are you?"

"Around the side."

He didn't have to look to know she was standing there, watching him. The small hitch in her breathing was the only sound she made.

"Did you come up here to badger me with more questions, Domini?"

"No."

"Then you came to finish what got started yesterday."

"I didn't say that."

"Hell, I know you didn't say it. You haven't said a damn thing."

"I missed you. I had . . . had to leave the house. It makes me feel smothered. And I keep trying to understand how you can be so . . . alone, Luke."

"Why not?" He grabbed the whiskey bottle and tilted it to his lips. Wiping off his mouth with the back of his hand, he held out the bottle to her. When she shook her head, he shrugged, then set the bottle back on the barrel cover.

Luke tilted his head back against the cabin wall.

His unbuttoned shirt hung free of his pants. Without looking at her, he said, "When I was little, I would search the skies when the wind came up wild. I couldn't understand why the stars weren't shaken loose. But I would dream of catching them when they did and having my every wish come true. But I never did find a wind star."

"Did you stop looking?"

His head angled down and to the side so he could look at her. "In a way. I grew up learning that wishes and dreams are for fools. I don't need anyone, Domini."

Taking courage Domini stepped closer to him. "I'm afraid that I do." She fought the burning tears that sprang to her eyes. How could she make his pain go away? "No one can survive without people to care and love them."

"I wouldn't know about that," Luke answered in a blunt, harsh voice. "I've never been able to count on anyone, and no one, sure as apples start green, ever loved me enough to care what happened to me."

"That's not true! Mulekey and Ellamay care a great deal what happens to you. Toma, too, although you'll both deny it." He was hard and harsh, yet in moments like this, Luke touched her so deeply, ensnared her tightly with need by revealing his vulnerability.

"And me, Luke, I care about you."

Intrigued by the look on his face, Domini reached out to touch him, only to jerk her hand back. There was a blaze of ripe anger in his eyes, ready to rip into her. But in the seconds that she stood frozen, his look changed to one she had seen the first night she met him. A look equally ripe, equally ready to rip into her hard-won control. The look was desire.

"What the hell does it take?" he muttered. "You want to be scared?"

"I am. I don't think you know how much courage it took for me to come here to you."

"Christ! Stay the hell away from me." This time Luke couldn't hide his desperation. She wanted too much from him. His hands curled against the wall, fingers pressing hard. Seconds that seemed forever long counted the savage beat of his life's blood.

"I'll help you, Domini. I'll help you keep away from me. If you don't, I'll swear I'll take you right here."

One look convinced her that he meant it. Domini shivered where she stood. If she turned away from him now, she would never find the courage to come to him again. Despite Toma's command that she marry one of his sons, Domini didn't want Matt. Luke was all that mattered. Her stomach lurched threateningly. She couldn't let fear take control.

"Still here?"

"I was afraid to come and now, Luke, I'm afraid to go."

He moved so fast she couldn't evade him if she

had wanted to. Domini had learned what she wanted. She submitted without any show of resistance when he grabbed her by the shoulders.

"I'll put the fear of God into you and keep you the hell away from me." He gave her a rough little shake. "Stop making me want too much."

"I don't fear God, Luke," she answered softly. "I was taught that's not what He wants. And I don't fear you." But the quaver in her voice belied the words. She did fear him. Feared that even breaking the very code of morals, committing sin by coming to him out of the bonds of marriage, Luke would still turn away from her.

"Then you're a fool, Domini. A damned fool. You should be running as fast as you can away from me." His fingers tightened. He searched her face for a sign of fear and found himself drowning in the gift of her trust.

Drugging, sweet, potent, he couldn't forget his first taste of her. The first woman he had ever wanted to share the intimacy of a kiss with. Tangled in his senses were her scent and her taste. The kind a weak man could drown in wanting them for his own.

But Luke wasn't a weak man. He wouldn't let himself be one.

"Luke?"

"Damn you." But there was no heat in the words. "You seduce a man's mind long before his body gets involved. You don't know what you do to me. But you're gonna know. No more running, Domini. Not for you. Not for me."

She had despaired of breaching the wall around his emotions. Now she could see the need in his eyes. She understood the need as she found an answering desire build inside her. His look was a mirror of her own. As was the hunger behind it. For the hunger whispered of more than desire, it beckoned with a promise of completion. The power . . . the very complex layers of need pierced her soul.

She stood gazing at him, and Luke, for reasons of his own, allowed it. How many times had she longed for someone to simply hold her? To know there was one person to offer comfort? Compassion? To have someone answer the need within everyone of knowing another cared deeply, that he would always be there to lean on? For herself there had been too many times when she had been as alone . . . as with Luke. He claimed she had seduced his mind and his body. There was nothing simple about her feelings for him. Luke had seduced her heart and soul.

And still he fought against it.

With his fingers biting through the cloth of her gown to the skin and bone beneath, he pulled her against him. Anger flared in his eyes. Hard and punishing, his mouth covered hers.

Domini waited for the anger to burn itself out. God help her, she could no more turn aside from his anger than she could turn away from Luke himself.

He jerked his head back and stared at her. "What the hell does it take? I'm no good for you. Forget Toma's crazy scheme. I sure the hell have." A storm of emotions shifted in her wide green eyes. "Can't you see that, Domini? I'm no good."

All she heard was a plea underlying the words for her to deny it. She did so without effort. "Luke, if there wasn't any good in you," she murmured softly, pushing aside his open shirt to place her hands on his bare chest, "would you keep warning me away? If there wasn't any goodness in you, Luke, would you have stopped yourself from having me that first night?"

"You pulled a knife on me. I didn't have a choice."

Domini raised her head. The move brought her lips closer to his. "We both know what stopped you. It was not your knife, Luke. And I came to you tonight because I need you. Not an easy admission for me to make. But you, if only you'd let yourself believe—"

His mouth closed over hers again, stilling the words, stopping the thoughts. She welcomed him this time, hungry for his kiss. Whiskey and smoke flavored the wet heat of his mouth. She savored the potency as she savored the masculine texture of his lips. If Luke wouldn't listen to her, wouldn't say the words himself, she could only show him.

Hunger too long denied was contagious. Reason

was stonewalled behind the barrier created by desire. Domini couldn't think of anything but her need for him.

"Luke," she whispered the moment he lifted his head, "there's so much good in you. So much love. I swear to you, if it's the last thing I do, I'll make you see it, too."

# Chapter Nineteen

⤳

"Honey, that's one crazy notion to have now." With the rough pad of his thumb he shaped the generous curve of her bottom lip, watching her reaction with eyes of midnight. The telltale shiver of desire, the hitch in her breathing, and the small sound she made ignited the heat running heavy in his blood.

"Being good, Domini, isn't what I had in mind," he murmured with a voice that could have persuaded Satan toward an act of charity. "No, not the kind of good you mean at all. Not when you've got a sultry voice that'll make a good man go bad just to hear you call his name in passion."

He worked his hand slowly down the length of her back. Once more he felt the telltale quiver that she couldn't hide from him. He bent to take her mouth again.

"Open for me, Domini. First your mouth that's got me so hungry I can't think straight." He brushed his lips against hers, his eyes narrowing when she turned to follow his lips.

"You feel it, too, don't you? Like a wild storm that's gathering strength to sweep everything in its path?"

"Hunger. That's what it is." She gazed at him, all dark hair, dark eyes, dark angles in the secret shadows of the quickening night. Even his voice was a dark murmur as he called her name.

"Domini. Open your mouth for me. I want you to give." He took her lower lip between his teeth and flicked his tongue over her lip. She leaned into him, closer, wanting more, a deepening tremble whispering of desire.

Luke spread his hands until his thumbs coasted up from the curve of her hips, shaped her waist, and then slowed to measure each quickened breath as he raised them to gently press the sides of her breasts.

"Frightened?"

"Yes. Not of you. The things you make me feel are too powerful, Luke."

"I know." His mouth kicked up at the corner. "Scares the hell out of me. I want you so much. You've got a body that'll make a bad man damn proud that he'll never, ever be good."

She tilted her head back against his powerful onslaught, willing herself not to panic as he kissed her with a force and passion that overwhelmed her.

Domini didn't dare let herself think about the

step she was taking. She felt as wild and reckless as one of the storms she loved to watch. This time Luke made her feel she was caught in a storm's center, spinning out of control.

She knew her strength of will was no match for his. If Luke could, he would make love to her and walk away.

They would both lose.

She couldn't let that happen.

Her fingers caught the back of his head, entwining in the still damp length of his hair. Domini opened her mouth for him, just as she opened her heart.

Luke gathered her closer to the heat of his body. He cupped her buttocks, bringing up against his hard, aching flesh. He rocked against her heavily, making sure she was certain of how much he wanted her. A small whimper escaped her lips, a cry that he stole.

"That's it, Domini, give yourself to me. Nothing held back." Open and hungry and demanding, his mouth covered hers again. His hips ground against the cradle of her hips, needing to sheathe himself in her softness.

He loathed his own lack of control. Emotions battered him like the storm he said he would unleash. He wanted her with a passion that blinded him to all else.

But within the desire churned a deep resentment that Domini, with her innocence and trust, dared to make him want, dared to make him feel again.

His fingers clenched the cloth of her gown while he fought not to tear it. She made him wild. His need for her was so intense he thought he would explode from it.

She didn't fight him, didn't plead for gentleness. She came to him like a willow to the wind, bending but not breaking.

With a groan Luke tore his mouth from hers and threw his head back. *Breaking?* Sweet Christ! He didn't want to break her. And while threads of resentment lingered, he knew he didn't hate her.

"Luke?" She cupped his cheek, frightened by his withdrawal. She burned and Luke was the only one who could satisfy the passionate need she had learned from him.

It was her soft, trembling whisper of his name that undid him. He wouldn't allow the word to form in his mind, the one word that encompassed what he felt for her, but he could find the strength to temper his passion.

He hadn't reckoned on Domini needing more from him.

Her lips brushed against his rigid jaw, scattering kisses that were a healing balm. Her lips glided down the bare, strong column of his neck with sighs of pleasure. Her hands fell to his shoulders with a kitten-like kneading that brought a groan from deep inside him.

Domini pulled back. "Did I hurt you?"

"No."

The word was clipped and harsh. Domini tilted her head back to gaze up at his face. "Did I do something wrong?"

"The only thing you're doing wrong is stopping. It's so wrong that you'll hurt me. So bad," he murmured, using his lips, teeth, and tongue to return the pleasure against the smooth, silky length of her throat, "that I don't think I'll recover."

"I'm glad, Luke. I . . . like touching you."

"Then touch me. And when you're done, I'm going to touch you. Like I've dreamed about." He freed her hair from its loose braid and spread the heavy, straight satin thickness down her back.

"Do men like to be touched?"

"Don't you know?" he caught himself and grinned. "No. How could you? But you will, Domini. Go ahead. Touch me." He could barely make out the sheen in her eyes, for true night had laid a blanketing cover across the land.

He sensed her hesitancy didn't come from reluctance but from not knowing where to begin. He didn't trust himself to lead the way. If he took hold of her hand he was likely to teach her how to caress his violently aroused flesh. A move like that would cheat both of them.

Seeing the tip of her tongue caught between the edges of her teeth, Luke coaxed her again to touch him.

"Wherever you want, Domini. There is no right

or wrong way. There's only what makes you feel good."

"I thought you didn't want to be good."

A teasing grin creased his lips. "Then be bad, Domini. Be as bad as you want."

He expected shy touches. Once again she surprised him. He even remembered wondering what surprises she held for him. When she eased his shirt off his shoulders Luke stopped thinking. A brush of her fingertips brought the sleeves down and the cloth settled behind him.

Domini let out a deep, shaken breath. She smoothed her hands over the curve of his shoulders. His skin was hot, blazing hot. And she told him so.

"You feel hard and strong. Like a hot, smooth, polished stone that the sun has caressed with its warmth." She looked up to find his expression intense, night shadows cloaking his eyes.

"But you're not stone. The Lord made you of flesh and bone and muscle. A pleasure for a woman's eyes. Even more . . . so much more of a pleasure for her to touch."

Her fingertips skimmed the strong length of his arms, then rose to his chest. Domini murmured surprise to find small nubs as hard and tight as her own nipples felt. Luke's breath hissed out from between his clenched teeth when she kissed first one, then the other.

One hand caught her hair, drawing her head back. He held her away from him for a long mo-

ment, then took her mouth. His lips were hot, hot
and wet in a kiss of fierce, burning hunger that
allowed no shyness, no hesitation, no refusal. He
could feel her trembling, or maybe he was the one
who shook from the force flooding his body.

Domini surrendered to the mounting passion
Luke freed. His widespread palms pressed against
her shoulder blades, the small of her back, her
hips, her buttocks, molding her body against the
length of his, letting her feel the strength of his
arms, the tension coiled in his muscles, his hard
masculine flesh. Pliant and willing, she pressed
against him. Hot and sweet, desire flared
through her.

Luke broke off the kiss. His hands retraced
their path up her back to thread the thick, silky
length of her hair. His breathing was as harsh as
her own. Without a word he scooped her up into
his arms. Domini closed her eyes as he walked
the few steps to the front of the cabin.

"Last chance, Domini," he said in a whisper.

She kissed his hard, hot chest, then looked up.
"You'd let me go? Now?"

"I'd rather use my own knife and peel off strips
of skin than let you go."

"Good. I want you too much to turn back."

He kicked the door open. The room was dark;
only the glimmer of dying coals in the fireplace
relieved the blackness. She could barely stand
when he set her down. She heard the scrape of
his boots and the sound of a bar dropped into

place across the door. There truly was no turning back from the risk she was taking.

"This time I won't open the door for anyone."

"I d-don't want you to."

"Second thoughts now?"

"No."

Luke went to her, but he didn't touch her at first. "No?" he repeated, leaning close to brush his lips against her ear, his voice a breath of sound. "No, you don't want this after all, Domini? Or no—"

"Luke, please."

"I want to." His teeth caught her earlobe gently, the tiny pressure shivering through her with pleasure. He backed off, the only sound their harsh breathing and the slide of leather from his belt. She had forgotten his knife and heard the thud of it falling with the belt on the wood plank floor. Minutes later, his boots followed.

"How many ways can I tell you yes, Luke? I came to you. I've told you that I want you. I—"

"You can show me, Domini. Show me how much you want me."

Domini didn't realize that she had backed up until the edge of the footboard stopped her. Luke came closer and she sidestepped as he caught her shoulders and bore her down to the bed behind her, following her down on the mattress, covering her with his strong, hard body.

This is Luke, she told herself, feeling the first wave of panic. Luke who's scattering sweet, heated kisses across your face. Luke whose body you're touching.

He rolled to his side, looming above her, his hand resting on her hip. "What's wrong?"

"Will you be gentle with me, Luke?"

"I don't know if I can. I've never been any woman's first lover before you. An' I've never wanted any woman the way that I want you."

"I trust you, Luke." To prove to him that she did, Domini didn't hesitate before hiking up the skirt of her gown, the move taking her petticoats with it. Freeing her other hand, she untied the knife sheath from her thigh.

"Here," she said, holding it out to him.

He took the sheathed weapon from her trembling hand, knowing the cost to her. This weapon was her protection, and giving it to him made her totally vulnerable to him. *Trust.* This was another measure of her trust in him.

Solemnly he leaned over and placed it on the floor, then turned back to her. "You won't ever need that again. Not with me. Not as long as I'm around."

To silence her question of how long that would be, she reached for him, drawing him down to her waiting lips, to a body flushed with passion as he settled his weight to her side.

Gentleness demanded a high price from him. His body was tense and seething with need, but he forced himself to open the buttons of her gown slowly, to kiss each bit of flesh he revealed.

Gentleness brought him rewards. Domini arching up the moment he lifted his head, her soft murmured plea for more a song of desire he silently echoed.

"I've undressed you in my mind more times than I want to remember." He slid the sleeves of her gown down her arms, trailing his lips behind. Her hands tangled with his in her need to touch him, and together they rolled to the side and back. Luke tossed the gown aside. With his fingertip he traced the edge of her camisole.

"You're so soft, Domini."

"And you sound so surprised, Luke."

He wasn't sure if she could see his grin in the dark. "I am. I never gave much thought about a woman's body being more than a way to slake a need. But with you . . ." Words failed him. He kissed the skin above the ribboned edge. Using his teeth he pulled the end of the ribbon until the bow was undone. Watching her, he hooked his finger into the first ribbon cross to work it loose.

The tug of his finger on the laces pulled her camisole lightly against her swollen breasts. Each small tug of cloth sent heat currents from the aching peaks of her breasts to her stomach, her thighs and knees. Restlessly she stirred beneath him. She moaned with the ply of his fingers brushing the valley between her breasts. Again and again he repeated the sensual caress, until Domini thought she would go mad from the fever flushing her.

When he was done, he slid the soft cotton cloth
back to reveal her breasts, then tugged the ties of
her petticoats free.

His hands touching her were gentle, and he
watched her as the rough texture of his work-
hardened palms covered her breasts. Her eyes
closed briefly, and a breath of need escaped her
throat as the first intimate touches released a
flood of sensation. His thumbs barely brushed the
sensitive, hardened peaks, and she arched upward, crying out his name.

Domini tried to unclench her hands from the
blanket beneath them and couldn't let go. Her
stomach muscles were taut with anticipation as
he peeled away the rest of her clothing. Luke's
hands were trembling against her bare flesh, and
he dragged in hard, shuddering breaths when she
lay naked. Domini fought not to cover herself
from his gaze. She ached and felt her body swell
with desire. His rough fingertips grazed her skin
with light touches that did nothing to ease the
tension holding her; if anything, the pleasure
intensified.

One hand slid beneath her back as Luke bent
his head. He felt the wild shivering that ran
through her, tightening the nipple that nuzzled
against his lips. Her hands rose to his shoulders.
His tongue flicked out, circled her, drew her into
the heat of his mouth until her breath broke and
her fingers were digging hard into his skin. She
cried out again when he closed his teeth over her

with exquisite care, her body twisting slowly as the wild passion matching his own sang free.

He ached to tangle his fingers in the black silk that hid sleek depths, longing to know if she wanted him as much as he wanted her, needed as much as he needed to join their bodies. Her hips were moving with the same rhythms of his mouth on her breast, her legs shifting restlessly against his.

He wanted to taste every bit of the golden skin he had dreamed of until he woke sweating from fevered heat. But Domini was reaching out, touching him, her fingers trembling as she stroked the taut muscles of his stomach. He caught his breath when she hesitated, and then he pressed his hand over hers, dragging it down, covering the hard masculine flesh even soft demin couldn't hide.

She tried to jerk her hand away.

Luke held her tightly. "You wanted to touch me, Domini. That's part of me, too. And where I want your touch most of all."

She was shocked by the shape and size of him. But when he moaned deeply and arched against her hand, Domini was tantalized by the thought that she could give him the same pleasure his caresses had brought to her. The heat of his lips, the light sting of his teeth grazing her shoulder, sent heat flooding her. She rubbed her cheek against the damp skin of his chest, trying to still the shaking in her hands as she sought to open the buttons on his pants.

She returned the same open-mouthed kisses, his skin as hot and damp as her own. She freed one button, but the pressure of his hard flesh against the buttons made it almost impossible for her clumsy fingers to open them.

Luke fought the temptation to strip off his pants. He rolled over on top of her, kissing her senseless, fighting for control, so afraid that the hunger of his body would make him hurt her. He wanted her too wrapped in passion to feel fear, too fevered to fight him when he claimed her as his.

Domini felt as if she were a helpless pool of need and want. He kissed every thought from her mind but him. Nothing existed but the hard body covering hers, the heat of him pressed between her spread legs, his hands taking his weight as he loomed above her.

He was gone for long moments, stripping off his pants, and she closed her eyes, suddenly feeling shy to to look at him.

"Open your eyes, Domini," he whispered as he stretched out over her. "I want to see you when I make you mine."

He lowered his body to hers slowly, savoring the feel of his hot, damp, naked skin on hers. He could feel every beat of her wild pulse. It echoed his own. Every quiver of excited pleasure that coursed over her caressed him.

His kiss was wild, possessive, and demanding. Domini's answer was no less. She twisted beneath him, stroking the length of his back, feeling the tension riding his body increase. She was lost in the scent and taste of Luke. The weight of his body both eased and fed the need that spiraled through her. Her tongue dueled with his. She spread her legs beneath him, lifting her hips, wanton as she rubbed against him.

"Christ! You'll burn me alive, Domini."

"Yes. That's what you're doing to me."

He touched her then. Stroking her until her body drew taut, her cry a plea mixed with his name as her head was flung back and she opened to him. He had never felt as male, as powerful as he did now, with Domini sobbing his name as she convulsed against him.

He lifted her against him and came up against her damp tightness. He wanted to take her slowly. He wanted to be tender. Pressing into her, feeling the sleek heat begin to give way, yielding to him a little at a time, Luke knew he couldn't give her what he wanted. He was too hot. Too hard. It seemed he had wanted her forever.

Her fingers bit into his arm. She tensed against the pain. There had to be pain before there was pleasure. Someone had told her that. Tossing her head from side to side, she could feel how tense she was. He was so still and she couldn't stand the waiting.

"Luke, please . . ."

He bent as if to take her lips, only his teeth caught her earlobe. He bit down hard as he thrust through the fragile barrier.

His tongue soothed her earlobe, his murmurs lost in her cry as he sank into her, heavy and hard and deep, filling her with his strength, stretching her until she denied him, then showed her she could take more. She clutched him tightly, their bodies slippery with sweat, and he pulled her legs around him as he pushed into her, slamming her against the mattress until the rope springs were strained. His mouth claimed hers, his tongue delving in the same demanding rhythm as his body, as he filled her again, and again.

She clung to him, his name a litany of need and demand. Domini clamped her thighs to his powerful hips as he brought her more pleasure than she had ever believed in. She was frightened of the tightness that held her, more savagely than Luke's surging thrusts.

"Come to me, Domini. You can't hold back," he whispered as the tremors began for her.

"No. It's . . . oh, God, Luke . . ."

"I know. Christ, I know." But he didn't stop, there was no mercy in him, no pity to let her retreat. He breathed her name, drunk on the power of what she made him feel, and drove deeper inside her. He let go of all constraint, his thrusts deeper, uncontrolled, his only thought to take possession of every bit of her.

He rolled over on his back to the edge of the

bed, taking her with him. She flung her head back, the long, damp, silky length of her hair gliding against his skin as he let his strong hands settle on her narrow hips to teach her the motions. He knew the sensations were intense and she tried once to pull away, but he wouldn't let her. He rolled back and she bit his shoulder as he felt her come apart in his arms. She clutched his his rigid body as he followed her.

Tremors racked her body. She had Luke. Sweat-slicked. Shuddering. As breathless and stunned as she was. "Mine," he had whispered at the end, over and over.

*Mine*, she thought, holding him tighter.

# *Chapter Twenty*

&

Luke couldn't summon the strength to move. He knew he should, he was too heavy for Domini. But he'd never felt so complete, so at peace. The feelings were heady.

Domini. He closed his eyes, not that he needed to. He would hear and feel her no matter how far he ran. Domini, all soft moans and sighs, trembling, frightened, but reaching for him with desperate hands. Hesitant, innocent, arousing him until he thought the fire would burn him to ash. She'd given him everything, nothing held back. And he'd been savage with her. Losing his control, plunging deep and . . .

Christ! Luke tensed. He'd lost himself in her hot, clinging tightness. Lost himself in every tremor he called forth, tremors that stroked him and lured him deeper. Lost himself until he forgot to pull out and spill his seed where it couldn't come back to haunt him.

"Luke?"

The uncertain whisper gave him the strength to move. He rolled off her, left the body that still tempted him to begin all over again, to repeat the one mistake he'd never, ever allowed himself.

The feeling had been incredible. Despite the panic trying to take hold, despite feeling trapped by his own unruly passion for her, he wanted to know again the one pleasure he had denied himself. Hell, who was he kidding? He wanted Domini. Again. And again. She left him raw and aching. Once more making him want too much.

But he couldn't force himself to get off the narrow bed. Tearing his body away from hers was enough punishment for any man.

Bewildered, hurt, Domini lay there beside him for long minutes, listening to their harsh breathing. She opened her eyes and turned her head. Luke was a pale outline in the darkness. Whatever light the moon provided filtered through thick-leaved trees outside the cabin. Very little light entered through the open windows. She sensed him withdrawing from her, even if he didn't move, shutting her out as only Luke could do.

She was still held in the throes of passion's aftermath and had to fight the trembling to force herself to move. Rolling to her side, she raised herself up on one elbow and tentatively reached out with her other hand to touch his hard, sweat-sheened chest. It took all her courage not to flinch when his breath hissed out.

"L-luke? W-what's wrong?" Domini hated the betraying quaver in her voice. She swallowed and tried again. "Did I do something wrong? Didn't I . . . please you?"

"Honey, if you pleased me any more I'd be dead."

*Honey.* She almost hit him. As it was, her hand slid down and away from his tempting skin.

"Are you sorry, Luke?"

"Yeah. That about sums it up."

Shadows. Hate and anger. Domini leaned down, her long hair brushing against his skin, and kissed him. Sweet and chaste, and far too brief.

"Are you going to run away from me, Luke?"

"I'm thinking about it. Only it's not . . ." He took a deep breath and released it. His hand caught hold of her hair, crushing the straight, damp, silken strands. "It's not you. It's me, Domini. I keep running away from myself. I made a mistake—"

"Loving me was a mistake? Giving me more pleasure than I've ever known was a mistake?"

"You're pushing me."

"Yes." She smiled, but doubted that he could see it. "I won't let the past come between us."

His arm rose between them to slide around her neck, but he didn't release his hold on her hair. "Don't you understand what happened? I spilled my seed in you. I've never done that with a woman. You know how babies—"

Her fingertips silenced him. "I know, Luke.

Once before you said you could walk away. Will you do that now? And before you answer me, I want you to know that isn't what I want to happen."

"What in God's name did I ever do that was so good to deserve you?"

She leaned closer, her sigh of longing whispering over his mouth. "You loved me. Here and now. And you will believe how much I love you."

"Domini?"

"Kiss me." But she took the choice from him. From Luke she had learned to tease, coax, and sweetly torment with a gentle ply of her lips on his. And when breathing was a ragged effort they both had to make, she lifted her head.

"Stay with me, Domini," he said, drawing her up to cover him. "I don't want to face another night alone."

"I'm here, Luke. I'll always be here for you," she answered, loving the feel of his hand on her hair, loving the feel of his body wrapped around hers. She was safe in his arms, the slow, burning tendrils of arousal blazing inside again.

Domini tasted his slow smile as she straddled his hard body. His strong hands took her hips to lift her over him, pulling her down onto him, filling her. The shattering began almost immediately for her, sensations shimmering as he arched up into her. She put her hands on his sweat-slicked shoulders, leaning forward to brace herself, her long, straight hair a curtain of black surrounding and sheltering them.

Sultry heat and Luke's whispers beckoned her with each surging motion he made.

"That morning at the stable, Domini, I wanted to set you on Devil facing me and slide into you like this. I couldn't stop thinking about your sweet body that didn't know when to quit teasing a man."

"I wasn't—"

"I know. That's what made it so hard . . . oh, Christ. . . ." He lost his desire to talk as the heated tremors began again for her. And he knew he wouldn't stop this time, either. She was his. And no one could tear them apart.

"Luke?"

"I'm right here. I'll always be here for you."

She was lost in the spiral of blazing passion, lost in the haven of the strong body that left her dazed and shaking. She didn't know how long she lay on him before he tenderly lifted her to her side and wrapped his arms around her, sheltering her, whispering to her until sleep claimed her.

At first Domini wasn't sure what woke her. The air was still, almost suffocating. She opened her eyes, her fingers curling against Luke's skin. His body was rigid, drenched in a cold sweat. She lifted her hand to touch his mouth and found his lips pressed tightly against his clenched teeth as if making an effort to still a cry.

Tears filled her eyes, in despair of whatever demon held him. She hated Toma, Amanda, and Matt at that moment as she had never hated anyone.

She wasn't going to let them win. She'd fought Luke awake, she'd fight his night demons, too.

"Love," she whispered, cupping his cheek, stroking the rough stubble that darkened his face. "Luke? Wake up."

Soft as her whispers were, light as her touch had been, she knew by the new tension gripping him that he was awake. She closed her eyes, praying for guidance, and lay her head on his shoulder.

Domini's soft, murmuring voice had called him from the darkness. He lay bathed in a cold sweat, afraid to move, afraid to close his eyes again. He wrapped his arms tighter around her, burying his face against the curve of her neck.

"Do you want to tell me what you dreamed, Luke?"

"I can't. I don't know." The admission should have shocked him. He'd never told anyone about the strangling blackness that came and held him but never let him remember what it was. The even rise and fall of her chest soothed him, and he snuggled lower, his cheek resting on the upper curve of her breast.

Domini held him against her, wishing she was wiser, wishing there was something she could do to make him trust her.

The answer came immediately. And before she thought about it, she began telling him of her own nightmare, of the attack and the murder that still haunted her.

And when she was done, Luke whispered, "I'll make you forget anyone ever touched you but me." He made love to her, sweetly and slowly, cherishing her with his mouth and hands and body as he couldn't do with words. He took her with the tenderness he had never given to another, and found a balm for his soul within her.

In silence he cradled her against him, feeling the glide of hot tears that she cried for both of them. And he stayed awake, guarding her against the dark places that hid their memories from him.

It wasn't only protection he offered. He was protecting himself from Domini ever finding out that the nightmare which haunted him had begun the night after her father died.

Dawn crept on cat's paws into the cabin as Luke kissed Domini awake. He helped her dress, reluctant to part from her just as she was reluctant to return to the house.

He held her close at the bottom of the path, forcing himself to be the first to walk away. He could feel her watching him until he disappeared behind the barn.

Domini touched her lips, regret deep in her eyes. Luke's kiss had tasted of good-bye. A foolish notion for her to have after the night spent making love, but one that stayed with her as she went into the house through the back door. There was no point in hiding. She couldn't disguise lips swollen from his kisses, nor did she want to.

Thankfully, Ellamay was alone in the kitchen, but Domini didn't linger after wishing her good morning. She headed straight to her room.

The curtains were drawn, but she was sure that Meta or Lucy had discovered by now that she hadn't slept in her bed. They'd likely told Amanda, and Toma, too, if he asked. With a shrug Domini dismissed worrying about it. They would all know soon enough that she had chosen Luke.

"I don't need to ask where you were last night, do I, Dominica?" Matt rose from her bed and came toward her.

"What are you doing here, Matt?"

"I came back last night, rather late, but I'd hoped to surprise you this morning by asking you to ride out with me."

She refused to let him see how his presence upset her. She hid the small wince a normal walk cost her, and went to stand closer to the fireplace.

"Does your father know that you waited in my bedroom?"

"My father wouldn't care if I spread you out on the dining room table and—"

"That's enough! Leave my room, Matt." She turned her back on him, gripping the edge of the mantel, willing him to leave. She wasn't ready for a confrontation with him.

When he wished, he could move quietly. He

came up behind Domini, grabbing hold of her shoulders to spin her around.

"Don't you ever dare order me in this house. You spent the night with Luke, didn't you?"

His hateful voice penetrated the mist in her mind. Domini didn't struggle against his punishing grip. She already sensed that Matt would like nothing more than a reason to physically hurt her.

"Since you already know the answer, Matt, why ask me?"

"Answer me!"

Her head rocked from the force of his shaking her. "Yes. I was with Luke. And I'll be with him—" She cut herself off. His eyes blazed with fury. In the next moment Domini blinked, wondering if she had seen that much emotion in his eyes, for he had mastered whatever rage he felt.

His grip gentled and she steeled herself for the stroking of his hands where he had bruised her shoulders.

"I'm sorry. Truly, I am. I didn't mean to hurt you, again, Dominica. You can't know how difficult . . . no, you wouldn't believe me anyway."

He released her and stepped away to open the drapery on one window. Domini stood where he left her, only turning to stare at his back. *Don't listen to him. He hates Luke. He'll try to poison you against Luke if he can.*

She wanted to listen to wiser counsel, but sensed that Matt knew something about his brother that she needed to know, too.

*Don't!*

*I must.*

"What is it that you know, Matt? You've hinted at some secret—"

"Forget I mentioned it. I have no right to tell you. Blame it on my being upset that you never gave me a chance, Dominica."

"Toma was wrong to pit you against each other. He had no right to force me to choose between you. I was half in love with Luke before I came here, Matt. I—" She stopped, sensing that he wasn't listening, or if he was, she wasn't saying what he wanted to hear.

"I think it would be best if you leave, Matt."

He turned and with his back to the light, his face was shadowed. "Answer me one thing, Dominica."

"Matt, please."

"Just one question. Did he hurt you?"

"Luke? Luke would never hurt me. He's not what you and your parents think. There's goodness in him."

"I'm his brother, Dominica. I've known Luke longer than you have. I've protected him and lied for him." It took a great deal of effort to stand and plead with her, but Matt knew he had no choice. He could see everything he wanted, everything that should by rights be his, slipping out of his grasp. Violence seethed inside him. But he didn't dare make another mistake in letting her see it. She was wary of him. He had to change that. Raking one hand through his hair, he used the charming smile that had never failed him.

"I truly can't apologize enough to you, Dominica. I wish you would trust me. But I also know that I must redeem myself in your eyes. Despite what you believe, Luke is my brother, and I want him to have everything that is coming to him. But before you tell my father of your decision—you did make one, didn't you?"

"Yes. You know I wouldn't have spent the night with Luke if I hadn't, Matt." He nodded as she watched him, a strange dread forming inside that she didn't want to hear what he was going to tell her.

*But you asked him.*

*Yes, she had asked.*

"I don't quite know how to tell you this. Unless Luke already confessed to you about his nightmares? The ones that he claims he can't remember when he's faced with the evidence of what he's done?"

Domini was too shocked to speak.

"I've taken you by surprise, haven't I?"

She was too shocked to answer and too stunned to catch the gloating tone of his voice. Domini grabbed hold of the mantel while the room appeared to tilt and swirl around her. Matt was lying. But why? Why would he lie about this, something so easily disproved? *Or proved?* a small voice countered.

"I might have known that he wouldn't tell you."

He stared at her pale face, her glazed eyes that lifted in mute appeal for denial. He shook his head. "Dominica, why would I lie? We've found everything from small dead animals to fires. When confronted, he denies he had anything to do with them, even when he reeks of blood and smoke. It's one of the reasons that my mother refuses to allow him to live in the house. She'd afraid she'll wake one night and find him in her room.

"I can see that you still don't believe me. But ask anyone here."

A knock and Lucy's voice calling Domini stopped her from answering him. Matt went to the door. Domini saw that he was beckoning Lucy to come inside.

She closed her eyes briefly. It couldn't be true. Luke would have told her.

"Lucy, tell Dominica about Luke's nightmares."

"Tell her, Mr. Matt?" Confused, the young woman looked from Domini to Matt.

"Yes, tell her," he repeated impatiently. "Tell her about the nightmares and what happens when he has them." Matt directed his piercing gaze at Domini. "You realize she has no reason to lie to you?"

All Domini could do was nod.

"Mr. Matt, you know your mama don't like us to talk about that. She'd take my place from me—"

"Tell Dominica, Lucy. Let me worry about my mother."

Twisting the edge of her apron, Lucy stared at the floor. Very softly, she said, "Mr. Matt, I can't say it. If your mama don't find out, your daddy will. He never wants anyone—"

Matt grabbed the girl's upper arm. "Listen to me once more," he said, the words slowly pronounced as he fought to keep his temper. "I want you to tell her why he's forbidden the house."

Lucy's wide, frightened brown eyes locked with his.

"Tell her!"

"Matt," Domini protested, starting toward them. "Stop this. Can't you see that you're hurting as well as frightening her?"

"Stay where you are," he ordered. "You won't believe me. Lucy has nothing to gain by telling you the truth. Do you, Lucy?"

"No, Mr. Matt." She held his powerful, frightening gaze a few seconds longer, then looked at Domini. "He left dead rabbits near Miz Amanda's door. Sometimes she'd find blood smeared on the handle."

"Finish," he demanded, giving her a little shake.

"She found a fire burning a hole in her drawing room carpet. And—"

"That's enough, Lucy. I don't want to hear any more."

Lucy stopped, but she didn't move until Matt released her and told her to leave them.

Matt smoothed down his hair. His expression was contrite. "I'm sorry you forced me to go to such lengths to make you believe me, Dominica. If you still have any doubts, I'm sure I can supply others who will tell you the same story about Luke."

"No. That won't be necessary." She wrapped her arms around her waist. She had known from the first that Luke had secrets. It hurt that he couldn't trust her enough to tell her. Hurt so much that when Matt came and put his arms around her, Domini didn't even notice him until he spoke.

"I keep saying that I'm sorry for hurting you, when it's the last thing I want to do. But you must admit that I had no way of making Lucy lie to you." He ignored her push, and stroked her hair back from her face with one hand and kept the other wrapped around her shoulders. "Stop fighting me."

"I tried to tell you how wild and dangerous he was and still is, Dominica. Luke thinks he's a law unto himself. Can you imagine how my mother has felt all these years? Being frightened of him and what he might do? It's true we don't want anyone to talk about it. He's a shame to our family. I know how deeply you think you feel for him, but Luke has caused a great deal of grief for all of us."

"Mulekey said the same thing about Luke," she murmured, trying to sort out what Matt has just said.

"About what?"

"He said that Luke was a law unto himself just like your father."

There was no emotion in her voice, and it couldn't have pleased him more. "I'm afraid that's true. The apple does not fall far from the tree."

*That makes you as ruthless as Toma.* It remained a thought. She knew Matt was lying to her. She had denied it first out of love for Luke, but there was something more. Luke's had been an open defiance. These things that Matt claimed Luke had done just didn't fit with the man Luke was.

He had told her he was curious and went into Amanda's room, was caught and broke her china doll, and Amanda had beat him for it. She knew the cruelty that children were capable of. Luke wouldn't have left dead animals or blood to frighten Amanda. The boy would have been no different than the man he'd become.

If Luke had wanted to retaliate for Amanda's many punishments, he would have broken every bit of her lovely porcelains, and what's more, Domini thought, his defiance would have made the act an open one. She could almost see him do that. But to kill an innocent animal? No. She wouldn't believe that of him, not even in the grip of a nightmare.

It was an act of a coward.

But why was Matt lying to her?

# Chapter Twenty-one

~

Domini suddenly realized Matt's touches had turned to caresses.

"Don't." She reinforced her protest and tried to pull away from him. "Let me go, Matt," she demanded, raising her head, ready to kick his shin when the door crashed open.

"Luke!"

"You bastard!" he hissed at Matt. "Get your goddamn hands off her!"

"And if I won't," Matt returned in a cool, goading voice.

Seeing the mask of murderous fury on Luke's face, Domini struggled harder. She landed a few kicks against Matt's legs.

Luke didn't answer his brother. He tackled him, tearing Matt away from Domini. Luke managed to land a solid punch to Matt's jaw. He ignored Domini's plea to stop. He had eyes for no one but Matt, eyes that promised him death.

Matt darted to his left, but Luke was there and he brought his brother down. They rolled from side to side, landing blows on each other wherever they could.

Matt twisted free. He scrambled to his feet, swaying where he stood.

Luke came at him again. He grabbed Matt's shirt front in his right hand and landed a solid left to Matt's jaw that sent his head snapping back. Luke released his hold on Matt's shirt and let his fist connect with his jaw again. Matt lifted his hands, instinctively protecting his face as Luke drove sledging blows to his midsection with brutal efficiency. Every time Matt tried to get a punch in, Luke easily dodged him.

One more blow and Matt hit the floor. Luke, chest heaving, for he had come on a run when Lucy fetched him, stood over his brother.

"I . . . w-warned . . . you. Told y-you to stay . . . away." Luke wiped off the blood from his cut lip with the back of his hand. "Get out. Come near her again and I'll kill you."

Matt painfully rose. His voice was harsh, his gaze no less furious. He didn't attempt to wipe the blood dripping from his split lip. A bruise darkened on his cheek.

"You think you've won it all, Luke. You're wrong. You're a bastard who's always been and will remain a loser."

"No!" Domini went to Luke. She drew his left hand to her lips and kissed his grazed knuckles.

"You're wrong as ever about him, Matt," she said calmly, facing him. "Luke hasn't lost anything."

Straightening, Matt's face creased with pain as he moved to slick back his hair. "You think you have him figured out? Why don't you ask my brother where he was the night your father died?"

"Stop it, Matt." Dear Lord, she wanted to know, but not like this. Not with Luke rigid at her side.

"Ask him," Matt demanded.

"No. I'm sick of your hints of secrets, Matt. If you know how my father died, if you know anything, then tell me. Tell me or do as I asked and Luke ordered. Get out."

"You can't ask him, can you?" he taunted. "You're afraid of what you'll find out about your precious Luke."

"Shut the hell up!" Luke ordered. "Get out of here, Matt. You're not wanted."

There was a note of desperation in his voice that forced Domini to look at Luke. Her breath caught when she saw the tormented expression he wore. Was he hiding something from her? She didn't want to give in to Matt's goading.

"Luke?"

"What the hell is going on here?" Toma demanded. His powerful stride carried him into the room, drawing their attention as he studied each one in turn.

"I want an answer. Matt?"

"Luke attacked me."

"No! You wouldn't leave my room, Matt. Luke

did no more than to protect me from your unwanted attentions."

"So, you made your decision. Luke's the winner."

Domini rounded on Toma. "Damn you! There are no winners in your schemes and lies. You want to know what's going on here, Toma? Your sons are doing what you want. Fighting each other. Hating each other. And you won't be satisfied till one kills the other!"

"That's enough out of you."

But Domini had the satisfaction of seeing Toma pale. He roused himself quickly, but for those few moments she was sure she had given him reason to think about what he was demanding from his sons. Tight-lipped, he surveyed Luke.

"You gonna be in any shape to finish that horse you ran off an' left?"

"Yeah."

Domini couldn't let him go. Matt had aroused a need to know the answer to his question. "Luke, wait. Do you know something that you haven't told me?"

Once more she lifted his hand to her lips. Her eyes searched his, hating the shuttered look that tightened his features. With her other hand she reached out to touch his cut lip, but he jerked his head back.

"Stop trying to mollycoddle him. Luke doesn't need it."

Without turning, Domini answered Toma with

all the bitterness she felt on Luke's behalf. "What would you know about Luke's needs? Have you ever seen to any? Have you ever once held your son? Did you ever tell him that you love him?"

"Domini!"

"No, Luke. He's got to hear it. You're not like him. You're not cold and hard. You can even tell me whatever it is that Matt keeps goading you about. It won't make any difference in my feelings for you."

She could feel him withdrawing from her although he had not moved. She suddenly felt chilled by the tension in his body. Releasing his hand, Domini stepped back.

"Don't you trust me?" he asked with infuriating calm.

"I trust you," she answered softly. "Now I'm asking you to trust me and what we shared last night. Were you there when my father died? Do you know who killed him?"

"What the hell difference does the past make?" Toma demanded. "It's over. Finding out isn't bringing James back, Dominica. Leave this be."

"No. Let him tell her," Matt goaded.

"Shut up." Toma stepped in front of Matt, his gaze targeting Luke. "The hell with these infernal questions. I'm not paying you to beat the hell out of your brother. I ain't paying you to get mollycoddled. There are horses waiting that need breaking. That's all you got to worry about. Break a man's bones when you're done with the job you gave your word to complete."

"Stop encouraging the rivalry between your sons!" Luke grabbed hold of Domini's arm to stop her from moving toward Toma.

"Give me a minute," Luke said, shooting a furious look at Toma. "And take Matt with you."

"A minute's all you're getting or I'll haul you out myself." Spinning on his dust-laden boots, Toma shoved Matt out ahead of him.

Luke released Domini the second she tried to pull free of his grip. Fury tightened every muscle in his body. The carpet barely cushioned his hard stride to the door. After he slammed it closed, he stood there staring at the door.

Dread filled Domini. "Why won't you look at me, Luke?" He didn't answer and she backed away until the wall stopped her. "Why?" she repeated in an agonized whisper.

He turned then, his gaze a scathing indictment as he studied her. "So much for trust," he muttered, raking his hands through his hair.

"That's not true! I do trust you. Why did you come here?"

"I went back to the cabin, but you'd gone. I saw that you left the hummingbird and figured you were mad. I just wanted to know why you didn't take it. Stupid, huh?"

"No. I wanted you to have the carving." She glanced around the room. "It doesn't belong in this house."

"I'd better get back to work."

"No!" She clenched her hands, hiding the move from him by sliding them behind her back. "Is it so much for me to ask for answer? Are you protecting someone?"

"What if I can't answer you? What if I said that Matt's lying? That he's stirring up trouble for me like he's always done?"

"Is that what you're saying? Matt's lying?"

"Let it be."

"I can't. You won't answer me. I thought trust had to work both ways. I was wrong. Am wrong about you. You don't want to trust me or anyone. What hurts me, Luke, is that you don't even want to try."

Luke remained where he was, staring at her. He felt torn. Fury and fear vied for dominance. He had used his fists to solve a great many problems all his life. Not that he would use them on Domini. Hitting a woman was one thing he'd never done. Hurting her would be hurting himself. Matt was another matter. His brother had increased the debt he owed him for years of hell by putting that doubt in Domini's eyes.

Seeing the way she was looking at him helped Luke to leash any need for violence. He reined in his emotions and tried to think calmly. The hope that had sparked last night was still too new for him to depend upon.

But Domini was wrong. He had trusted her. He had let her stay with him, allowed her to see the haunted sleep that woke him in a cold sweat. She didn't know how much trust that took.

And she didn't know because he couldn't tell her.

His word of honor and his pride kept him here on the ranch. He wanted to bolt and run with Domini, wanted to believe he could have her and a fresh start. He wanted to believe in her love.

Luke admitted to himself that he was scared. There was weariness underlying her words. If she stopped fighting for him, he didn't think he'd care what happened. And that frightened him even more. He had allowed Domini closer than anyone had come to him in more years then he wanted to remember.

He couldn't lose her now.

But he couldn't tell her what she wanted to know.

He just couldn't.

The door behind him beckoned. He could walk away. He'd done it before. Too many times.

"If you walk away from me, don't come back." Until Domini actually spoke, she didn't think she would say those words to him. But she sensed he was going to turn his back on her, and if he did, he would shut her out of his life.

"What the hell do you want from me? Blood?" He stalked across the room to stand in front of her. "Here," he said, swiping the back of his hand across his cut lip and holding it out to her.

To his shock, she leaned forward and kissed his

hand. The tremor betraying his turmoil was so slight that she couldn't see it. But Domini felt it. Her insides were tense and she fought not to show that to him.

"I want your love, Luke. Not your blood. Not to see you hurt. Don't fight Matt. He taunts you into it. You can't give in to him or to Amanda. All they know is hate. You're not like them."

"You sound so certain. Yet we're the same blood." Leaning closer, Luke placed both his hands flat against the wall on either side of her head. The move imprisoned Domini and kept him from grabbing hold of her and holding on tight to what he thought was slipping away.

"That may be true, but they're driven by a need for revenge against each other, Luke. You're driven by the pain they've caused you."

"You're asking for too much. For what I can't give you."

Domini touched his clenched jaw. "That's one more lie I've heard today."

He closed his eyes, his head dropping forward until his forehead touched hers. "Why are you pushing me? Why are you looking for what I never promised? And you're blind besides. You keep forgetting Toma hates me as much—"

"No! Oh, no, he doesn't. You don't see the fierce pride in his eyes when he looks at you. He—"

"He's got a hell of a way of showing how much he cares. And I don't want to talk about him." He leaned his head back and lifted her chin with one hand. "Leave it all be, Domini. I'll finish breaking his damn horses and—"

She planted a quick little kiss on his lips. "Don't ask me to forget about finding the truth, Luke. I don't believe I can."

His grip on her chin tightened slightly. "The hell with it! You wanna know why I didn't answer you? I can't. I don't know what the hell happened."

"Don't know?" she repeated, her gaze searching his. "Then why," she asked in torn, pleading voice, "did Matt—"

"He's a bastard. I've been telling you that. He knows you were with me last night. He can't stand having anything that he thinks he wants taken away from him. He said that to make you doubt me." His gaze, intense and penetrating, targeted hers. His hand slid from her chin and curved over her throat. Her pulse was wild, too wild for him to count its beat beneath his thumb.

"And Matt got what he wanted, didn't he? You're full of doubts about me."

"No, I—"

"I can see it in your eyes. Don't you start lying to me."

"I'm not lying. I have no doubts about us. Or you," she hastened to reassure him. "I may have denied what I felt from the first when I saw you, but I don't believe there was ever any doubt that I would—that we would—" She swallowed, unable to say it, longing to look away from his hard stare. But she had to bear with his scrutiny, for Luke had to be sure of her. Just as she had to be sure of him. Deep inside herself, she knew it would be the only way for them to love. She wasn't sure where this certainty came from, but it was firmly implanted.

"Now he's got you lying to me and yourself. Christ!" He started to back away and found himself hauling her into his arms for a kiss that was raw with desperation.

Domini answered his kiss with total, honest giving. It was all that Luke would accept from her now. All that he could accept.

Luke broke the kiss and pushed her away from him before he did something he would regret. He wanted to restake his claim on her. And Domini wouldn't fight him. But she might hate him afterward.

"Luke?"

"For the last time. I don't know what the hell happened that night!"

Bewildered by his quickly shifting emotions, Domini tucked her hands behind her to hide their trembling. She didn't dare move, just stared at him.

"I don't know," he repeated in a harsh, tortured voice. "I can't remember."

She watched him spin around and head for the door.

"Luke, don't go!" Her plea was lost beneath the slam of the door.

Minutes later a soft, hesitant knock sounded. Domini roused herself and looked at the door.

"Go away," she said.

"Miz Colfax wants to see you," Meta said.

"I don't want to see her, Meta. I don't want to see anyone." To make sure that she was given some time alone, she fled to the door and locked it.

"Are you all right?"

"I'm fine, Meta. I'll see her later."

Pacing the floor, Domini shoved her loose hair back from her face. *Think!* she ordered herself. But her pacing brought her close to the floor-length pier glass. The mirror's reflection showed a wild-eyed, wild-haired woman, lips swollen from kisses, her cheeks flushed and her gown wrinkled as if she had slept in it. The image blurred, and she closed her eyes for a moment, then turned away.

What she saw in her mind's eye was Luke as he'd been last night. His long-limbed body rigid, sheened in a cold sweat.

Could his nightmare have something to do with her father's death?

The question stopped her cold. She didn't know the answer. The only thing she was sure of was that Luke, whose raw, masculine sensuality left her breathless with a passion she had never envisioned possible, was as tormented as she was.

Her spirit felt battered. She couldn't cope with the web of lies and betrayal that shrouded the Colfaxes.

Wrapping her arms around her waist, Domini stood in the middle of the room, rocking back and forth as she struggled to sort out the truth.

She couldn't believe anything that Matt told her. Not about the incidents of finding dead animals, but who had been responsible for them. Lucy not only had been frightened into talking, she had been bewildered by Matt's insistance that she tell.

The lies had served Matt well in the past. She was very sure of that. His mother's favorite, Matt would have her believing anything he wanted to tell her about Luke. And Amanda, nuturing hate against her second son, would be anxious to have another weapon to use in her plan of pushing Luke out of their lives, mostly away from his father.

Matt had overplayed his hand. He'd been too desperate to have her believe the worst about Luke. In the short time she had been here, he had done all he could to discredit Luke. He'd had years to work on his parents. And their pride couldn't, wouldn't make allowances for anyone who brought them shame.

More important, she realized, was that since Matt had lied about this, he had lied about Luke hiding something about her father's death. She had to be right. Luke was a man so elemental in his passions that he couldn't lie to her. With a heartfelt sigh Domini felt the tension that gripped her ease away.

She had to get Amanda to tell her the truth. But would she? The woman had her own web of deceit that she spun with cunning.

What purpose would it serve to lie any more now that she and Luke were lovers? She understood Luke's fear that Matt would try to hurt her. Would Amanda goad her son into killing her?

It had to be Amanda. If Toma had wanted her dead, Domini had no doubt that it would have been accomplished quickly to keep her from making any claim to the original mine he and her father had discovered.

She fought the urge to run and find Luke to convince—no, to beg—him to leave here right now.

The unanswered questions of why her father had left them and the matter of his death had haunted her for too many years. Domini couldn't leave without knowing.

And Luke, she reminded herself, with his own honor and pride that was as every bit as fierce as the father and mother he denied, had given his word to Toma to stay. That despite Toma's treatment of his own flesh and blood. Why wouldn't the man admit that he loved Luke? Not that it would matter. Luke wouldn't leave here until he had tamed every horse contracted for delivery to the army.

This last incident with Matt had left her shaken. She wasn't sure she could avoid him. Not in this house.

It wasn't just for herself that she feared. Her hand curved over her belly. She had risked everything last night. Risked her love, risked the possibility of carrying Luke's child . . .

She had to be safe. Glancing longingly out of the window, Domini thought of the cabin overlooking the ranch. Luke's cabin. He had said nothing of wanting her to stay there with him. She wished she could tell him of her fear. She yearned to tell him that she understood how hard it was for him to share himself with her.

As she stood there, staring outside, a group of men rode out. She couldn't see who they were individually, but assumed they were going to relieve those hands who had stood watch last night. In the midst of everything else that was happening, Domini had forgotten the threat of the raiding Indians.

Would that she could forget that she was trapped here as easily.

If only Amanda could be trusted. The feeling grew stronger that she knew what had happened the night her father died. Not only knew, but perhaps contributed to his death.

Amanda had hinted that they were lovers. Toma wouldn't have stood for that. He was capable of killing.

Domini shrank from a confrontation with Amanda.

So many questions remained unanswered.

Amanda had to hold the key.

How else could she find out the truth and set Luke free?

# Chapter Twenty-two

～

"Come in, Dominica. I have been waiting for you." Amanda was seated on a white brocade settee near the window in her drawing room. She was dressed in pink taffeta and pink on pink embroidered silk. A cameo was pinned to the high collar of her gown. With her icy blond beauty, Domini couldn't help but draw a comparison between the etched profile of the cameo to the woman who watched her entrance with a cool, calculating gaze. She decided that the shell-like perfection of the cameo had more life than the woman who wore it.

"If you expect an apology for my keeping you waiting, Amanda, there isn't going to be one."

"I see."

Domini, far too restless to sit, strolled the room, trailing her fingertips over the cool, polished surfaces of the delicate furniture. "I've come to a decision," she said after a few moments. Moments when Amanda's gaze increased her tension.

"Have you? Will I be the first to hear of it?"

"You already know that I spent the night with Luke. There's no need to pretend otherwise. I love him. If I could convince him to leave here now, I would."

Amanda's silence forced Domini to look at her. In spite of her dislike for the woman, she was drawn closer. She remained as still as one of the many porcelain figurines decorating the room.

"No comment?" Domini prodded.

"Would anything I had to say change your mind?"

"Yes. You could tell me why Matt taunted me that Luke knows more about my father's death."

"He does."

Whatever Domini thought she had expected Amanda to answer, she wasn't ready for the soft admission. Her hands closed over the folds of her calico gown. *Bide quietly.* Her breaths were shallow. From the past came Sister Benedict's voice. *Patience is the companion of wisdom. Be long-suffering and prudent, and you will obtain mastery over wickedness and accomplish all justice.* And Domini needed justice, not only for her father, herself, and her mother, but for Luke.

"You prove to be stronger than I was led to believe. Sister Benedict wrote that you were obedient, Dominica. I believe she lied."

"Believe whatever you want, Amanda. You will

despite anything I tell you. All these years you've schemed for your own revenge against Toma regardless of the hate you've sown. You never cared about me beyond what use I'd be."

Domini threw her head back, praying for both the strength and patience she desperately needed to see this through. When she faced Amanda again, the woman had not moved.

"If you had followed my wishes, Dominica, I would have cared a great deal for you. The path you've chosen sets us at opposite points. You will have none of the Colfax wealth now."

"You think I care about money? I want the truth about my father. Was he your lover? Is that why he died? You claim that Toma didn't kill him, but he knew, didn't he? You made sure of that. It's the only thing that makes sense to me." Resuming her pacing, Domini felt her head clear as she continued, almost as if she were speaking with herself.

"What I don't understand is why. Toma was your husband. You had two children with him. Unless my father was the latest of a great many men in your life?" She waited expectantly for an answer.

Amanda let her wait. She studied Domini, carefully veiling the hate that swelled inside her when she thought of her carefully made plan gone awry. Her body ached from the rigid posture she maintained, but she refused to allow Domini to see how furious she was.

"Do sit down. We can be civilized about—"

"No, Amanda. I don't want to be civilized. Not if it means to be like you. Don't you have any feelings? Can't you see what you've done to your own family? Don't you care?"

"Stop shouting at me. If I did not care I would leave you this very moment. You were to be docile, sweet, and grateful to me for rescuing you from a life of drudgery. And that's all you would have in that convent. Toma had to approve Matt's wife or he refused to let him inherit. You were perfect—"

"But I'm not! I love Luke. And I don't want revenge. Do you hear me? I don't want it!" Domini hadn't realized that she had moved closer to Amanda until she found herself staring down into her chilling blue eyes. She backed up, shaking, the way her voice shook, with the force of emotions seething inside her.

What did it take to rip that perfect concealing mask from Amanda? What could she say or do to get the truth from her?

When she saw a thin smile crease Amanda's lips, Domini had to force herself back a few more steps. The woman had to know how frustrating and how painful this was for her. Amanda would use it to her advantage. She would continue to withhold the truth until Domini either gave up or gave in. She couldn't allow Amanda that power over her.

"All right, Amanda, you win."

"Win? You have changed your mind about Luke?"

"No," she said, fixing a sharp gaze on her. "I won't stop loving him. But I will stop asking about my father. It's your secret."

The hardest part was turning and forcing herself to walk across the room. At every step Domini expected Amanda to call her back. Silence accompanied her to the door. She couldn't falter now.

Domini pressed her thumb on the gleaming brass latch, cupping the smooth, cool handle of the door with her other fingers. *Please, God . . . please . . .*

"If you walk out of that door, Dominica, you will never know how your father died, or why."

Rigid with tension, Domini faced the door. "I can't play your tormenting games any longer. You've enjoyed it, Amanda, and I'll leave you to the Lord to decide your punishment."

"You were right about James, you know. He was in love with me. He planned to run away with me."

Pain slipped through Domini's guard. Why? she longed to scream. Why would he love you? But silence had become her weapon. She waited once again.

Amanda smiled. She chose her words carefully, her eyes pinned to Domini's back. She didn't want to miss her reaction.

"Luke knew, of course. He was there the night we planned to leave."

"If Luke knew, then Toma and Matt did, too."

"Did they?" Amanda taunted.

Need to be done with this turned Domini around. She gripped the handle behind her back, leaning against the solid door while she fought her desire to shake the rest out of the woman calmly watching her. She refused to raise her voice, or allow the denial that sprang to mind to be spoken.

*I don't know. I can't remember.* Luke's words. His nightmare.

"If you will not believe me, there is nothing I can do to convince you. Is there, Dominica?"

"I haven't heard anything from you but a veiled hint that Luke had something to do with my father's death."

"Oh, Luke had more than *something* to do with it. He killed him."

"No!"

Amanda rose then, but not toward Domini; she faced her own portrait. "You are a foolish, stubborn young woman if you continue to deny the truth. It is what you wanted. You cannot deny it simply because what I said is not what you wanted to hear. Luke," she repeated in a firm voice, "killed your father and stole any chance for happiness that I had."

Domini couldn't think. It wasn't true. Everything within her denied it. Luke couldn't have killed her father.

"You're lying, Amanda."

"Would you like me to describe—"

"No. God, no." Domini's whisper reflected the fear that took hold of her. She didn't dare allow herself to waver in her belief that Luke was innocent.

*I don't know. I can't remember.*

"You are not dealing very well with this, Dominica. Would you care for sherry?"

Domini's eyes went from Amanda to the painting. How could she remain so calm when condemning her son as a murderer? Her mind supplied the answer. Amanda had hated Luke long before her father ever joined Toma in his search for gold.

"You're still lying to me," Domini said softly. "My father had nothing to do with the hate you hold for your son."

"He's not mine."

"Luke is *your* son." Domini knew she had to press her advantage. Amanda's calm facade had slipped. She saw the way her hand clutched the skirt of her gown. What Domini found herself fighting now was a well of pity for Amanda. But just the thought of Luke helped her to stifle the feeling.

"Why did you hate Luke? Did you see him as a rival for Toma's affection?" Domini mused, then answered herself. "But you weren't in love with Toma. And he was poor then. Matt was firstborn, that would always ensure his place. Why hate

Luke? For that matter, Amanda, why didn't you leave Toma if you hated him so much."

"Look at her!" Amanda demanded, pointing at the painting. "Do you think she had the strength to fight a man like Toma? Do you believe she could deny him?"

"Living in a convent with women taught me how strong those women could be."

"I was never given that choice. I married Toma. I bore him a son. It would have been enough for any other man." Her hand fell slowly to her side, but she continued to stare up at the painting. "But not Toma. He had to have another son."

Compassion swamped Domini. She didn't want to feel it for Amanda, and she fought down the urge to offer the woman comfort. She never expected it to be so hard. The pain that Domini sensed coming from her reached out. All she could do was imagine Luke, and keep the pain of his feeling unloved and unwanted foremost in her mind.

"Haven't you punished everyone, including yourself, long enough?"

"It will never be enough for what I suffered at his hands."

"But you stayed with him, Amanda. Surely his wealth means a great deal to you. You're surrounded with it. You used it for me."

"I deserved some compensation for the humiliation he has caused me."

"Was my father really in love with you? Or did

he pity you?" Domini took a deep breath, then slowly released it. She was afraid to move as Amanda lowered her head and turned to her.

"Have you ever truly loved anyone, Amanda?"

With a lost look, the woman gazed around the room. "I knew there was a little risk when I sent for you. But I thought I could prevent Luke from interfering. I never knew what he would do."

"Then you'll be happy to see the last of him. And of me."

"He will never make you happy. He will never love you. He does not know how to love. He is his father's son. And that has been part of my revenge against Toma. He will never have the love he wanted from Luke."

Cold encompassed Domini. For the first time she wondered if Amanda was insane. Surely no sane woman could say these things and maintain a state of calm?

"Amanda—"

"Silence, Dominica. You wanted to know, now you must listen. I told you Toma dragged me and my young child from one mining camp to another. Matthew was sick most of the time. Despite my every plea Toma refused to understand that he was not a weakling but a child in need of good food and a warm place."

She paused, her fingers toying with the cameo pin as if it would supply the words she needed to continue.

Domini bit her lip and waited. She had to let

Amanda tell her story in her own way. How else would she find out the truth?

"I begged that man and he would not believe me. He would not admit the possibility that his own stubbornness could cause Matt to die. Toma is never at fault." Amanda took a deep, shuddering breath, then another. She gazed up at the painting. Very softly she continued.

"I lost a child and was ill. Before I was fully healed he was demanding his rights. I swore that if that child lived I would have nothing to do with it."

"Oh, my Lord, Amanda! You not only hurt Luke terribly, but you punished yourself, not Toma."

"Save your pity for someone who cares to have it. Once he was sure that I would carry the child to term, he left me with his friend's widow to await the birth. He took Matt with him, refused my every plea to leave me my son. My boy was terrified and Toma did not care. The man was and is an animal.

"Can you understand what it was like for me to be forced to take care of myself while his child sapped my strength? When all I wanted to do was die?"

"No, Amanda. I've suffered other things, but I can't begin . . ." Domini faltered as she became aware of the rage shimmering in Amanda's eyes.

"But I couldn't die," she went on as if Domini had not spoken. "I had to be strong to get Matt away from him. I made a vow each day that I would never care for his child. And I kept it."

"But Luke is your son, too! You can deny that all you want, but you gave birth to him. How could you punish an innocent child for what Toma did? He needed your love every bit as much as Matt. How **could** you destroy him like that, Amanda?"

"I did not want him. Toma saw to his needs. He found a woman who had recently lost a child and was willing to nurse him. The small claim he was working provided enough money for those first years so that I remained in one place. And I had Matt back with me. It was all that mattered by then. All I cared about until James came to us."

Domini was torn between hating her for what she had done and filled with an overwhelming compassion for what Amanda had suffered.

"I know how much this hurts you, but did Luke ever know this?"

"I never told him."

Domini believed her. She couldn't say why, she just did. But she also sensed that Luke knew, knew and blamed himself. It was the way a child thought. She had blamed herself when her father never returned. If she had been good all the time, had never asked for more than he could give her . . . Shaking her head, Domini stopped herself. This was old, beaten territory she couldn't return to. It wouldn't change the past. Nothing could. But old hurts and hates could be ended.

Amanda moved to the side table and poured a small stem crystal glass half full of liquor for herself. To Domini's surprise, she tossed the drink back and refilled the glass, this time sipping it.

"Would you—"

". . . finish? Of course." Amanda shot a chillingly brilliant smile at her. "Your father was unlike any man I had ever met. He was kind, thoughtful and made me laugh. I told him. He insisted that we had to leave."

"Did he ever mention me or my mother?" The question burned inside Domini, and she held her breath until Amanda answered, half dreading what she would say.

"At first. He never really loved her, you know."

Denial sprang to Domini's lips, but she swallowed it. "You could be right. If he had truly loved my mother, he never would have left her. Or he would have sent for her."

"You are a continual surprise to me, Dominica. I believe we could have been friends."

"Not with the way you hate Luke. I told you I love him. And in listening to you, I've discovered that his love means more to me than the past. Knowing the truth will not bring my father or mother back to me. It won't undo the years I've been alone. and I don't want to end as you are, Amanda, bitter and alone."

Domini knew she spoke the truth. The past didn't matter anymore. She turned to open the door and found Matt waiting.

"I was afraid that I would find you here," he said, pushing Domini back into the room.

"Matt!"

"Don't worry, Mother, I promised you I'd take care of her."

Domini saw that he was dressed for riding. The well-worn clothes lent him a harder look. Her gaze locked on the gun belt strapped around his hips. "Matt?"

"You and I are going for a ride. Pity you refused to consider the Indian troubles. I had no choice but to accompany you."

"You're going to kill me?"

"I do believe I've managed to shock you, Dominica. There's no other way. Luke can't have you. And I'm afraid that my mother has been under a great deal of strain these last weeks. She told you too much."

"She didn't tell me anything." Domini started to back into the room, although she knew there was no escape that way. She thought of screaming, but the gleam in Matt's eyes warned her that he would enjoy hurting her.

Domini looked toward Amanda and realized she would be no help. Her gaze was once more fixed on the painting. Her voice was chillingly soft as she spoke to her son.

"Are you sure that he'll come after you?"

"Once Luke sees that I have her, nothing can stop him. Caully and Grady are waiting. He won't live this time."

"And Toma? Will you rid me of him?"

"No one will question my story. She came here for revenge and got Luke to help her. After killing Toma they ran into a band of Indians. There's no one—"

"You're crazy! Both of you," Domini yelled. "I'm not going anywhere with you!"

The gun slid into Matt's hand in a move almost too fast for her to follow.

"Of course you are. You're going to do exactly what I tell you."

Domini stared at Matt—and then she knew. "*You* killed my father, didn't you?"

# Chapter Twenty-three

❧

"No!" Amanda screamed, fists against her chest as she rounded on Domini.

"You can't deny it." Domini was shaking. "Luke liked my father. And my father cared for him. Luke knew about me. He told me my father wanted him to meet me. But I can't believe that my father loved you. I think he pitied you. He might have agreed to help you get away from Toma, but I can't believe he betrayed his friend by becoming your lover."

Her gaze darted from mother to son, then back. "You wouldn't have wanted her to leave, would you, Matt?" She had thought that Amanda had the most chilling gaze she had ever seen, but Matt's bore a cold fury that sent shivers up her spine.

"Matt? Tell her that cannot be true. You know how much I counted on James taking me away. And you saw him. You told me," she cried out with a rising note of panic, "that you saw Luke kill him. I believed you. Matt? Tell her! For pity's sake, Matt, if you love me at all, tell her that Luke killed her father!"

Matt's cold, hard stare and his silence were all the answer that Domini needed. She ignored Amanda's hysterical sobbing as she collapsed on the sofa, and pinned her gaze on the gun that Matt used to motion her closer.

Domini's hand slid over her thigh in a nervous gesture. She managed to hide her fear when she realized that she didn't have her knife. Last night . . . She had taken it off and handed it over to Luke. And this morning, she reminded herself, she had forgotten all about it.

"What a-are you g-going to d-do?" Amanda half sobbed as she lifted her head and looked at her son.

"Get rid of everyone who stands in my way," he returned in a calm voice.

"Dominica?" she asked him.

"And Luke. Then Toma. You'll never have to answer to him again, Mother."

"Matt, are you sure—"

"There's no other way. She won't keep this quiet, and I wouldn't trust her to do so."

Domini wasn't sure who would come running if she screamed. She couldn't think, not while both Matt and Amanda discussed killing her. She needed to do something, not just stand here waiting. Edging to the side of Matt's vision, she wasn't really surprised when he followed her move.

"Don't move, Dominica. It would be just as easy to shoot you here."

She must have shown her fear, for he nodded as if satisfied. Domini started toward him, her steps dragging.

"Be careful, Matt," Amanda warned.

"I will. Don't worry. Toma's down at the corral watching Luke. They won't see us ride out until it's too late to stop me." In a sudden move he reached out and snagged hold of Domini's wrist, throwing her off balance. She fell heavily against him, but he quickly righted himself and yanked her up beside him.

Pressing the cool barrel of the gun beneath her chin, he urged her out the door and into the hall. All she could do was to obey him now and watch for a chance to run.

"Open the door. Slowly. Don't try anything."

Domini had to wipe her sweating palm on her skirt before she could get the door opened. Two saddled horses were tied to the rail in front of the porch. She forced herself not to think of the gun Matt was pressing against her skin. A soft breeze, filled with the scent of summer grasses, blew against her sweat-sheened face. She could feel the sweat trickle down her back, soaking the cloth between her breasts and under her arms.

Through the fear she heard the pounding beat of her heart. For a few moments Domini heard a roaring sound in her ears and thought she would faint.

Matt jerked on her arm. "Don't try any foolish tricks, Dominica. It would disturb my mother to have me kill you here. Let's move down the steps carefully."

She couldn't have spoken if she wanted to. Her throat was parched as she realized that Matt was sick. Sick and crazy. He shoved her forward so that she stumbled against the rail.

"Mount up."

She turned and eyed the gun, her gaze going no higher than his bare throat. Righting herself, she slipped beneath the wooden rail and went to the horse's side.

"Move, damn you!"

Even as Domini set her foot in the stirrup, she gave thought to running. But she wasn't ready to die.

And Matt would shoot her right here. She had to go along with him. Somehow, some way, she'd find a chance to escape him.

She made a move to gather up the reins before she lifted herself up into the saddle.

"Leave them. Just get mounted."

Even with her height it was difficult to pull herself up. Her slippery hands didn't help matters. By the time she sat in the saddle, Matt had mounted his horse and grabbed hold of her reins.

"If you do anything, call out to anyone, bring

the least bit of attention to us, there's a bullet waiting."

"Now or later. Makes no difference." Her voice had a rusty sound, and she wished she had never spoken.

Matt smiled. "But if anyone comes near us, there will be a bullet for them, too. You don't want any innocents getting killed, do you?"

A quick shake was all she could manage.

"Good. I'm glad we understand each other now. Shame it couldn't have happened sooner."

Domini ignored his comments. She hid her surprise that he was heading around the back of the house. To leave the valley they would have to cross the meadow. Someone near the barns or the corrals would surely see them.

She eyed the way he held his gun in his right hand, hiding it from sight by resting it inside his thigh. He kept her reins and his own secure in his left hand. The bay he rode crowded close to Domini's horse. She knew it would present a cozy picture to anyone who spotted them riding across the meadow at an easy canter.

Domini was also well aware she had little hope of ripping the reins from his grip.

She directed her gaze straight ahead. On her left they were approaching the path that led to Luke's cabin. If she could make it up there, Matt would be exposed if he came after her. Luke was sure to have a spare gun up there. If not . . .

She wouldn't think about failure. With care she

slipped her right foot free of the stirrup, pushing against his horse's side to gain a little room. When she made her move, she had to be fast.

As fast as her heart was pounding. As fast as the seconds sliding by.

Now!

Domini's foot lashed out, making his horse start with alarm. She didn't wait around to see. Tumbling down to one knee, she was up and running for the path. The moccasins helped give her purchase on the uneven ground, and with her skirt and petticoats scooped up in front so she wouldn't get tangled in them, Domini thought she had a fair chance of making it to the path.

She hadn't counted on Matt coming after her on his horse.

The pounding hoofs tearing up the earth sent a stream of terror through her. She ran faster, feeling the sweat pour from her skin. She thought she heard a shout, then more, but the roaring was back and it blocked everything from her hearing.

Mulekey's shout alerted Luke that something was wrong. He was down and across the churned earth of the corral in moments.

"Matt's chasing that filly of yours flat-out on his horse!"

"Christ! I warned him." There were no saddled horses in sight. Luke ran back for the green bronc he'd been working with and leaped for her back. Using the thick, long mane and his legs wrapped around the horse's barrel to control the dun mare, he rushed the pole fence gate that Mulekey and two other hands hurried to unlatch.

Luke sailed right over them, the half-wild horse tasting freedom in the way the rider crouched on her back. Her hoofs tore the earth and grasses, sending them flying out behind her. Luke cursed himself for having taken off her halter not minutes before. With one hand secure in her mane, he leaned forward. His body slipped, but he persisted and managed to grab hold of her ear.

The mare was startled by the yank on her ear and mane, startled enough so that Luke was able to turn her toward the path. He looked up and caught a flash of Domini's gown.

Matt had closed the distance between them. But his horse was stumbling on the loose rocks on the path. Luke swore when he saw his brother abandon the horse. He intended to chase Domini on foot.

Filled with a cold fury, Luke watched his brother use a savage twist on the reins to turn the bay around. A hard slap on the horse's rump sent the bay flying down the path straight at Luke.

His half-wild mare easily handled the climbing, rock-strewn path. But not with another horse coming at her in the opposite direction.

Clinging to his mount until the last possible moment, Luke dropped off. His boot missed the edge. He grabbed a young sapling to stop his downward slide and for a few seconds swung free.

As he regained his footing on the path, he heard

the mare scream and rear. A quick look showed her kicking out her front hooves as the bay closed with her.

Luke barely spared a moment's regret for the horses. Domini needed him. He took the path at a hard run. He couldn't see her. Fear filled him that Matt would get to her before he could.

He had felt fear like this once before. That helplessness that he wouldn't get there in time to stop Matt. Luke saw a hazy mist in front of his eyes. Images formed. He shook his head. He wasn't going to let Matt hurt the one person he cared about.

But no matter how Luke tried, he kept seeing himself running after Matt. Almost as if he had done this before. Sweat poured over him. *Remember!*

*I can't.*

*You won't. Not even to save Domini.*

Not now! He couldn't fall into that bottomless nightmare. But there was that gut-cramping terror come to take hold of him. It always began with the shouting. He could hear them up ahead, and he had to get there to stop them.

No! There were no shouts. It was a crashing sound he heard, followed by curses from the woods sloping up the mountain. Luke veered off into the cool shadows of the massive trees.

He had to find Domini. He had promised her that he wouldn't let anything or anyone hurt her again. It was all that mattered to him. Matt couldn't be allowed to kill again.

*Again?*

Think of Domini. Only her.

But when he looked ahead, he saw darkness. The dark of his nightmare. And he knew it was still daylight.

He felt himself slip back in time despite his will, despite the effort he made to stop the images forming in his mind.

He tripped over a thick, exposed tree root and fell sprawling onto the leaf mold covering the forest floor. He clawed the earth with his hand. He couldn't draw a breath.

Helpless. He was helpless again.

"Domini?" Her name was a hoarse croak. Blood trickled from a cut on his forehead. Luke struggled to his feet, swaying where he stood as his mind replayed a scene of a rocky ledge ribboned with moonlight and shadows.

For a moment his vision was blinded by the images. Domini's scream tore through the air. He turned wildly, trying to determine where the sound came from. The wealth of foliage shrouded the earth in twilight. A wave of queasiness jarred him. His ears rang with the remembrance of another scream. But not a woman's. It had been a man's. A man who had been pushed over the edge of the rocky ledge above him on this mountain.

He shook off the nausea and felt the light-headedness fade. On the move again, he felt a sharp, cold clarity come over his senses. The rush of his blood brought an exquisite, almost painful tension that made him feel as if he were walking on the edge of an abyss.

The feeling called to him, lured him as he darted between the trees, shoving aside the low-growing, thickly leaved bushes. He tried to listen to the sounds, but none came to guide him.

Domini! Where was she?

He caught a glimpse of pale sky up ahead. The overpowering smells of pine and rich, rotted leaf mold filled his lungs as he fought to breathe. He tried to control the wild rush of his blood with his willpower. Recklessness could get him killed. Who'd save Domini then?

He scrambled over a massive fallen tree trunk. Before him the saplings thinned and he could see the rocks and huge boulders that marked the beginning of the ledge.

A sob that could only have been Domini's tore through the air. Luke thought his heart would stop. He fought the urge to make a sudden appearance. Not until he was sure that Matt didn't have Domini. He cautiously wove his way between the young trees and crouched behind a boulder.

Peering around the side, Luke saw his brother's back. His stomach heaved when his gaze found Domini. She was flattened against the bare rock face, her arms spread wide from her sides, fingers digging for purchase on the rock. Wide, terror-filled eyes dominated her face.

The edge of the ledge was a mere side step away.

At the same moment that Luke saw Matt motion with his gun for her to move toward the fall that would mean her death, he realized that he had no weapon.

He had to distract Matt and at the same time make sure that his brother didn't fire his gun at Domini.

He forced himself to shut out the sound of Matt's voice goading and taunting her to jump. He wasn't about to question why Matt didn't just shoot her. His brother was insane if he thought he would get away with killing her. Luke welcomed the icy calm that blocked out the sounds from the woods behind him. Keeping to a crouch, he moved around to the other side of the boulder. There was barely a foot's span of solid rock for him to inch his way around. He would be totally exposed. Totally at Matt's mercy if his brother turned suddenly.

But it was the only way he could come up behind Matt.

Sweat dripped into his eyes. A rough shake of his head was all the warning he gave Domini as he made his move. And he knew she saw him, knew she understood what he was going to do, for her pleas rose loudly.

"I'm begging you, Matt. I don't want to die. You can't believe you'll get away with killing me. You can't. Someone saw us. They'll be coming for you."

"And they'll find me. But you'll be gone. Crazy over finding out that Luke killed your father. I tried to stop you. But you jumped. And you're going to jump."

He moved forward just as Luke leaped for his back. The gun went off, chipping bits of rock above Domini's head.

Matt twisted and managed to roll to his side. He swung the gun at Luke's head. Shifting his weight saved Luke from the blow, but Matt's strength was behind the punch that landed on his shoulder. Fire streaked down his numbed arm. Before Luke could move, Matt twisted and turned, brought up his knee and used it to pin Luke in place.

Luke landed a punch to his brother's jaw. When he brought his right hand back for another blow, his elbow hit the edge of the ledge and rock crumbled and fell. Matt shifted his weight, as if he had become aware of how close they both were to going over the edge.

"I'll kill you," Matt muttered, sliding back off his brother's body.

"No!" Domini launched herself at Matt. She used both her hands to grab hold of his with the gun. Pain from the ankle she'd twisted threw her against Matt and carried them with slamming force against the boulder.

All Domini could think about was stopping

Matt from shooting Luke. His fingers tore at her hands. She tried to block the pain but could feel her grip weakened by the maddened strength Matt had.

Matt ripped one of her hands free, and she used it to claw his face. There was icy fury in his eyes. She screamed when he caught her hand and bent her fingers back. Snapping her head to the side, she saw the gun he was holding aimed at her head.

"Let her go, Matt. It's not Domini that you want. It's me. It's always been me that you've hated. Now's your chance, Matt." Soft, taunting, Luke forced himself to continue. He swallowed bile as Matt froze. He spared a moment's glance at the gun and his brother's finger on the trigger. *No, God! Please don't let me lose her!*

"Domini won't tell. No one will ever know what happened up here. Look at me, Matt. I'm unarmed. You could shoot me now."

"Luke?"

"Shut up, Domini. This is between me and my brother. That's how it's always been. Let her go, Matt. You don't need her. She's not in your way to having it all. I am. Just me, Matt."

"Damn you!" Matt's scream of rage as he shoved Domini at Luke echoed down the mountain. Gripping the gun in two hands, he brought the barrel around aimed at Luke. His mouth thinned as he saw that Luke had pushed her behind him.

"That's not gonna stop me. One bullet will finish off the two of you."

"No, Matt. You're not going to kill your brother." Toma inched forward the barrel of the rifle he held. "I want you to set your gun down, Matt. Don't make me shoot you."

"He's always been your favorite. Bastard, hellraiser, troublemaker. You always took his side."

"Put the gun down, Matt. Then we'll talk. But you're wrong."

Matt's response brought the click of the hammer being pulled back. "It won't matter if you shoot me, 'cause he's gonna die, too."

"You can't kill your brother!"

"Watch me, Toma. Watch me kill the only thing you've ever loved besides your damn gold and power."

"I'll give it to you. I'll give it all to you. We'll go back to the house right now and I'll sign over everything. You'll be the Colfax in charge, Matt. Everyone'll have to answer to you. You won't even have to stay around here. You could travel. You always wanted to travel, didn't you? Now you can. All you need to do is set the gun down. Luke won't try to take anything from you. Right, Luke?"

"Yeah. Right." Luke's gaze remained locked on his brother's eyes. He didn't know if Toma's shaken voice and the promises he was making even reached Matt. All emotion had disappeared from his brother's eyes. Behind him, he felt the uncontrollable shaking of Domini's body pressed against his back.

And he felt the sharp edge of the rock she was forcing into his hand. The brush of her fingers, the small squeeze she gave his hand, lent him the added courage to risk it all. He couldn't let her die. He only wished he could warn her what he was going to do. Matt's eyes were clouded with rage again. He'd be making his move . . .

Luke yanked Domini to the side with one hand, and the momentary distraction of her fall drew Matt's attention. Before he could squeeze off a shot, Luke threw himself at his brother, grabbing the barrel of the gun with his hand and smashing it against his upthrust thigh. He heard bones crack with the forceful blow of the rock landing on Matt's fingers. With an unholy scream Matt released the gun, spinning quickly as he tried to lash out, and the edge of rock beneath his feet gave away.

Both Toma and Luke tried to grab hold of him. The ledge crumbled beneath their weight, and Matt was gone.

# Chapter Twenty-four

❧

Domini drew Luke back from the edge. His shaking hands covered her ears to hide the sounds of the death cry that was still a moment later. He closed his eyes against the pain that tore through him.

"I almost lost you," he whispered against her lips. His thumbs brushed the tears from her cheeks, only more fell, faster, until he cradled her head against his shoulder and held her tight. He didn't know how much he loved her. He had never loved anyone this much. And all he could do was rock her against him, holding her as if he would never let go. *Soft enough to ease a man's pain.* He remembered the thought, remembered his rejection of needing a woman's softness . . . a woman's love.

And he'd almost lost her before he ever found out.

And he needed . . . God, how he needed her.

Luke wasn't sure how long he stood there hold-

ing Domini before he became aware that Toma
was talking to him.

He met his Father's bleak expression.

"I was afraid that I had lost you, too. I blame
myself for his death, Luke. Matt was insane."
Toma cleared his throat, feeling the moisture in
his eyes. He turned away from Luke, brushing
aside tears. They were a weakness. He couldn't
remember the last time he'd cried. Couldn't remember when he cared enough over the loss of
anything to cry.

"Go to him, Luke," Domini said, lifting her
head from Luke's shoulder. "He's hurting. Just as
you are."

Her tear-filled gaze was steady and direct in
meeting his.

"Domini, I love you. But don't, oh, God, please
don't ask that of me."

Her joy at hearing what she most wanted from
his lips was doubly clouded with tragedy. First
Matt's death and now Luke's refusal to make
peace with his father. And she couldn't add her
plea to Toma's for forgiveness. When Luke was
ready, if he ever was, the forgiveness for what he
had been made to suffer had to come from him.
Freely given as he had given her the treasured gift
of his love.

If that love could heal . . .

"I can't blame you for not wanting to have anything to do with me—"

"Toma! Give him time." Domini looked at the

broken old man as the hand that reached out to touch his son fell back to his side. A fierce protective urge made her want to scream at him that it was too late, but pity for Toma's pain at losing Matt stilled her tongue. Her love for Luke refused to allow anyone to rush him now.

"Luke needs time. We all need it." Shivers racked her and Luke tightened his embrace, his murmuring voice bringing calm when she felt herself about to splinter apart in the aftermath of violence.

She watched Toma as he stood and stared at them for a few minutes, then nodded, picked up his rifle, and started down the mountain.

"It's all right, love," she crooned, her hold every bit as hard and protective as his. "He's gone."

"I know." He released a shuddering breath. "Just let me hold you, then I'll take you back down. I need to know that you're all right. That I haven't lost you. I couldn't stand losing you now, Domini. I couldn't live with that loss."

*Too*, she finished silently, hurting for this man she loved.

His fingers slid deeper into her hair until he cupped the back of her head and tilted her face up. Within his eyes was a plea for understanding. Love shone in her green eyes, and yet he struggled to put his feelings into words.

"I need you, Domini. Need you to teach me how to love. I said the words but—"

"Oh, Luke—"

"No. Let me finish. I'm not sure I know what love is. But I want to learn. I need you in my life. I never knew how empty it was." His voice broke and he closed his eyes briefly. "Domini, I can't really explain. I've never felt like this for anyone. When I heard you cry out and knew he was hurting you, I thought I'd die if something happened to you. I know," he whispered hotly, "that I would have killed him for touching you."

"But you didn't kill Matt." Her hands lightly shaped his face. She rose on tiptoe to kiss the cut on his temple. "You didn't do it. His own crazy greed caused his death. Love, please don't blame yourself."

She brushed her lips against his, wishing with all her heart that she could take the pain from him. All she could do was pray that her love would be enough.

Looking into his black eyes, she saw that the shadows had receded. They might never be gone, but although Luke didn't believe he knew how to love, Domini could not mistake the blaze of light that shone in his eyes.

"I love you. I will always love you, Luke," she whispered.

Trust, hope, and love, most of all love, gleamed in her eyes. He scattered kisses across her cheek. "When you whisper my name like that I'd go through hell itself for you."

"No more hell, Luke. My love is waiting. I'm

waiting. All you need to do is reach out and I'm yours."

His mouth opened on hers, hot and hungry. But in moments he gentled the kiss, sipping at her lips as if she were pure, sweet water and he needed the life-giving taste of it. He had known need with this woman, but none like this. Each tremor of her body rippled over his, and she was all giving softness as he slowly rocked her against him. Fear and shame rose along with anger. He should have protected her. Rage that he hadn't ate through him as his lips gave nothing away of his inner turmoil and offered her cherishing kisses.

He broke the kiss, pressing her face against him.

"Let's go down the mountain, Domini. I want you away from here. I want to be away from this place."

She took a few steps at his side, and he saw that she was limping. "Matt do that to you?"

"No." She squeezed his hand. "I tripped and twisted my ankle."

"Same thing. If he hadn't been chasing you—"

"Leave it be. It's over."

And because her gaze pleaded and she so desperately needed to believe that, he nodded. "Yeah. It's over." He scooped her into his arms, wanting to hold her, needing her touch to make him believe, too. Slowly he made his way down the mountain with his precious burden.

Toma waited by the cabin. Luke brushed past him and set Domini down on the bed.

Being ignored by Luke was not a new role for Toma. But he didn't shout to demand his son's attention. He didn't even talk to him at all as he went out and returned with a basin of water from the barrel. He looked at Domini, found her direct gaze disconcerting.

Clearing his throat, Toma stepped closer to the bed. "I've a few things that need to be said to you."

"Not now you don't," Luke warned.

Domini touched his hand, stilling his move to wash her face. "It won't hurt us to listen. Listening doesn't mean you have to act. All of us are hurting now. Please."

He opened his mouth and shut it. He couldn't deny her. Shooting a look at his father, Luke let his warning show in his hard expression. "Go ahead. Talk."

"I wanted you both to know that while I had my doubts that Matt had told the truth about Luke killing your father, I let the matter be. It was easier not to question. A bad habit I had fallen into when it came to Luke. I know my wife thought she was in love with James. But Amanda never really loved anyone but herself.

"The night he died, James had packed to go back to you and your mother. Amanda didn't believe me when I told her. We had a terrible fight. She told me she was leaving me, and I couldn't let her go. She claimed that your father was taking her with him."

He stared out at the twilight that blanketed the trees beyond the window, remembering the shouts and the accusations that had flown back and forth that night.

"Toma?" Domini gently prodded.

"Yeah." He raked one hand through his hair, the very same gesture that Luke often made. "I'm not excusing my part in this. When she showed me her packed bags, I went after your father. We fought and I left him barely able to walk. Happened right down at the bottom of that path. I saddled up and rode out for most of the night. When I got back in the morning, he was dead.

"I mourned the loss of my friend. He tried to tell me that if I kept on, I was going to lose Amanda. But I know he never betrayed me. He was a kind man. Too soft, I'd tell him. Maybe that's what Amanda built her dreams on. Could be he figured that time apart would help the two of us. That's something I'll never know." He looked at Luke.

"I can't be sorry enough for allowing Matt's veiled hints that you had something to do with James's death. I know you loved him. Loved him as you never did love me. But you know I made sure those whispers never went far, Luke. To my face no one denied my story that his death was an accident.

"That guilt will follow me to my grave. If I

hadn't beat him up, Matt wouldn't have been able to kill him."

"You finished?" Luke demanded, rising from the bed.

"Guess I—"

"If you're finished, get out."

"Luke!"

"No, Domini. Leave my son be. You just remember that your father was coming back to you."

Luke walked away to stand with his back toward them near the fireplace. Domini sighed and glanced up at Toma.

"Thank you for telling me that. I always wondered."

"I want you to have his share of the mine," Toma said in a gruff voice. He wanted to make peace with Luke and didn't know how.

Helplessly, Domini hoped that Luke would say something, but he remained silent. "Luke, do you want—"

"Nothing of his. Not a damn thing."

"All right. Toma, I won't take the money, but if you could, send it to Sister Benedict at the mission. There are so many needy children she can offer food and shelter to if—"

"Consider it done. But you don't understand how much money is involved."

"And I don't want to know. There was a time when I thought the money from my father's share of the gold mine was important, when my mother was alive. It's not important now. I found something far richer and more precious to me."

"You knew we'd found gold? He'd told me he was gonna surprise—"

"Toma, my father couldn't keep a secret. He wrote to my mother. One more secret I kept from Luke and from you. The letter was faded, and creased, and stained with my mother's tears." Her voice broke on the last, and she clasped her hands together in her lap, ignoring the pain of the rock scrapes on her palms.

"When I finally learned to read, Sister Benedict gave me my mother's book. I found the letter there. My father was worried about you. He thought you'd changed, a man possessed by greed. He felt sorry for you, Toma."

"Sorry for me?"

"Yes." Her smile was small and sad, "You see, my father knew how to love, and all he wanted was to bring the gold to my mother so he could hear her joy as she whispered his name." She studied him in the fading light and realized that he didn't **understand**. A small noise made her glace at Luke. He was staring at her, and she waited, hoping, praying, and as his smile came, Domini had her reward.

Luke understood.

Toma shook his head. He saw that their gazes were locked on each other, and he felt shut out of what they shared. He had no choice but to leave them.

The door closing roused Luke. "Did you tell him the truth?"

"Yes."

"That business about hearing your mother call his name?"

"What he wrote to her was, 'I hear you whisper my name in my heart, Consuela, but soon you will have me near when you call. All that I promised will be ours.'"

He hated the sadness that crept into her voice. Just as he hated the fear that still lurked within his mind. What if he couldn't learn to love?

"What had he promised her?"

"His love, Luke. It was all my mother ever wanted."

"I'm not big on making promises. I don't think—"

"The promises in love are to be there when needed. To hold someone through the night. To be there to wake and share the joy of morning. Love," she said, rising and waving him back as she limped to his side, "is knowing in your heart that someone cares for you. That you'll never be alone. Love is what I feel for you."

She lifted his bruised hand to her cheek and gently rubbed it against her skin. "Love is my pleasure in your touch, and my touching you. It's knowing how much you hurt and wanting to take the pain away. Or if not away, then to share it. Love is strength, for there is power within its giving. To me, as to my mother, these are the things of love.

"The passion that we share, Luke, is a flame so bright that it dims a fire's blaze. Love is a healing balm for the soul. A gift that is freely given. No rules. No demands that it be returned. You only have to reach out and take the gift that is offered."

Leaning closer, she brushed a butterfly-light kiss on his chin, then rose to touch her lips to his. "Love, Luke. Soft and sweet or fierce with need. When you love, you'll find it brings its own rewards."

His fingertips shook. He shaped her features as if seeing her for the first time. Luke thought he was. Strength and gentleness. Truth and honor. And love . . . so much love awaited him.

Her belief that all he had to do was reach out and take her gift became his.

And only the rising moon witnessed the whispers that followed as sighs and murmurs became the whispers of each other's names. Whispers filled with love.